IN THE SEAT OF A STRANGER'S CAR

IN THE SEAT OF A STRANGER'S CAR

a novel
by Beau Flemister

—

NETWORK

Honolulu, Hawaiʻi

Grateful acknowledgement is made to the following for permission to reprint
previously published material: Penguin Random House LLC: Excerpt from
Henderson the Rain King by Saul Bellow (Penguin Classics Reprint edition, 2012),
"I Am A Child," words and music by Neil Young, Copyright 1977 by Broken
Arrow Music Corporation, Copyright Renewed, All Rights Reserved, Used by
Permission, Reprinted by Permission of Hal Leonard LLC.

Book design and illustrations by Noa Emberson

First Printing, 2019

Library of Congress Control Number: 2018914814

ISBN 978-0-578-42800-0

SECOND EDITION

NMG Network
36 N Hotel St Suite A
Honolulu, HI 96817

www.nmgnetwork.com

V. 1.3

For Mom and Dad

Note

If you are unfamiliar with certain words and phrases, please refer to the Glossary on page 303. Often, due to accents found among Pidgin English speakers in the novel, the "r" is dropped and replaced with "ah." Like: fakah, frickah, or triggah.

Contents

Part III: Journey to the Edge of the Earth

I am a child, I'll last a while
You can't conceive of the pleasure in my smile
You hold my hand, rough up my hair,
It's lots of fun to have you there

—Neil Young

WHAT A STRANGE GAME THEY ARE PLAYING

When the woman placed the small child into the trunk of the 1997 Cadillac Deville, the boy could hear it breathing: the perpetual slush and sigh of the sea, inhaling and devouring the shoreline with each vast gulp. This endless panting was the sound of his home, as was the detonating crash of waves breaking in the distance. And beer cans crinkling in men's clutches. The random pop of a thrown bottle on the naked, low tide reef. Chained dogs barking anxiously and the wedge-tailed shearwater chicks crying in their nests at night like hungry human babies. Then the trunk swung shut with a metallic crunch, and the boy felt like he was falling underwater. Suddenly he was submerged—suspended—and all of those sounds were muffled, nearly unrecognizable. The breath of the lunging shorebreak was but a faint whisper and anything above surface, obscured. The trunk clicked open and swung skyward with a hydraulic hiss. The woman looked in as if to say, *peek-a-boo*, and the boy giggled instinctively. She tossed in a king-sized Snickers bar and a half-empty Dasani water bottle.

And shut the trunk again.

What a strange game they are playing, the boy thought, and before the first ghosts of fear surrounded him, he waited for the trunk to pop open again. Moments passed and the boy held his breath as one would below the surface. He strained his ears, which adjusted to the sudden darkness as one's vision would, and listened to the crashing shorebreak mumbling somewhere above the surface. He heard voices of the woman and a man, like talk smothered in pillows.

The boy waited. He had no idea where this game was going. Then finally, he gasped in a breath of air, though still submerged. Frustrated, he kicked at the small room's ceiling from his back and received an abrupt reply, violent and loud. Three hollow slaps to the top of the trunk door, like gunshots punctuated by the piercing treble of a ringed finger. The gunshots frightened the boy stiff. So again, instinctively, he held his breath.

He squinted in the darkness, now unsure whether they'd forgotten him in there or not. It hadn't been but a few minutes since the woman dropped him in, and he wondered if her memory could be so poor. He began to holler in the pitch, but it felt like yelling underwater.

The driver turned the keys in the ignition, and the child's bones rattled within his slight body. His hollering bended, now elastic with the vehicle's jarring stutter. The deep engine roar replaced the whispering surf, and the car accelerated over a bumpy dirt road. The boy rolled backward inside the trunk, nearly somersaulting. The vehicle ramped onto asphalt and the boy popped into the air. His forehead hit the carpet-lined trunk ceiling. Instantly, he felt nauseous and respired slowly. He braced his body and sat propped on his elbows, wedged in a corner of the shuddering space.

After countless, sudden stop and gos, after tumbling to and fro in his cave, after the vertigo of braking and the shake of acceleration, the road beneath the whining tires felt smoother. The sharp turns and dizzying bumps leveled out and the boy felt like he was floating. Above the surface a premium outlet mall, Pearl Harbor, Aloha Stadium, and Honolulu International Airport shrunk behind the Caddy. Though the trunk was barely large enough for the boy to sit upright, to counter the nausea from changing lanes he remained on his back. And though he lay blinded in the dark room, he glared persistently into this strange, rushing night. He was too terrified to close his eyes.

Then, for a moment, the boy smelled something wonderful: freshly baked bread, the scent penetrating the depths of his underwater chamber. A brief break from the nightmare, then quickly evaporating. The vehicle slowed, merging onto a highway, and the engine hummed louder, turning with effort. The darkness became hot and smothering.

The child peeled off his t-shirt and swallowed. He inhaled thick, stale air. The heat was draining, wringing him out like two giant hands would with a wet washcloth. The stops and turns continued until, at an unexpected break, the engine drone ceased. The boy felt footsteps thumping over concrete. He heard doors slam and new voices with kinder tones, welcoming guests. The motor turned again, and the vehicle lunged forward, tipping down a small hill, then screeching viciously to a halt. The child breathed in short gasps. The wheels spun, shrieking hysterically beneath his trembling body, followed by another burst of motion, the vehicle zigzagging from right to left. Another halt, and then for the first time on the journey, the boy's cave moved forward, the Cadillac reversing. The engine cut, a door swung shut and the stench of burnt rubber crept into the child's room, so pungent he could taste it. And then total silence. All but his short, desperate gasps of breath. *Snatching...snatching...snatching...*

PART I

A PECULIAR DISCOVERY

1.

"Make me dynamic."

Valet parking is a lot like stripping: you'd like to get out of it, but the money's just too goddamn good. You never knew valets made bank? Well, now you do. We clean up. Maybe not all the time, but some years, some locations, some gigs are indeed better than others. Yet still, just like stripping, there's a stigma. An odd, and might I add unwarranted, reputation. I mean, you can see it in their eyes. Literally watch a customer go through three of the five stages of grief handing their ride over to a valet. As if every attendant is related to, or influenced by, those two greaseballs in *Ferris Bueller's Day Off*. By the way, thanks for that, John Hughes. That sweeping generalization and basically *only* living portrayal of valets in popular culture has really done a number for our image. Those two goons are pretty much our blackface.

But I get it. That instinctual doubt in handing over

your vehicle to a complete stranger. Giving some kid in a tacky uniform with a name tag an $80,000 piece of machinery. That, or getting to a place where suddenly, there's no self-parking. Where you're suddenly no longer in control. And worse yet, handing over your baby to someone who might look a little rough around the edges. Someone obscured in a cloud of e-cig vapors with a long-sleeve athletic compression shirt on that you get the feeling he's wearing to hide his prison tats. There's that quick look. We all know the one. They give us that look like they're dropping their kid off on the first day of kindergarten, and the teacher looks like...well...a valet parker.

I can tell you one thing: trust your instincts.

Because maybe we're rifling through the glove box, searching for a Kleenex to blow snot into while you scarf down your seared ahi tuna platter at Roy's Waikiki. Or not. Maybe we're pulling out your car on an early morning shift, still drunk from the night before, sweating out those Vodka Red Bulls and Long Islands all over your plush leather seats, going forty-five in reverse in a concrete underground garage. Or not. Maybe we're flipping through your iPod, or rearranging your presets, or sniffing those stray panties from the backseat, or maybe we're taking your hideous Ford Mustang rental out for an afternoon lunch run. Or not. You just never really know, do you?

For the most part, here's what you *should* know: enjoy your meal, look your date in the eye, screw your "instincts" and ask the hostess to split that twenty for spare bills on the way out. Which begs the age-old question: What's a good tip? Christ, what's that saying, *If you have to ask...*

One dollar—don't even bother. Three bucks—getting warmer. Five's a fair starting point (it's 2018, pal) and beyond that—you have our undivided attention. Trade secret: a valet will do just about anything for a 20-spot. A valet will damn near bury a body for fifty.

Thing is, you hear about strippers saving up their tips to pay their way through law or medical school, but how many doctors or dentists have you ever had that actually looked like they could work a pole? No, really, is that bit just a rumor? Maybe dental *assistant*—I've definitely seen some of those gals that could moonlight at a strip joint. But what stripper has ever said they were shakin' it to become one? Just doesn't add up. But at the same time, I sure haven't heard any valets say, "Oh, I'm just parking to save up for Stanford Law." Does that mean that strippers have more ambition than us? Maybe they've got daddy issues and we've just got Caddy issues. Or, maybe valet is the job that was so cush and comfy as a kid—you just never really grew out of it. Valet can go from college job to full-blown career if you mess around and let it. I dunno, it's like you're sitting pretty, and then a decade goes by, you're thirty-three years old with bum knees and asking yourself, *How am I still fetching cars?* Which brings me to another point. I said a decade of honest to goodness employment, but here I am, maddened by the thought of it. Us valets got dreams, though.

And, when you really think about it, it's not the worst gig. You'd be surprised what parking cars could get you. We got guys supporting families, owning homes, paying mortgages, subletting—on this gig. Sure, a lot paying child support and maybe even some alimony, but *valets*, for Christ's sake!

Guys putting their kids through private school. Yeah, cheap Catholic schools, but still private. That's some forward-ass thinking. Take Nelson, for instance:

First-generation American from the Philippines, Nelly's been working for the company eight years. He works seven days a week and most times double shifts. That's back-to-back eights (eight-hour long shifts), half-valet, half-bellman at his hotel. On those hours, including hourly wages, minus taxes (plus tips, of course) he's pulling in about $450-plus a day. He's twenty-seven years old, owns two homes, a few vehicles, and to top it off, has a wife and two kids. But then again, I guess you gotta ask yourself, what kind of life in the P.I. did you have to leave to be totally cool with working sixteen hours a day? Hell, I've worked a few double shifts before, and all I can say is they're either the best way to own a home or, in my experience, lose a girlfriend and a goddamned toenail. Screw doubles.

One time I asked him, "Nelson, what's next?" And he's all, in this thick Tagalog accent, "Well, I deed carrs. I deed homes. Now: Da sea. I goin' buy one yacht, I tink, next." He says this to me at work, like, *while* we were working. Then he kinda looked out to space, nodded as if to say, *so shall it be done*, hopped in a hotel guest's rental car, sped down the ramp and parked it.

We might as well address the elephant in the room right now too: the one about the valet that copied some guy's house key while the customer was out to dinner, found their address off some mail on the passenger seat, then a week later broke into their pad and robbed them blind. Have I seen anyone pull this type of shit? C'mon, what are we, savages? Sure, this is America, so stranger things have happened...but this is also Hawai'i—which can feel pretty far from the New World sometimes.

You know what most people commonly start a conversation with us about? What the average tourist or guest comes to us for and thinks is an appropriate exchange for our job title? Dining suggestions? Nope. Road directions? Nope. Cultural happenings? Yeah, right. It's the same every time. They kinda sidle up next to you, barely look you in the eye, glance both ways to see if anyone else can hear them and ask, "Hey, you guys know where I can score some weed, right?" Which comes out more a statement of fact than an actual question.

Downright insulting. That or, "Which street has the best hookers?" Or, "Is there a number I can call for...you know..." Or, "C'mon, man, you goootta know where I can buy some..." As if our kind would inherently know. Now, I'm not gonna say one or two of us *isn't* into a clandestine activity or two, but what kind of moron would actually risk getting caught selling a customer weed? And c'mon, we can't *all* look like stoners. But shit, if they palm me five or ten bucks, I tell 'em Gary, the graveyard-shift guy, will take care of them. He definitely *always* looks stoned. Either that, or really tired. Overnight shifts must be exhausting.

Here's another thing to consider: many times a valet is a company's very first impression. From a five-star hotel to an Anthony Bourdain-blessed mom and pops to a senator's fund-raiser—we're the ones greeting you and helping your spouse out of the door. One of our guys, Kainoa, often sniffs the seats that women have been sitting in. Like, just because. Another one of our guys, Gene, has a borderline psychopathic temper. Another kid can barely talk he's got so many tongue piercings. All said and done: Just trust us. You take care of us, and we'll take care of you.

"Fakah!"

"…"

"Fakah! Watchu doing ovah dea, haole?" says Palani irritably. Palani is almost always irritated—it's pretty much his only look. Probably because he houses five kids from three different mothers and rocks a fade that looks more Semper Fi than barber shop chic.

"Just taking notes, dude."

"Fo' wat." Palani also has an absurdly deep voice for how slight a frame he has. He's the kind of guy that barely weighs a buck-forty and can't stop bragging about his high school football days. *Brah, could've played fo' Wyoming if nevah had my firstborn*, he harps.

Wyoming's got a program?

"I'm writing a book, P-Diddy."

"*Haaah*, you still doing dat? Feels like you wen tell me dat fo ages, brah. Maybe time fo geev up da ghost, ah? Nah-nah-nah…I goin' be in um?"

"Yeah, you, Gene, Kainoa—all the boys. But it's a novel, so it's kind of fictional. Of course I'll change the names to 'protect the innocent,'" I assure him, signing bunny ears. He scowls back at me and mimics my air quotes with his own, then hides his index fingers, turns both birds and flicks me off.

"No need, bu. Ainokea whatchu mention; jus make me handsome," he says, strolling over to a hotel guest's rental, buried deep within the garage.

"Jesus. So I could talk about all the shit you pull over here. The rock you found in that crackhead's car two months ago, and all you want me to do is portray your character as physically good looking?" (He found an extremely dirty bag of crack rock on the floorboard of a customer's car, took it, asked me if I wanted half—which I declined—and then sold it a few days later, justifying that he was helping the man kick his habit.)

"Yups. And super akamai. If get room in da story. No ways, actually...make me *dynamic*, bu. I no like be one-dimensional, you fakah. Put some thought into me."

By the way, right now what Palani was doing is what's called "lingering." Depending on the customer's deliberate or inadvertent transgression—a failure to tip, smelly car, overall sour attitude, etc.—the valet takes his sweet little time. He smokes a cigarette, has a quick bite to eat, shoots the shit, and eventually, brings the car around. What took so long? *Gosh, Mr. So-and-so, I'm terribly sorry; we're really backed up.* We even have a squirt bottle to simulate fake perspiration.

Maybe I just call it that.

Kainoa sees the two of us talking, wanders over (also probably lingering) and interjects skeptically:

"Ho, Captain Cook, you writing one book?"

After haole, that's another thing they call me—Captain Cook. As in the eighteenth-century English explorer that invaded the Hawaiian Islands and, for most Hawaiians, is remembered alongside the likes of guys like Hitler.

"Uh-huh," I say.

"Brah, I nevah knew you could read," he jokes.

"Says 'the guy,'" I snap back.

"What 'guy,' haole?"

"Say the guy who writes 'Nissan Prius' on the valet tags—"

"Eeeeasy tygah. Ho, cherry, so one more book by one haole about da Hawaiian experience," he says, rubbing his palms together, his sarcasm palpable. "Can't wait fo da unique perspective."

"Fakah! You on stay-cation, o wat!?" shouts Gene menacingly, head-butting into our conversation. "Kay, 'kay, 'kay, 'kay, 'kay…" he says, shuffling toward us like a boxer, or maybe more mixed martial artist in a cage. Gene, aka Mean Gene, either always has two loose fists up, sparring with an imaginary opponent, or one hand down his cargo shorts, adjusting his genitals. Somehow, he's doing both at the moment, simultaneously. Gene is all-bark and all-bite but has been in two separate altercations with customers in the last month. Our company works on a three-strike method. Apparently, his sister is twice as tough, too. "M.F.Kayyyyyy…Sherry at da front desk, Christy da waitress from Sea Bird…or da nerdy hapa-haole chick from Starbucks?"

"M, F…K.?" I ask, puzzled.

"Marry, Fuck, Kill," Palani clarifies.

"Brah, no can play dat game anymore, coz," scolds Kainoa. "Da times wen change already. Das fricken premeditated sexual assault, dat game."

"Brah," says Gene, suddenly serious. "You no tink wahines play da same one wit bruddahs?"

"Which Sherry?" chimes Palani, confused. "*Hāpai*-Sherry or Japanee Sherry?"

"Frickah—*hāpai* Sherry, coz!"

Oh yeah, Gene also has an odd fetish for pregnant women. "Fine den, you party poopahz. Marry, fuck, killlll... Joe Moore...Howard Dashefskys...or Robert Kekaulas." "Ho, tuff, dis one," says Kainoa. "Is Dashefskys one anchor or one reportah?" "Das da haole dat sound like one Hawaiian, ah?" asks Palani.

I leave the boys and walk toward the car that Gene has parked and left halfway down the garage ramp. Gene trails behind me.

"I goin' be in your book, too, or wat?" he asks...or orders...it's hard to tell with Gene.

"Of course, man."

"An wat I goin' be?" says Gene, staring me right in the eyes. I wasn't sure if this was a test or not.

"A fricken' character," I make out, trying to match his energy. "I dunno, man, just another name."

"Den make sure you gimme one cool name...like..." Gene thinks about this for a second, slapping the side of the car with his paw-like hand, "*Mac*. Yeah, Mac; I always wen like dat name. Das mines."

"You got it, Mac."

I pull out my Moleskin and pretend to make the note.

Because despite how lucrative the gig can be, every valet has dreams of something bigger. Something else. Even a valet putting two kids through private school and paying a mortgage on a house refuses to consider this job a career. Even after twenty profitable years of it. Really, the only ones who've accepted being in it for life are the owner (who's now a millionaire) and a few managers floating around locations that don't actually have to park cars anymore but somehow see six figures on their pay stubs. They've graduated from parking to, simply: management. But, believe it or not, valets are a resourceful bunch. And there's always a side hustle. That being: attempting the thing that you dream of becoming (full-time), or doing something to simply supplement the gig. The side hustle is the hope, and even the most deranged and puerile valet has some of that somewhere inside them. Doesn't everyone?

2.

Like a snake devouring its own tail

So. What's strong, and/or weak, about this piece?"

"I dunno, the author uses a bit of passive voice, for starters. Which is clearly fricken' bush-league."

"*Really?*" I say, a little too surprised. "Like, where?"

"Like where he says: '*And so the boy was raised by a pack of wolves…*'"

"Hmm. Guess you're right. Well, what did you find strong in the piece, then? Anything that popped out to you, or kinda made you think?"

I glance around the classroom. A few students are looking into their laps, trying to hide the texting, the strain of it giving them bizarre double chins. A couple of them stare out the window, watching the hala tree leaves rustle with the trade winds. Does this shit really make them *that* bored?

"Eh, not really. Overall, it's pretty sentimental and,

like, the images are kinda vague at times. It's like, *show* me the place, don't just tell me about it, you know? And come to think of it, the author kind of switches tense at times, but I feel like it's not on purpose, as if he's using some kind of post-modern device like some writers do these days. I mean, really, who edits this shlock?"

That smug little prick. I swear to God. The answer to that one is *him*. He's the editor. And it's always this one with the snobby-ass comments and critiques. A perpetually disinterested, albeit sharp-as-a-tack sophomore named—I shit you not—Kaito Wolf Quest Doschberger. Wolf Quest. Friggin' prep schools. He's got a shirt on that reads, in bold Helvetica: *I listen to bands that don't even exist yet*, burgundy stretch-skinny jeans and dons a bleached-out haircut that's clearly Bieber-inspired.

Thing is, I figured I'd kill two birds with one stone, and while I taught these little shits how to write, maybe they could teach me a little something, too. So, yes, I have them edit my work—mainly articles and stories that I've submitted to local and international magazines—mixed in with their own work. Fine, by international I mean in-flight, but many that, with their help, have been published around town. I pass it off like I'm giving them exercises from "anonymous" authors. Anything from grammar and punctuation to tone, structure, voice, narration, plot and character development. As of late, we've been workshopping my book...without them really knowing that. Occasionally the feedback's positive; most of the times it's not. They really get a kick out of ripping on those-with-no-name. But then again, there's no room for softies. We're living in a cut-down-comment world, baby.

Really, I more or less got the job for street-cred. Like, *what do you do?* "Oh, I'm a writer…but I teach at Punalani on the side." Punalani, being *the* premier prep school in the Islands and alma mater to some of our state's greatest minds. Anything but "full-time valet-parking attendant." Sometimes, I don't even really know how I was hired. Just kinda slipped into the po-zish. I guess technically, I'm not full-time. I get two slots during summer school and then sub as much as they'll let me during the regular school year. It's been a few years and there still hasn't been an opening. At least that's what they keep telling me.

But I had some friends that were actually qualified—local prep school grads, valedictorians, NYU film school with honors, now screenwriters. They taught there during summers when they were getting their own starts as grunts doing spec work for the studios. Then, basically they hooked it up and got me into the fold, teaching a creative writing course during summer school. Summer courses—which is more or less diet school year. It's kinda like saying you're published…online. But whatever, a job away from the 'lot is still a respectable step in the right direction, even if it feels like I've been speed-walking in a straight line for a few years now.

They must have been pretty hard up that summer, too. I think my buddies told the director that I was away researching and writing a novel in Indonesia, which I'm guessing seemed really romantic and boho to the guy. I've been kind of "writing a novel" for the better part of a decade now. But I *was* in Bali…surfing and hitting on Scandinavian broads midway through their gap year experiential phase. And, I *was* published by a few small-time mags in Hawai'i. Long story short, I suppose the director figured if I was some sort of traveling "novelist" (all travels funded by valet tips, mind you), then I could teach creative writing to high schoolers. Even at our great state's policy makers' alma mater. So I was in.

"Can you just flick on the second half of *Rounders* already? I think we've had enough of these 'editing exercises,'" says Brandon, signing the quotations to the class, now suddenly captivated by Kaito's interruption. This dickhead *never* raises his hand. And who does bunny ears anymore?

"Ya'll ain't ready for the second half yet," I retort.

"It's gotta be better than the second half of *Il Cinema Paradiso*. And, by the way, can you tell me where to find those two hours of my life? The school lost and found doesn't seem to have them."

"Hey-yoooo!" cries a boy in the back. The class roars supportively.

"Don't act like you weren't crying at that end scene in *Cinema*, dude," I frown.

This newer generation is ridiculous, too. "Old" for them is mid-90s and beyond. Usually, only one out of twenty of them has seen *The Breakfast Club*, my go-to character development film. None of them has seen a Wes Anderson flick on purpose, let alone Tarantino, Scorsese or Coppola. So it's pretty easy to explode their little minds. You show these bitches *Good Will Hunting* and you're an instant legend. But you can't blow your load; you gotta save that one for the end of the course. Also, pay-wise for summer courses, you can't complain, either. You pull in about $50 an hour for four hours of work, you're out by noon, and you've got the rest of the day to enjoy the summer sun. Taxed to hell, of course, but still, that's not bad cash. Even for a valet. Plus, it's honest, cerebral money. No skulking for a tip, or lingering because they didn't, or waiting in the wings in case the guest needs directions to the tourist luau. No fetching, no running, no sweat. Literally: no sweat.

Another nerd, Kawika, calls out from the back of the class. "Yeah, this is some wanna-be Garcia Marquez shit!"

Others nod their heads in agreement.

"I'm not following, Kawika—"

"Yeah, magical realism without the magic is just freakin' *boring*," says Kaito Wolf Quest, cutting me off.

"Well, can you at least get a sense of any themes the author tries to convey through his writing? And if so, what are they?"

Wolf Quest flips his bangs back, doesn't even raise his hand and snaps, "Themes? What themes? The protag just seems like some entitled loser. And, how do we even know that the writer is necessarily a *he* if this shit is 'anonymous'?"

Well, fuck me.

"Uh, I guess one can assume…through tone and the way the protag portrays the women around…" I stammer. "Okay, how 'bout this. Keeping in mind the qualms you have with the story, for homework tonight I want you all to rewrite this piece, aaannd…come up with some suggestions to drive the plot forward. Give me some end points for the protagonist. Let's craft some bottom together, people. Turn it in tomorrow with your *own* twist; your *own* voice and tone," I coax.

Listen, I'm not saying that I've published *a lot* of work around town under my own name that might use some rich sixteen-year-old's intellectual property, but if I don't push it...who will, right? And some of their shit is pretty genius, too, I swear to God. On the other hand, me not getting caught yet probably says a lot about the current state of the publishing biz. Or, readers in general.

But I'm at the whiteboard right now and dammit, that means business. A couple of sighs ring out from the crowd.

"I don't know if you guys are really getting this," I say smoothly. Teaching, subbing, summer schooling, whatever you want to call it—it's all about acting. And if there's anything I've learned from valet parking, it's putting on a show. Make 'em think you've got it *aaalll* under control. I tuck my shirttail in some more and scratch a "strengths" and "weaknesses" column on the board.

"Okay, first: can anyone describe the writer's style? In what *way* does the writer convey his ideas and images to the reader? Talk to me about the language..."

Ralph, a soft spoken, clean-cut kid who often combats this seventy-two-degree room with various fur-lined parkas, calmly raises his hand. Ah, Ralphy, always my voice of reason. Definitely the brightest bulb in the class, if I ever had a protégé. But, seriously, a friggin wunderkind. Definitely a better writer than me and totally published and doesn't even know it.

"King Ralph, whattya got?"

"Well, like Kawika said, the style does seem to be quite Marquez–inspired, but if I could describe the way the author structures a lot of his or her sentences, honestly, it resembles a snake sort of devouring its own tail."

"Oh, so, like, that symbol thingy…of, umm…infinite wholeness? What's that thing called?" I ask, snapping my fingers to remember.

"*Ouroboros!*" shouts someone from the back.

"Right! *Ouroboros*," I repeat, "and *language* guys. Don't take advantage of my benevolent chill, fellas."

A little lost in the moment, I've begun drawing a rudimentary cartoon serpent on the board, scales and all, mouth agape, consuming the tail end of itself.

Well, fuck me.

"Yes, exactly like that," says Ralph. "Granted, I understand the author has his or her own specific narrative style, and maybe this structure is deliberate, but some sentence breaks could fix things. And it could read a little easier without compromising tone."

I take a step back and look at the accusation of my style. It wasn't a compliment. I feel my face reddening but am hidden from the pompous peanut gallery behind me. The bell rings, and laptops, textbooks, and folders clap and cram into book bags. Zippers whiz and a cloud of voices erupt. Tennis shoes and flip-flops scurry and squeak into a queue out the door. A mass exodus from the punch line that is my class.

"Don't forget your homework, guys!" I call out, half-plea, half-command.

Kaito and Kawika are the last to leave and vibe off each other's irreverence. Their voices snipe me from behind, feigning encouragement.

"Thanks, teach, I *really* learned a lot about writing—and you know, come to think of it—a bit about myself today," croons Kaito.

"Indeed, another *extraordinary* class. I shall count the hours till the next one," he snickers.

My eyes mouth, "Screw you," and I smile curtly. "Thanks, guys. See you next class."

I wipe away the vacant pros and cons columns, my style snake, and stare numbly at the blank whiteboard before me. Pros, Cons: 0-0.

3.

Fucking James Franco

'm not one to normally shit where I eat, but there's this one flower girl in particular—a half-Salvadorian, mainland-transplant bombshell named Marisela—that's seriously making me rethink that silly ass policy. I'm working Morton's Steakhouse, my main at-work reading/grading/writing spot, and I'm not counting the minutes until she comes by or anything...but I do know this is one of her days here and I've scheduled myself accordingly. Our company, Royal Valet, is not only contracted by various hotels in Waikīkī, but also by several upscale restaurants in the greater Honolulu area, as well as for some private parties. Royal's even got a budding chauffeur service. I know, snazzy, right?

Anyways, since Morton's is a restaurant, you have, like, three or four hours of downtime between the "dinner in" and the "dinner out." And, yeah, by downtime I mean crickets and tumbleweeds slow. Now, if you were a smart valet, you'd multitask and use that between-time wisely. Learn a language on YouTube, read a novel, get to know the stock market, I dunno, invest in cryptocurrency, what have you. But most of us squander that precious block on Instagram or Netflix or high-stakes online poker. I, however, am striving for excellence. Did I mention you could also undercut the valet service at the Neiman Marcus around the corner when their lost clients show up at our booth? None of those rich cougars are there past nine p.m., so you just park them free of charge, point to the sliding doors down the way, and when they return, you get a fat tip that's all off the books. Honestly, if you've got a halfway official-looking roller booth and valet tickets (all of which any schmuck could find on Amazon), you could park anybody and no one would know the diff.

"Wow, car boy, new all-time low?" She catches me off guard.

"Huh?"

"That right there," she says, pointing at my literature. "What, are you reading the new James Franco book to make you feel better about yourself? Like, at least you can write better than this big hunky, famous movie star? Like, there's some hope for you, right?"

God, she's good. That's exactly what I was doing.

"You wanna just get out of here with me?" I counter pathetically.

"Dream on. And, I thought we've gone over this before: I don't date valets."

"The hell's wrong with valets?"

She squints and looks off as if to say, *How can I phrase this gently...* "Valets..."

"Are the male version of flower girls?" I interject.

"Aaaaah, silly, little car boy; we women of the petal at least have brains...and don't have to wear some demeaning colonial era, subservient-chic uniform...and can actually leave the parking lot...and undoubtedly make more money."

"Honey, hate to break it to ya, but flower girls are like one rung above a Keʻeaumoku rub-and-tug on the 'ladder of demeaning jobs.'"

She winces. It was a little harsh. "Which is why I feel we're *perfect* for each other!" I salvage.

She hands me her keys, places the bouquet on the ground, and looks down at my work. I gently grab her free hand.

"Aww, and is that a little notepad by your brand-new hardcover?"

"Why, yes it is. I'm actually a writer. I'm working on a novel—this isn't my full-time job."

"Riiiiiiiiiight. Which is why I only see you at least five days a week at various booths all over town. You do know that plagiarism *is* a crime in a court of law, right, and that plagiarizing bad literature is just a crime against culture."

"I'm flattered that you've been paying such close attention to my work schedule, babe, but you better watch that mouth before I kiss it. Also, do tell me about these mysterious 'Crimes Against Culture,'" I air-quote. "Are, like, food blogs and Crocs and illegal downloading on a Most Wanted List?" I ask, chin in both palms, elbows on the valet booth.

"Good one. I think I'll add that 'watch your mouth' bit to *my* book," she says.

"What do you mean, *your* book?"

"I'm writing a book."

"About what?" I scoff.

"Stories I've experienced while slinging flowers. Pretty

much an exposé. I've already published a few one-offs in some local lifestyle mags. *Bamboo Ridge* is gonna publish a story in their next issue, actually. Excited about that," she says, arranging her bouquet by color, snipping a stray thorn off a white rose. "I'm sure you're familiar with that one; I remember seeing you lurking around Kuykendall at UH some years back. Glad to see you've made some progress," she nods, looking my booth up and down.

No. *I* was writing a book about my experiences in the service industry. *Me.*

"Ha! A short story collection? Good luck getting that printed. You're just a regular Latin Jhumpa Lahiri, huh?" I say.

"I'll take that as a compliment. But yeah, I am getting it published. My agent's been communicating with Scribner *and* Random House. 'Kay, I gotta make some money now, car boy, but it really was very engaging convo... Oh, and remember, just because he played Allen Ginsburg in a movie doesn't actually mean he can write in real life, bye-eeee."

Speechless, I have no comeback. *She* has an agent?! Where the hell do you get a goddamn agent? And I bet she is getting published in *Bamboo Ridge*. They *only* publish ethnic people. And she isn't even from here; she just looks like it! God dammit! This has ruined my night. Still feels good to write better than James Franco, though. She nailed me on that one. *Palo Alto* sucks.

4.

Like that time when he was five

Inside the trunk, the boy hollered hysterically until his voice felt like claws scratching his throat. He kicked the carpet-lined roof in the dark, suffocating room until his heels felt raw, and he pounded the metal behind the license plate until his small fists bled. He was exhausted and frightened, and confused and so thirsty. In between feeble kicks he listened, sweaty and still, for someone to come for him, but all he could hear was the faint sound of a stereo blaring music, flashing intermittently, and then muting again with the crash of a slamming door. *Skyscrapers bloom in A-MER-i-caaa, Cadillacs zoom in A-MER-i-caaa, Industry boom in A-MER-i-caaa, Twelve in a room in A-MER-i-caaa!...* CRASH! Tires screeched occasionally like violent screams, horns honked angrily, distant sirens rang out, footsteps squeaked. The boy had to use the bathroom terribly and was holding on for dear life. But hours passed, and he could hold it no longer, whimpering shamefully as he relieved himself, for surely he'd be scolded—slapped, most likely—when his mother discovered what he'd done. But where was she? He hollered into the black once more...

The boy was used to being alone, but he'd learned to pass the time, as all young children do. He'd always had a fascination with animals. With all the frustrated dogs, chained up, tied, barking and whining around him. With barely any other boys his age living in that settlement of tents on the beach, indeed, the animals were his only friends. From the mangy, scar-faced poi dogs to the needy bush-house cats to the mongooses and mother hens, the boy had company and, mysteriously, seemed to tame them. He'd wander over to neighbors' guard dogs yapping incessantly at the highway, and he'd caress their fat heads, quelling them momentarily. The animals would practically bow at his bare feet. He'd catch ghost crabs peeping from holes near the shoreline behind his shack and diligently inspect their fragile little bodies before placing them back into their respective caves. He had no pinch marks on his fingers, no dog bites or cat scratches on his arms, just a few fleas now and then crawling through his thick dark hair. A couple discolored tattoos from over-itched mosquitos bites spotted his olive little arms.

The boy was familiar with moving. Familiar with upheaval and panic and survival. Familiar with neglect. And being ignored. And being left. And being used. He was barely eight and there was already so much that he'd forced himself to forget. So many "that time whens" he'd had to purge from his mind like puss squeezed from a festering boil.

Like that time when he was five and auntie fell asleep at a Starbucks table while waiting for him to finish up in the bathroom. But he'd accidentally locked himself inside, the automatic lights cutting off, and he was unable to figure out how to get the lights back on. An employee finally heard his frantic sobs through the break-room walls, bringing the key to unlock it, only to discover him crumpled on the floor by the crack of light shining through the foot of the door, eyes bloodshot, literally dry from crying them out. And the woman—still facedown at the checkerboard table, oblivious to the commotion.

Or that time in first grade, when the boy itched for months until the school nurse took him to a physician at Queens Hospital, who discovered that the boy had scabies and who knows how long he'd been living with the condition untreated. Or that time just last year when an uncle snuck him into a UH basketball game and used him to retrieve the spare change and any other fallen effects that dropped behind the rows of seats in Stan Sheriff Center. How by the end of the night he could barely walk, his knees were so bruised and scraped from crawling down the narrow aisles.

Or that time when they stayed at an auntie's house in town. How she took sick pleasure in flicking him with a formidable middle finger in the center of his forehead every time he tried to climb up on the couch to watch TV next to her, or attempt to snuggle up by her feet, or when he'd laugh at a funny part in the show, or more or less make a peep at all in her stern presence. Or that one time when they finally got into transitional housing out at Barber's Point, and just when the boy began to sleep soundly and feel a modicum of comfort, they were kicked out because Uncle got caught stripping the copper wire to sell off-property.

Or that time last year when that goofy man from Big Brothers Big Sisters would come out each week for a couple months with his cousin's Big Sister. How even though the boy wasn't remotely a part of the program, they would include him, take him on excursions to Makaha Beach, and bring him lunches each time. How the man always had an ukulele with him and even free-styled a rap about the boy that would make him collapse with laughter every trip. How just when he thought maybe he would keep coming back—he didn't.

But he had a home, or at least that's what he believed it to be, even if it was one that took in rain like a leaky ship with every storm, along with rays of light every hour before dusk. And occasionally, the woman who had placed him in that trunk was near him in that home, next to the man who was driving. Mostly, they were gone and he was not taken with, but sometimes, just sometimes, they were around and they'd notice him in the room he mistook for a home, where he could hear the sea pulsing nearby, dogs yapping, and footsteps just outside the thin walls, crunching through the gravel and kiawe brush. He'd crawl between the two at night on their pitiful, filthy futon, flattened by years of bodies and even heavier souls. They'd be asleep, or in and out of it, surrounded by paperbacks and VHS sleeves. Surrounded by blackened, burnt spoons, random syringes, and countless neon BIC lighters, some still glow-ing red at the metal mouth. He would crawl in between these perspiring zombies, who were numb, motionless, or moving like sloths. The boy would ask Uncle to put on the TV, the remote lost somewhere in the pile of shit, and they'd turn to him in slow-mo and sigh and shake their head. So the boy would settle for the nook between two damp bodies. And somehow, that was enough.

In the morning when he'd wake up, he'd smell like cigarette butts and heroin sweat, but a morning smelling like that meant that they had come back to him. It was a deranged and fleeting kind of "family time" that he'd look forward to, sometimes for weeks. That nook was all the boy had. Lying there in that trunk, in his own fear and urine and sweat, the boy imagined that space between those two. He imagined the animals, the dogs and the way their eyes squinted when he scratched their dusty necks. He thought of the lizards he'd find that would magically change colors in his small palm—that would happily surrender when he'd pet their small, pale bellies. The boy began to breathe slower and thought of the sea near his home, how it seemed to breathe, too, rushing up the beach, then back out again. He waited calmly, hearing voices echoing off the walls outside the trunk. He waited.

5.

"Fakah, you telling me you hate La-La Land?"

Underground, in the valet key room, beneath the lobby of the Waikīkī Sands Hotel, Kainoa Carrera is dancing and singing. He shimmies, snaps, sways, and spins to a song that sounds vaguely familiar in the neon-lit, windowless office much too small for his frame. Some try-hard DJ on the college radio station has suddenly decided to divert from her normal avant-garde, indie-pop playlist, and is now airing *West Side Story* in its entirety. Ironically, I think. I pass by on the way to a car and see Kainoa flailing his arms, reenacting a fairly intricate, choreographed routine. And closer to the door, his voice a falsetto, crescendoing in sync with the play, simultaneously at war with the ancient A.C. unit attached to the office, which moans incessantly like a dying animal.

Most hotels with a valet service have these valet office-*cum*-key rooms. Not to be confused with Security's office…which we don't share a space with. Christ, that'd be painful. I mean, you think valets are rough, pretty sure the job requirement for security is: a pulse. And even that can be hard to prove. We've commonly referred to a few of them as "Bernies." You know, like, *Weekend at…* They're pretty talented at sleeping upright. Anyways, just as "all happy families are alike," so are most key rooms, designed to be the stopping base and safe haven for keys, with the crew in the lobby radioing down for outgoing guests. Besides a wall of hooks and keys, conditioned air that smells faintly like farts, a boombox, mini-fridge, desk, chairs and a couple *Maxim* mags—not much to mention. There was this one time, though, when an off-duty valet paid the graveyard shift guy to let him have the room for ten minutes to bang a Tinder date he just met. That ended horribly, as we couldn't get the stink out for days. People eat on their breaks in a key room too.

Anyway, while this apparent interest in art theater surprises me, Kainoa is also a tough cookie to crack. Pushing forty and denied a management, or even valet captain, position, due to a few too many accident report sheets, Kainoa usually isn't Mr. Sunshine at the workplace. In fact, he can be a moody son of a bitch. Blame it on the child support, I guess. But what's always kept me wondering about the man are those little blonde hairs. Certainly, I have heard of Kainoa's prowess in the dating field. A handsome Hawaiian-Puerto Rican mélange, on the rare moments he's forced to flash a smile at work, it brings the toughest of customers to their knees, and women of a certain age range to his beckoning will. I swear, the guy has some kind of fresh-divorcee radar device. But without fail, every single time I've worked with him, like some serial killer's calling card, entangled in the raven, gelled crew cut spikes, is a different, stray blonde hair. Evidence of a fresh kill. Varying lengths and textures, clinging to a different area of his scalp, so imperceptible you'd have to be quite close to him to truly notice. But for emphasis (and indeed he is one emphatic son of a bitch) Kainoa can be a bit of a close talker. So spotting those faint wisps of gold isn't too hard.

Assuming that he was just messing with me—some elaborate show so he could tell me how horrible the channel was—I swing open the door. "All right, all right, I'll change it," I say, throwing my hands up in defeat. "The station is bogus, I know…"

Most times, if the valets aren't absolutely loving the music I'm playing, then they're telling me how lame I, and the station, am, "*you sucking haole*." But before I can reach the button—

"BRAH! You know what dis is? Fah-king *West Side Story*! I LOVE dis shet!"

"Really?"

His expression turns from pure ecstasy to reticence, like a Rotweiller whose tail has suddenly stopped wagging.

"Bruddah, if could redo 'um again, aftah I wen grad from high school, I woulda tried out fo' Broadway theadah."

He inches closer to me, locking eyes to secure his point. He was getting emphatic again.

"All chru school on da Big Island, I wen join every single play and musical. 'Coz, I *loved* dat shet. *Cats*, *Phantom*, fah-king *Les Mis*! I felt like one *star*, bu."

Now, even closer, his hot Marlboro Menthol-ridden breath tickling my nose.

"You hea my voice?...Was *made* fo' dis shet."

"Totally," I agree.

"Coz, you watch *Glee*?"

"Is tha—"

"I watch *Glee* religiously. I heard you ask da kine what he like do if not one valet."

I guess this was my cue. He holds his stare and I can see a curly blonde...wait, is that a *pubic* hair clinging to his goatee? Christ, he gets a lot of play for a forty-year-old valet. I think for a moment on this. How does he wrangle this seemingly endless army of blonde, and/or peroxide blonde, women? What about this silver-tongued Puerto Rican titillates them so?

"I *said*, I heard you ask Palani what he like do if—"

"Right. Why, what would *you* like to do, Kainoa?"

"Fah-ken Broad-way, haole. Broad. Way."

"What, is your 'aumākua, like, Laurence Olivier, or something?"

"Nah, Lin-Manuel Miranda, you fakah," he snaps back. "And no get too comfy, haole, you cannot dis-respeck 'aumākua lai dat. *Reverence*, brah. Reverence." He toe-spins away from me, shifting attention back to the boombox.

"You hear dat shet?! MEAN, bah!"

I could see the dream bubbling within him, his six-foot two hundred-pound frame practically vibrating with excitement. "BRAH. Das what you should do!"

God, what.

"What?"

"You writing one book, ah? Fuck dat, make 'um one *play*! Brah, da kine *Singing Valets*—fo' Broadway! Mean, yeah?"

I hate theater. Hate plays, hate musicals, hate slam poetry, spoken word, hate all that crap. And it's hard to hide your disgust sometimes. Hard not to think to yourself, *I am surrounded by idiots.* But that's just it—here I am, running for cars just like him. Dreams and laments, just like him. I slip out of the door as he stares at the stereo, entranced by the song, by the story, the production, the stage and spotlight. By visions of actors snapping and dancing and spinning on an imaginary set in his head. And shit, if done right, maybe *Singing Valets* would make a great play. I mean, seriously, how was his dream any more absurd than mine? Who was I to judge?

"Bruddah. I see da stinkeye you stay geeving me inside," he says before a long, serious pull on his vape pen.

What, is this guy clairvoyant or something? I stop and spin around to give him my attention.

"If you not goin' write one book, and you not one actual teach-ah yet...try write one scrip wit me, you frickah."

"I told you, I *hate* musicals, Kainoa."

"Fakah, you telling me you hate *La-La Land*?"

Got me.

"Das what I taught, bu!" he says, with a pull so hard that the glowing electronic device begins to wheeze. "Listen. Even if you no like da kine—musicals—fakah, I jes trying for geev you one...impotence."

"You mean *impetus*?"

"Das what I said, haole. Write me one scene or sum-ting so I can act 'um out, den we run some lines lai dat. I dunno bout chu, but I going be one actah…what-chu like be?"

"A writer? But, like, full-time?" I reply, which comes out more like a question. How telling.

"So harry up, den, you frickah!"

Kainoa steps outside the key room shortly after me, half-humming, half-singing "*Ev-ery-thing free in A-MER-icaaaa…*"

Maybe it was somewhere around the eightieth rejection letter from a literary agent, or when my last classmate moved off the rock to get a real job—something I'd never really brought myself to do—when the dream started to slip away. Because it's easy to trick yourself out of dreams in paradise. Why leave Eden when you're pulling in close to six figures and showing, like, *three* on the books? But that was obviously my failing: the not leaving. It wasn't the rejection letters or slush pile that discouraged me. It's knowing that anyone here that wants to be anyone, or at least succeed in any creative field, must exit the Garden, naked and bewildered, dick in hand. It's the bold that leave and take chances over the Pacific. Sure, not everyone makes it, I've seen plenty come home with their tail between their legs, but I've also seen most of my classmates make 100K more than me because they've taken that chance. They've been able to come home precisely because they watched these islands fade away beneath the cumulonimbus clouds by not dilly-dallying too long after an undergrad.

And me? Maybe my window to leave has shuttered. Maybe the glass jalousies have fogged with sea mist and flipped shut. Closed. Kaput. Sure, I was still submitting here and there, but how many years in a row can you write about Kaka'ako's burgeoning street art scene, well... before it's inevitably torn down and developed? If those that cannot do, teach...Because it wasn't long ago that I remember wanting to go Thoreau on this scene. I once wished to "live deeply and suck the marrow out of life," and somewhere along the way, my metaphorical woods became a concrete parking lot. I used to get a hard-on just seeing two hundred words of my own (at ten cents a piece) printed on a page, and now I'm tricking sophomores into doing my grunt work.

Where are my woods?

6.

"Was one ex-tra or-din-ar-y experience, yeah?"

It's not like I actively try to isolate myself from the other valets, we're just into different shit, I guess. I'm definitely the social appendix of the crew at the various hotels and venues. As in, I can work perfectly within the group, but without me they're just fine. Hell, I might even be the tonsils. They definitely don't ever consult me when it comes to sports or MMA; they know I'm clueless in those departments. I don't own a vaping device. They see me reading *The New York Times* on break and go, "Haole! You pay tree dollahs fo' dat, an get da *Advertiser* fo' free at da bell desk? Smart, ah you…jack-ass!" I mean, technically they're right, but if I had to explain how you just don't get the same A. O. Scott film critiques in the *Honolulu Star-Advertiser*, I'd get a palm to the skull.

So, fine, they'll go out for drinks after work or make plans to catch a game at Yard House, and I'm normally not invited. Or they'll go dirt biking or drifting or diving, and I won't receive that call. It's not even because I'm a haole; that's honestly never it. It's all the little things I can't help doing that alienate myself from them. Sure, I'm always part of their conversations, our working relationships are strong. It's more my changing the channel from the Jawaiian music station to college radio to catch the bossa nova hour or plugging in a "Waking Up with Sam Harris" podcast episode that irks them. Reading W. S. Merwin poems and biblically thick short story anthologies in the key room on lunch break. Or asking a restaurant patron who pulls up with NPR on, "Is that Liszt's 'Un Sospiro'?" You could call it nerdy, but let's call a spade a spade—it's pretentious.

I swear I'm not fishing for sympathy, but there's always that disconnect. I'm not playing Nintendo DS at the valet stand or checking my iPhone for the spread or watching a Worldstar brawl or whatever the hell else some of these guys do to kill time when there's three hours between the dinner "in" and "out." I'm boning up on French and seeing what's new in *The Paris Review*. Geek-ass stuff like that, left over from my U of H days that still turns me on. Maybe the sad part is that I'm over a decade past those "days" and still clinging to some persona that was never actually realized.

A visiting Japanese family squeezes into their rental car, being seen off by another family, standing respectfully in a neat and smiling row. They do their bows, and the mother buckles her infant into the car seat, and then gets in and sits next to her baby. *Every* visiting Japanese family from Japan does this: the mother *always* sits next to the infant in the back seat. The other family sees them off and watches diligently as they pull away. They watch and bow until the rental makes its final turn out of sight eight blocks down the road. And somehow, this is beautiful.

"Fahkin Japanee fah-kahs no tip me, brah," fumes Gene, pacing in frustration. He punches his palm menacingly, his personal method of catharsis.

"Japanese from Japan never tip, Gene. How is that a surprise to you anymore?"

"Haole, you gettin smaht o' wat? Bumbai, I goin' stick you, coz." He throws his forehead at me, and I flinch. Then smiles, brings me in for what I mistake is a hug, but becomes a pressurized rear-naked chokehold.

"I'm just saying...I'm not surprised, that's all. And I think it's cool how the moms always sit next to the baby, you know? Americans never do that shit."

"Yeah, prolly moa safe, ah? Da mom was hot, but yeah?"

I make a gesture between a nod and a shrug.

"Haole, you evah been wit one mom still nursing?" asks Gene, switching gears.

"No, definitely not. I haven't really been with any older women."

"Brah, girls nevah gotta be old fo' nurse, dummy."

He's absolutely right.

"That's true...Soooo, lemme guess, you've been with a nursing mother."

"Yups, plenny-times. Jus' last night even. Was so *mean*! Dis girl I been seeing, she live Vegas, yeah? But she stay visiting right now, and stay at one hotel room off Kuhio."

"Uh-huh..."

"And so I go ovah dea last night, and we boning,

yeah? But she on top, jus' *riding* me," he says, thrusting his pelvis, eyes closed, one hand on his chest. Some hotel guests are approaching, a young hipster-couple, visibly perplexed at the gestures Gene is making.

"Okaaay," I say.

So aftah little while, I go fo' grab her chi-chi, yeah—all big from breast feeding, yeah? So, I go grab 'um, and day staht fo' squirt all ovah my face, and I was all—*whooooaa*!"

Gene shakes his head as if being sprayed with a garden hose. He spins around, as if he'd sensed the couple coming, switches tone and greets them warmly, "Well, good afternoon, sleepy heads! Brunch to beach, huh, folks? Last name: Del Monte, am I right? We'll swing that pony around in a second!"

The couple smiles back and the girl wearing what appears to be an ironic muumuu digs through her purse for a tip.

Gene turns to me and finishes. "But den aftah couple seconds was like, *yeah…mean*! And I jus' let 'um squirt all ovah me! Was one ex-tra or-din-ar-y experience, yeah?"

I'm losing it, doubled over in hysterics, barely able to keep it together in front of the waiting couple. And I can tell through Gene's vivid pantomiming that all the bell-men, even some of the taxi drivers lingering in the lobby, know exactly what he's talking about, too.

The way the boys can turn it on and off is pretty impressive. Every day I see Gene pull shit that'd make James Lipton start slow-clapping. And always in "the front," as it's known, what we refer to as the entrance/lobby of a restaurant, private estate, or hotel. "The front" is our goddamned stage. The front is *Inside the Actor's Studio*.

For instance, Gene'll be rattling off his usual bullshit to us, just totally into it, as if anyone wouldn't know what he was talking about just through body language. Like:

"Faaaahk, bu! Had dis chick da oddah night. Baaahhrr-rah! Just trying fo' work me out, you know what I mean, Hawaiian? And brah, was just da *meanest* Japanee chick, and she jus like bone *all* night, 'coz. An bruddah, was all-tired, but had to maintain, ah? Like aftah da second time, she still like fo hana hou, and I nevah knew what fo' do, 'cause I nevah like let her down, yea? So bruddah, had chopsticks laying around from L and L and I wen snap da chopstick in half fo splint my *boto*, like one broken fingah..."

Then turning to a guest, completely transitioning tone and dialect, tilts his head to the side and happily greets them, all teeth.

"Well, hello, Mis-ter and Mis-ses Rob-in-sonnnn," enunciating every vowel and consonant immaculately. "How was snorkeling at Hanauma Bay yesterday? Greeeat. Now, let me go and get that car for you. Oh! Did you folks need any travel directions or perhaps any dining recommendations?"

His enthusiasm teeters on condescending if it wasn't so heartfelt. And somehow he pulls it off. The best is when they're so impressed by Gene's service that they undergo that little internal battle you see guests go through—torn between feelings of shame for not tipping him and genuine obligation. So they'll kind of bring him in close and, under their breath, not knowing the exact protocol, ask, "So I'm terribly sorry, but what's the deal with tipping?"

Without a hint of irony, completely sincere, Gene'll reply, "Commonly five to ten dollars is the average gift..." Then, pausing to look in the air and 'carry the one' with a finger, "Yes, *definitely* that."

You see, as a valet you never tell anyone how much you *really* make. From lot to lot, a valet in the same company won't even tell another valet how much he or she makes. You don't even tell your friggin' mother. *Especially* if it's good. Those who ask are looked upon as spineless beggars. The question, *So what do you guys average on a night shift?* is interpreted as: "I know you guys are banking; let me in on it pleeeease!?" So really, unless you're a valet getting consistent shifts at the same spot, outsiders are given the same old, tired answer—a sour puss, ambiguous shrug, *Ah, kinda depends...*or *Mmm, well, ya know...* Or plain lied to, as in *Ho, shetty, bu. Like barely break dollah* ($100). And in actuality, $200-300.

"*Haole!*" shouts Palani, stepping into the key room. He says it like he'd say "*Boo!*" to scare a child. That child is me, though.

"Yeah, 'Lani."

"Fakah, no call me dat. I get one auntie name Lani, jack-ass. Eh, you park da Gypsy caddy dat came in here?"

"Nope, Kainoa did. And I think it was a local couple going to the Sea Bird for happy hour, not Gypsies."

"Brah, I swear I seen Gypsies come in dat car, bu. Ting almost nevah wen start, yeah?"

"I dunno, it sure sounded ratchet."

"Da car been hea past tree hours, but make sure you catch the charges, haole."

There's a three-hour-max validation limit for parking

non-hotel guest cars with us. After that, it's $5 an hour with a $30 cap. "Yeah, I'll make sure they cough it up."

"No park da Gypsies, haole. Dey no like follow da rules!" he clarifies.

"And we do?"

"Dey no like follow *our* rules, I mean."

Sometimes, you can hear the valets peeling out in the garage beneath the hotel lobby, ten feet above them. Not all the time, but sometimes you just need to feel something. We'll punch the gas to hear the engine roar. To hear the scream bounce off the concrete walls. Off the parked cars and through the dusty gray pillars. Feel that stationary tipping point of acceleration as the cars wobble from side to side, tires spinning, breathing smoke before we hit the brakes. Before any control is lost. Sometimes, we'll just floor it on a ten-yard-long straightaway. Committed. Pedal to the metal, RPMs teetering, quivering in that 7/8 red zone. Feel the sink of your body, the gravity pulling you backward into that leather seat, all the while accelerating. Sometimes you just need to feel *forward*. Until you punch the brakes to feel the jolt and bite of something more powerful than yourself.

To smell that chemical intercourse between rubber and concrete. We burn out just to *feel* something. Pull an e-brake to hear a rental car shriek, maybe even scream along with it. We aren't ruining any property, just test-driving its limits. These rentals are arrogant and tease us with that new car scent. They must be put through our initiation.

They are wild horses that must be broken. Feral dogs that must be tamed. Brakes are meant to be kicked. Pedals are meant to be stomped. A machine is made to be operated. To shape-shift. To become a blur.

We are underground. We are robotic. Zombies. Move cars, take tips, hear numbers, move cars. Repeat. It is a strange role and these garages are filthy. The constant exhaust and fumes. These vehicles are clean and sleek, but always excreting, burping, farting gaseous waste. They leave their excrement, that black film on the ceilings and walls of the lots, like toilet scum on a porcelain bowl. They leave their dust on my lungs, in the creases of my uniform. On this island these hotels, these parking lots, these caverns are its hidden hells. *Pave paradise, put up a parking lot...* And I work to sustain it. Shuffling the vehicles that carry the people that keep these hotels occupied and running. Thriving. We shuffle the vehicles that these guests drive around the island like lice infesting a body. I enable the blood sucking. I shuffle my own car to work to shuffle more. I understand this tragedy and have no conviction to change it. We are underground. Literally, underground and this complacency has become a livelihood.

I sit. In the seat of a stranger's car. And the stale, recycled air of the A.C. blasts its icy breath upon my blank stare. Ever so softly, the preset Hawaiian music station plays a tune. *I saw you in my dream...we were walking hand in hand...on a white...sandy beach...of Hawai'i...* But at the moment Bruddah Iz sounds like a song that authorities blare into a house full of perpetrators to smoke them out. My thoughts go numb. My body recedes into itself. I am liquid, sinking, further and further into the sponge of monotony. A moving sponge in idle, with gleaming rims and a new car scent. I begin to transcend. I feel as if I'm not moving forward, but just floating in place as the image of the car lot passes by me. The fluorescent lights float above my head like distant moons. Cars on both sides, reversed in stalls like soldiers waiting. What is my role in life? To move a machine fifty meters away from point A to point B, then a few hours later, from B back to A? The empty stalls, and the corners of darkness where the glowing moons don't reach. Concrete pillars streaked with the smears of misjudged turns like mottled blood stains. Like homicide. It all floats by me. To be sitting and still moving forward. To be moving forward and going nowhere.

Time passes. Seconds, minutes, hours, *years* in these cars.

I tell the students that I will "awaken" them with fine writing. By creating something *living* with their words. But am I even truly living myself?

I reverse instinctively into stall 302. I shove the shifter into park, still numb, and turn the keys counter-clockwise, drawing out this redundant ritual. In the distance Gene's shouts bounce off the walls like dog barks.

"*Wat bu?! You on stay-cation?! Harry-up haole, we get one rush!*" he says, trudging up the exit ramp, finishing a cigarette. And once again the vacuous silence from the inside a parked car.

And then a kicking…

Bmmf, bmmff…Bmmff, bmmff…

7.

Cough it up

A drawn-out, collective sigh reverberates through the classroom. The sound, like the roar of a seashell pressed to an ear, intensifies with each student that has caught onto the gig, all trying to outdo one another's distaste. The noise tapers off quickly, punctuated by various fart rips from a few jokesters in the back.

Behind me, evidence of a half-baked but earnest lesson plan on "Being Specific" clutters a white board in red and green dry-erase marker. Handwriting that vaguely looks like graffiti tags on the side of a subway car. They were supposed to read designated chapters from Tim O'Brien's *The Things They Carried* for homework, and today we made lists of items we carry in columns on the board labeled "tangible" and "intangible." Through this, were we figuring out what was considered concise and vivid in our writing, or vague and abstract. I'd lost the plot myself, so naturally we slipped into my "anonymous writing block" to work the kinks out of a passage I'd been prepping over the weekend.

"Okay. So, what's that? The writing? You're not into the writing. What's wrong with it?"

Ikaika throws up a hand, heavy metal devil horns, actually.

"Yes, Ikaika."

"It's not the *writing* really, more the narrator's, like, *attitude*, or something."

"What about his attitude?" I ask.

"Gawd...*Everything*. Or just mostly his, I dunno, naivete?"

"Wait? What?" I say, probably too defensively.

"Like, he's just this judgmental, entitled WASPy character, and we're supposed to *relate* with him, or, like sympathize with this hero?"

"*I'm a white dude and it's rougher than I thought it'd be for me out thereee*," whines Ikaika sarcastically, in a seemingly rehearsed five-year-old throwing a tantrum voice.

"*Yeah, how come they don't hand me the world any moreeee*," whines Kaito, the trend catching on far too quickly.

"*Awww, I earn higher wages than women for no reasonnnn*," wails a girl from the back.

"*Awww, I have a bachelor's degree but—*"

"Yeah, yeah, guys, we get it, but I think this is less about race and gender and more about mediocrity and how disabling it can be. And, how prevalent that is in this protagonist's or even *your* generation. And *why*."

"Meh," he shrugs and jacks off the air with an empty fist, a gesture that's now equated with "not buying it."

"From what I'm gathering, the speaker's an educated, white, able-bodied male. So like, what's his excuse? The guy's got, like, HBO *Girls* syndrome."

A hand flares up from center field. Travis. Kind of the class clown; it could be hit-or-miss with this one. As in, I usually try to ignore him and wait for Ralph to save the day. I was desperate to change direction, though.

"Yes, Trav."

"Well, what I want to know is," he pauses for effect, "do they make that shirt you're wearing in an adult size, because personally I really like it, but I've grown out of a youth-large, like, two years ago, and..."

The crowd goes wild. Goddammit. I glance down. I suppose it was a little tight. It's *slim-fit*, for crissakes!

"Hilarious, Travis. Hilarious," I nod.

The bell rings and the kids are frantic again. A few *yes*'s and *finally*'s ring out as the students scurry from the room.

"Just remember one thing, class!" I holler. "'Lovers and madmen have such seething brains, such shaping fantasies, that *apprehend* more than cool reason ever comprehends!' At this midsummer juncture, be that lover; *be* that madman!"

"Yeah, yeah, Shakespeare, we get it..." they retort, a couple yelling out "*Suck-a-diiiickkk!*" before escaping from view. Typical.

Not a bad class. Not bad at all, I reflect, grabbing the eraser to wipe away the chicken scratch from the board. I'm thinking next class we could get into "The Iceberg Theory," maybe read a little "Hills Like White Elephants"... I feel eyes on my back and turn to see that

Ralph has hung back, watching me. With a strange look on his face that I can't quite decipher...

"Hey, Ralph, what can I do for you?"

"Um, well...I was perusing a website last night..."

Aw, goddammit. I knew this moment would come. I was being too damn careless, flying too close to the sun. Shit. Shit. Shit. How would I *not* expect a prep-school kid to browse a local lit-site or two?

"Alohafiction or Ninth Island, or something-dot com— some local lit blog, and...I saw my story."

"*Your* story?"

The First Lady

On a warm and blustery midweek night, just two blocks from the water on Kaneohe Bay, an aging two-bedroom, one-story home dozes in its lot. On this night, like most nights, the salty trade winds whip off the shallow bay and dance among the houses and plants. They rock the traffic lights and avenue signs to and fro, dangling in the business district. The coconut trees banded with their silver bracelets arching high above the house rustle and shake. The louvers on the glass jalousie windows cloud and frost from the sea-coated breeze. The scent of plumeria flowers blossoming in the front yard wafts in, mingling with the smell of the briny Pacific and just a hint of foul sewage mixed in there too from the nearby treatment plan. But only a hint.

The four young boys snoozing in one of the rooms, on separate bunk beds, on opposite walls, don't smell these familiar scents. Nor does their dozing father in the adjacent room, his snores like intermittent dirt bike blasts accelerating somewhere in the distance. No one in the household smells these smells or hears these sounds, but Miriam Tanaka, a pudgy working mother who tosses and turns, anxious and hyper-conscious despite school and carpool duty the following morning. Beside her, her round husband, Wendell, twitches unknowingly. Lying on her side, she reaches her free arm out and rubs his boar-haired, broad shoulders. He purrs a little, a low, gurgling, animalistic sound in the darkness. Miriam gives her husband a soft kiss on the back, sniffing the faint odor of mechanic grease, or was it tire rubber? *Still smells like Napa*, she thinks to herself. No matter how hard Wendell scrubbed, it was never totally gone. They had two too many kids for what he earned. *Lucky his parents passed us down this house.* Somewhere in the neighborhood a car whooshes down a quiet street and the night sighs. Miriam sighs too and looks up toward the ceiling. A gecko waddles above her, clinging to the paint, digits fanned. It chirps loudly into the unknown, the staccato call echoing through the room and hall. Miriam contemplates an endless list of to-dos she needs to accomplish tomorrow, most of them by 9:00 am. But she calms herself, as she does often, by thinking of a place and time. By thinking of him...

She was a Punalani grad—she'll always have that. That, and that one night. She was kind of a catch back in high school. Well, she could choose. She remembers seeing him around campus at first, even going to a couple of the games to watch him play. Nothing special, but not terrible either. Just a little ironic that some of the haoles and a few Asian kids could outplay him.

Then visions of the '79 Spring Formal flash through her mind. Teenagers dancing with hair too big, pant bottoms too belled, minds a little too hazy off pot and swiped liquor. *What's she got that I don't?* thought Miriam. She pictures herself in those regal blue and black designer gowns that grace the covers of *People* and *Us Weekly*. Miriam pictures her own raven hair done up like hers. Pictures herself under him, teenagers again. Him digging, digging, sweat from his neck and brow dripping into her eyes. She, grasping his dark back, receiving those rhythmic motions, fingers splayed, like the gecko clinging above her. She sighs, breathy and exhausted, exhaling *ooooohhhh...Baaa-rr-rryyy*, and somewhere a car whooshes down the street, into the night. And now nails, clawing at his glazed shoulders, tearing at his satellite dish-like ears. His throat bending backward into oblivion, lips vaguely parting. The Washington Monument, erect and reaching on Capitol Hill. A big-boned, utterly striking woman standing beside him, on a Japanese airport runway, somewhere in Europe at a diplomatic dinner, in Chicago at the inauguration in front of a billion people kissing him like she was the only one who ever had.

Too cold, D.C. in the winter, she thinks with a surety that only an unsure mind could ever contrive. Was that above New York City or below? If above, then definitely too cold for her.

It was just a one-time thing. And just weeks later she had met

Wendell, a public school rebound (pretty exciting for a private school girl), and just months after that, graduation. Just in time to don an ivory robe scarcely loose enough to cover the small bump that was her first son, Barron.

The moist, saline trade winds whip through the screen and lick her bare thigh and forearm uncovered by the Ross sheets. Her skin forms goose bumps and Miriam shivers. The moonlight illuminating the room flickers with each racing cloud that hides and reveals it. Barron was dark, much darker than her other three sons, but Wendell was over a quarter Hawaiian. Or was it an eighth? She was a little unsure, and Miriam often wondered, *what if?* Miriam's thoughts steadily ease. She drifts out of consciousness. The palm trees above her tremble, and even a passing shower swirling off the towering Ko'olaus pelts the old roof of their home like a soft, fading drum roll. Almost involuntarily a mantra flows through Miriam's mind as she finally lets go and surrenders to the night. Something very certain, even more so than their family, than their livelihood, than this house. *I was his first.* He told her so. *I am the first one. Me. I am the First Lady.*

"Yea, Ralph abou—"

"And I just wanted to say thank you…Thank you so much for publishing me online. I mean…how flattering…But…"

"Uh-huh," I reply evenly.

"But I think you accidentally put *your* name as the author."

"No…*Ohhh*—you know what must've happened? The website assumed the contributor who posted it—me," I say, "was the same as the story's *author*…and…Dammit! I could've sworn I put *by Ralph Saito*. I am so sorry, these frickin' websites, you know?"

"Oh, no…mistakes occur, right? I mean, honestly I'm just so thrilled by all the positive feedback the story's getting. I think people are really enjoying it, judging by the comments, right?"

"Um, yeah...definitely." I couldn't quite tell if he was so sheltered and green that he was buying the "mix-up" or not. "So, I'll get that cleared up tonight, then, Ralph. And again, so sorry about that."

"Oh, not a problem...And...I think there's a couple other sites that you need to 'clear' things up with as well."

I smile and feel myself nodding way too many times for a person that isn't insane.

"So. How are we going to handle this?" Ralph's brow furrows, his jaw clenching. The mood in the room suddenly shifts.

"What do you mean?" I ask.

"Brah, don't play dumb wit me. I mean, how you've been *stealing* my work and publishing it under your name."

Brah? Ralph spoke Pidgin English? Where did my compliant star student go? My poetry-loving protégé?

"Listen, Ralph, I swear—"

He raises a finger and stops me cold. "That it was an accident, right? How dumb do you think we are?"

"I don't—"

"That was a rhetorical question," he snaps.

Well, there goes this job.

"The first time, I admit, I thought it was a mistake or something. But it's been like, what—two or three times now? Is that, like, your *thing?*"

Probably about five times, actually. I swallow hard.

"Listen, Ralph, I can explain."

"Nah, no need. How. Are. We. Going. To handle this?"

I do not like this new Ralph. Not at all.

"Well, how do *you* want to handle this?" I peep.

"Well, obviously I'm blackmailing you."

I nod.

"What do you want, Ralph?"

"Well, first I want you to take it down."

"Done. Easy," I chirp.

"I'm not finished yet. You still owe me."

"Ralph, I—"

"I have all the proof I need for the dean: the date and time of the original Word doc I originally sent to you. I want the money you've made off my stories, every one of them that was published, both in print and online."

"Ralph. That might be a total of, like, eighty bucks. And I'm being generous on that one. Small-time editors don—"

"Then cough it up," he says, extending a splayed palm.

"What, like, *now?*"

"No, Q4—*yes*, now!"

I retrieve my wallet and flip through a wad of ones and receipts.

"Ralph, I'm sorry, but most of it'll be in ones and fives—"

"What are you, stripping on the side?" he scoffs, shaking his head.

If he only knew.

"Just bring the fricken' money tomorrow, jackass. In big bills. That *specific* enough for ya?"

Ralph spins away on his toes and leaves the classroom. No, I do not like this new Ralph one bit.

8.

"I tink we get one situation, Hawaiian..."

Bmmf...Bmmf.

The sound is so close. Could it be coming from inside *this* car? Snapping out of my daydream, I pull the lever by my left ankle and hop around to the rear bumper. Nothing.

Bmmff...Bmmff...Bmmff...

The sound is coming from the car beside me. From the meth head couple's car, who parked for the restaurant at the beginning of the shift. I grab the trunk door, but the car is locked.

"GENE! PALANI! HEY!" I yell toward the valet office from a corridor in the lot.

Palani yells back, irritated. "Da frick you want, haole? Stay on da phone, coz.'"

"Get off the phone, Palani, and grab Public #302! Something...or *somebody's* in the trunk!" I holler back frantically.

"Ho, relax, auntie! I coming!"

Palani half-jogs over to me.

"Just press the fucking fob button from there!"

"Fakah, no need get—"

"Just PRESS it!"

He fiddles with the keys, the brake lights flash, and the trunk door levitates delicately, like steam rising off hot bread.

There, lying at the bottom of the trunk, is a small boy with one leg extended mid-kick. Then everything seems to freeze in the lot, everything but the sound of the boy's rapid breaths, his small chest heaving with every gasp. His wide brown eyes dart between us, confused, locked within his body, resembling a dog surrendering.

"Brahhh," utters Palani.

Kainoa strolls over to us, just having parked a car. "Chu guys looking at?"

"I tink we get one situation, Hawaiian..." replies Palani.

"Hah?" Kainoa peers into the trunk. "Ho, *nah*! Dis frickah stay lock inside da whole time?" he exclaims, shocked.

"Bah, I tink his maddah dem come in almos eight hours ago. Parked for da restaurant and nevah came back yet."

"Ho, dey going owe *plenny* charges fo' dis one, ah? Das like almos *terty* bucks pass time limit, ah? Chee!" Kainoa grins. He just can't help himself.

"Brah, you serious? What we going do about da kid? If dis not accidental, probably should call da cops, ah?"

We look closer and see a half-empty bottle of water that had rolled into the corner, next to a torn-open Snickers bar. The boy's mouth is smeared with melted chocolate. The trunk reeks of urine.

"I dunno. The candy bar, the water," I say, pointing in the trunk. "It looks like they left him in here on purpose. That's some serious-ass child abuse."

"Coz, das fahking psycho-lo-gi-cal damage," surmises Palani.

"Fo' reals. No can breathe too good in hea," adds Kainoa.

"Call Madero. He's an ex-cop; he'll know what to do. Kainoa, you parked this car, go into the Sea Bird and see if his parents, or whoever they were, are in there."

Turning to the kid, we could see his chest still heaving like a trembling puppy.

"You're okay, buddy. Everything's all right now," I say in my best talking to a six-year-old voice.

Palani reaches into the trunk and the kid finally breaks. He starts to sob, and at the same time holds out his arms to get carried from the trunk. Palani's got three at home, so I guess I shouldn't be surprised by how soothing he can be.

"No cry, boy, no cry. We getchu. You safe now, boy," he coos.

I watch the boy lock his arms around Palani's neck, rest his small chin upon his left shoulder, a tear-streaked frown settling on his tired, broken face. The kid must be exhausted—it was past eleven o'clock. I pull out my phone and call Madero, the Waikīkī Sands valet manager.

"Heeeyyy, Madero. Sorry, man, I hope I didn't wake you…Nothing's wrong, no accident. We just have a little situation over here at the Sands. We thought we should call you first about it…How are you?"

"Top shape, bu. Top shape," he mumbles, half asleep. That's his catch phrase (top shape)—which I absolutely love. "So what, something happen? Lost keys? Somebody wen crash?"

"Um…somebody left a kid in the trunk of a beater."

"Like one *keiki* kine kid?"

"Yeah. And they like *left* him left him. Like they're gone. Not in the restaurants, nowhere. It's been almost ten hours. I don't think they're coming back…"

Madero exhales and for a moment we share the violent white noise of his static-ridden sigh. "Bruddah, I not going come back tonight, you know I stay Kahalu'u side. But one of you guys—you, some-body—stay wit da kid and da graveyard-guy."

"Okay."

"Da car get plates an' registration lai-dat?"

"VIN number's scratched off, expired safety and reg. I'll look in the glove box for any more papers, but seems like the car's not legal."

"Fahk, bu. Das one situation, ah?"

"Yep."

"No call da cops yet, yeah? Jus' take care da kid. He all right?"

"I think so. They left him some water and a candy bar in the trunk—"

"Fah-kahs," he hisses.

"And he was pretty scared, but he doesn't look beat up or sick…"

"Kay, bah. I coming in first ting tomorrow morning. Tanks, ah, Hawaiian?"

"Yep."

I can hear Kainoa rounding the corner, coming down the garage ramp. He clomps toward me, shaking his head. "Brah. One waitress, Sherry, at the Sea Bird said one couple came in, ditched on da bill, like, four hours ago! *Had* to be dem, brah."

"Did you tell her about the kid?"

"Nah, just said dat dey left one shetty car wit us dat barely start. Dat we stay waiting for da owners. You told Madero yet?"

"Yeah, he said hang tight."

9.

She had to find a faucet

The owners of the 1987 Cadillac DeVille were certified pieces of shit. Not only did they abandon a vehicle with the Waikīkī Sands Hotel valet department, but they also bailed on their dinner bill at the on-site restaurant, the Sea Bird. And perhaps "inhabitants" is a better word than "owners" of the sputtering white Cadillac, since stained a grotesque blood orange from parking in red dirt and pineapple fields where the two would shoot heroin and pass out. A better word than "owner," because owning implies a degree of legality and the couple—a forty-two-year old Caucasian male and twenty-five-year old mixed-race woman—had neither title nor deed for the vehicle. Indeed, the car was purchased nefariously—cash in hand—and certainly, the car was on its last leg—Ford alternators—but they couldn't care less. The vehicle was merely a mode of transportation to score smack as well as a mobile shelter for nights in town. The man knew he couldn't flip the car on Craigslist, as he'd done with many others for tragically small profits. Whatever temporary fix he'd bought the DeVille with was wearing off completely, just like his high was, when the two of them slipped away from the building after politely asking for dessert.

Granted, this escape wasn't a difficult task, as the seats at the Sea Bird practically kiss the beach, with a four-foot barrier blocking them from the shoreline. Regardless, real pieces of shit. They'd ordered dessert after heaping surf and turfs (most of which the woman slid into her purse to squirrel for later), and when the waitress returned with a brownie à la mode—they were gone.

They booked it across the shoreline, west-bound, darting across Fort DeRussy park through the damp, just irrigated field that squished beneath their steps. They crossed Ala Moana Boulevard and followed the service roads behind the mall to avoid the HPD cops prowling the beach park. They took the back streets to Ward Avenue, slinking past the somber warehouses and miserable bars, onward along Halekauwila. The couple's bellies were full but they were fiending, a certain unending kind of hunger they'd come to live with, gnawing at them daily, propelling them forward, prompting every step, making every decision. Decisions like shedding dead—and live—weight from the mission. Even if that weight weighed forty-five pounds. Even if that weight kicked and screamed and clawed the door to get out. Even if that weight shared a hovel by the beach and DNA with one of them. They shed that weight and made the choice a junkie always does: get more. Naturally, they were going to Chinatown.

This meant passing the dozens of homeless Micronesians inhabiting the edges of Mother Waldron Playground. Passing that city block of tents and shopping carts, lean-tos and crying infants in that plain-sight slum, of sorts. They approached a stout mother of three from Chuuk who wore a dress down to her ankles, hand-embroidered with brilliant flowers and other traditional stitching. They traded her eight ounces of premium, luke-warm filet mignon and a scoop of garlic mashed potatoes for five cigarettes, as the woman had no narcotics. They left that bizarre favela lost in the city and continued down Queen Street, increasingly more desperate and, as always, dead broke.

There are modern nightclubs in Chinatown that sparkle and throb for their patrons. There's Manifest, and Tchin Tchin, Scarlet and Club Nextdoor. And there are increasingly pretentious haunts popping up every few months for the foodies. Restaurants with chic and shabby modern decor, spacious one-page menus and custom draft cocktails replete with well-aged small-batch bourbon. And there are the beat-up dive bars harkening a wartime era that collect the vast array of drunken scum. Smith's Union, Hank's, Amy's Place, Hubba Hubba. The dives with the giant stone-faced thugs with two braids policing the street and escorting the hookers and she-males. So many passed out and loaded, desperate doorway dwellers. Sidewalk sprawlers. Old deranged men, picking their infected scabs. And then there's River Street, with the huddled clumps of humans, tweaking on meth, sharing pipes and needles, eyes popping out of their greasy heads.

River is where the couple ventured, as they had many times before.

"Got any H?" asked the man.

"Twenty for a bag."

"No money," he said, glancing back and gestured to the young woman with hollow, lifeless eyes, "but she's down..."

She had to find a faucet to wet her mouth.

They split an eighth together in the nearby Zippy's bathroom. Two other couples waited in line behind them to do the same.

"*One Zip-Pac, extra mac*," sighed a tired voice over the open-lounge intercom.

The couple shuffled down Vineyard, took a side street to Beretania, and got to A'ala Park, where they fell asleep in the grass with the rest of the vagrants. In the morning the man awoke, but the woman wouldn't be roused, despite his nudges and prodding.

So he left her. He begged for change outside the nearest 7-11 and used the $2.20 to get on the No. 93 Wai'anae Coast Express. The young woman could find a way home. She always did, somehow.

10.

Sometimes the crowd just wants the hits

"Can anyone tell me what the author of this piece is telling us?" I ask. "What's he getting at? What's beneath the surface of this 'iceberg,' as Hemingway's theory suggests?"

Blank stares. Disinterest across the board. A couple gum-bubbles pop, piercing the silence like firecrackers behind mouths full of metal and ceramic.

"He's wondering, like, who's behind the wheel of this thing?" says Kawika.

"What thing?" I prod.

"Life, *duh*," snaps Kaito, out of nowhere, still looking down at his desk.

Totally thought he was zoned out and texting. Such an arrogant little bastard.

"So what, the narrator or speaker *isn't* in control?" I ask, drawing a rippled horizontal sea line across the board with a small triangle of ice poking through the surface, attached to a gigantic mass floating beneath.

"Well, he feels like he's not," says a kid mid-row.

"How does one lose control of his or her life?"

"You tell me, I'm just sixteen," frowns Emma, now suddenly concerned, eyebrows forming an upside-down V.

God, I love these little turds.

"Well, he says he's been doing the same thing for over a decade so..."

"Routine. Comfort. *That's* how one loses control. Getting too comfortable. They get numb," declares Kaito.

"Like the Pink Floyd song," I add.

"What's Pink Floyd?" asks...pretty much everyone.

"The rock band? *We don't need no ed-u-cation...? I have be-come, comfortably numb...?*" I sing. "No? Nothing...? Seriously?"

"This lesson plan's making my brain numb," snickers Kawika.

"What if there really is no true depth?" asks Ralph. "What if the tip of said iceberg is all there is, with no mountain beneath the sea?"

"All bark and no bite," adds Emma.

"Just the tip!" cries Kaito, collapsing in laughter.

That one catches fire and spreads across the room.

"Well, what would suggest that?" I ask, half-curious, half-terrified.

"I mean, the narrator has convictions and passions, I guess, but really no motivation," says Kaito. "Why, as readers, would we suspect him to change, or have any reason to reveal more?"

"That mutha-fuckah needs a wakeup call or sumthin'!" says Ikaika, doing his best, albeit racist, Samuel L. Jackson.

"And *what* exactly would he reveal?" says Ralph with a vaguely sociopathic smile.

"I'm not following, Ralph," I butt in abruptly. "Hemingway's Iceberg Theory is about the reader *implying* details and depth in a story through the strength of the writer's prose."

"Well, the Iceberg Theory is also known as the Theory of Omission. So what is the narrator omitting, or hiding, if you will, beneath that cute little tip?"

A few kids giggle and a couple even crane their necks, now unexpectedly interested in whatever it is Ralph is getting at.

"Umm, what's happening right now?" asks Kawika, for the class.

"Yeah, my cousin Robbie said he got to watch *The Big Lebowski* last year—when's *that* happening?"

"Well, ladies and gentlemen, I save The Dude for the second half of this course, but I was going to share with you a film today that's almost as interesting, and certainly as pertinent," I say, flipping on the projector and loading the DVD.

Sighs and groans of disapproval echo through the classroom. "Hope you twerps are ready for Nicolas Cage's career-defining role!" I holler.

Even they are puzzled. I dim the lights and the Columbia Pictures woman glows brilliantly through the darkness. The opening scene of *Adaptation* begins. I sit back and exhale.

"Now, I want you guys to take a look at three themes

here, okay?" I say, watching the screen, simultaneously digging through my bag for a sack lunch. I turn to my right and Ralph is hovering over my desk, obscured in shadows.

"*Jesus*, Ralph," I whisper, fairly spooked. "Ya scared me, pal."

"I could tell," he mutters back evenly. "It's fun to watch you squirm."

"Ralph, what was all that about anyway? I thought we were...you know—"

"Square?" he cuts me off. "Even? All good?"

"Yeah?"

"Eighty bucks not goin' cut it, brah," he hisses, switching accents again. "How much you got on you today?"

"Shit, Ralph, on a teacher's salary—"

"Puh-lease," he sneers, "I want the earnings from your *real* job. Cough up those singles, bitch."

"Ralph, what if I just help you publish this, like, with a solid university journal or review, and we can move past this like mature adults," I reason.

"Mmm, I'll take the cash instead, Nelson Mandela, but I appreciate your diplomacy. Poppa wants the new iPhone X come September."

"Ralph, I'm tapped out on—"

"I will rat you out so fricken fast if you don't put forty dollars in my palm, I swear to God."

"Fine, fine, fine, geez," I say, reaching into my pocket to find my wallet. "Can we just agree on a final price to end this charade?"

"It ends when I say it ends."

Nope. I do not like this new Ralph, one bit. And here I am, cat-fished by my own negligence. I'm definitely gonna need to pick up some restaurant shifts to get some work done.

"*Knock, knoo-oock...*"

Shit. Derek. My overly enthusiastic summer school director. The kind of guy that's still proud of the mustache he grew for "Movember" the following July. The kind of guy that actually says, "Knock, knock," at an open doorway instead of just knocking. When it rains, it friggin' pours, huh?

"Hey, Derek. What's the word?"

"*Nada mas, amigo.* Just checkin' in."

None of us are Latin, by the way. None of us speak nor teach Spanish. Another thing about him I loathe. He looks past me at the whiteboard, and his eyes scan what I haven't finished erasing.

"The Iceberg Theory again, huh," he says with a frown, stroking his pedophilic 'stache between his thumb and index finger. "Wasn't that part of your lesson plan last year?"

Of course it was.

"Sometimes the crowd just wants you to play the hits, am I right?"

"You know we gotta switch up the curric' each year, amigo. If the students notice a pattern, they'll sell the following year's class their course notes, and then you've got a room full of unenthused *estudiantes*, am *I* right?"

"But a graduated class full of savvy economists?" I retort, trying my best to weasel out of his trap.

"L.O.L.!" he says. Aloud. "But seriously. You can't recycle curriculum. Not at this school. How's that book coming?" A question that feels more like, *You feeling okay?* as of late. This goddamn day will not end.

"Coming along. Rewrites, revisions...You drop by for anything in particular, Derek?"

"Naahhh," he says breathily, like a lie. "Just want our students to be psyched. And teachers, too, of course. Are you psyched, *compadre?*"

"*Estoy* psyched."

"*Bueeeeeno, bueeeno,*" he says, licking the ends of his mustache by curling his tongue grotesquely over his upper lip. "You got a publisher for that book yet?"

"I've been shopping it around." I've been doing no such thing. "Why...you offering?"

"L.O.L.! Well, if you ever need any connections, I still know some people in the industry from my years at Northwestern."

"Thank you, Derek, I appreciate that. Listen, I'm gonna—I'm gonna go work on next class's lesson plan. You mind if I—"

"*Por supuesto!*" he erupts. "No more recycling, okay, *jefe?*"

I nod and slip through the doorway past him.

11.

Chemistry like You've Got Mail

The thing about flower girls is that they're not really selling flowers, they're selling pity. Just like valet parking, it's a totally superfluous job. Like, if a guy really wanted to get a girl a flower on a date, he should've had the class and foresight to buy one before he showed up, and then present said gift upon arrival. You know, like a friggin' gentleman. One would think. Just as if one needed to park a car, they'd just park themselves. Again, one would think...

"But this is the flower girl hustle. They find a location, usually one that's classy enough to hire...well, *us*. And then they'll arrive at designated times, say, during the middle of dinner, from 7:00-8:30, and then again later—midnight to two a.m. to get the guys that are nice and lubed up. They bat their eyes at our boys, who are suckers for flirts (shit, suckers for any girl with a heartbeat), and we park them for free. They're only in there for thirty minutes, so it's a mutual 'respect the hustle' favor we give them. Free parking for some fruitless flirtation. Then they get their bouquets together, hang that basket from the inside of their dainty little elbows, drop their keys on the desk (if we haven't already parked them), and saunter off, skirts just a few inches shy of their ass.

"Inside the bar, it's full-on 'Look for the Sucker' game, and flower girls are pros at it. They might feed you bullshit like, '*Listen, we're helping them find love.*' Or, '*We're getting those guys laid,*' but I'd really like to get an official 'bought flowers and got laid' statistic on that one, though. So they justify this bullshit job by dubbing themselves modern-day Cupids, but, c'mon! These girls have their 'insecurity radars' on as soon as they walk through the door. I swear, if they haven't first sniffed out the saps that are too drunk to say no to a beautiful woman urging them to buy roses for their equally as inebriated and vulnerable date, then they're doing the usual, which is looking for an awkward-ass couple on a first date, or awkward-ass guys in the midst of hitting on a stranger. *Just bought you a drink—and a rose while I'm at it? Sure, why not?* Just comprehend the implications of buying someone you just met a rose? The following expectations you've created for both parties? 'Cause even if you do buy one, the sheer symbolism is so goddamned layered and ancient, it sucks out any lightness and fun from a so-far-so-good-going first date. A trap by any other name, am I right?

"What's my beef? I dunno, it's just a parasitic job to me. Vampires in stilettos. They're like unlicensed, nomadic, snake oil aphrodisiac vendors. Temporary third wheels that roll into the middle of your conversation with a woman, offering you romance for an inflated price. It's like, I don't care about the gesture. I'm cheap and I was doing fine before you showed up and proceeded to ruin my game because my partner's too shallow to realize how forced this gesture actually is. Because therein lies the fallout: if one does refuse a flower, especially after glancing at their date and maybe mulling it over for a millisecond before brushing the flower girl off, that shit is the gorilla in the closet for the rest of the night. Your date just involuntarily switched from "your date" to the "girl you might like, but not *quite* enough to spontaneously buy a rose for." So literally, you're damned if you do and damned if you don't. No-thank-you-very-much, flower girl. That, or I'm just a cheap asshole."

"Are you finished?" asks Marisela.

"I've just started my thesis, babe. I've got at least three more courses of bitching left."

"I dunno, hearing this rant coming from a valet parker seems a bit 'pot calling the kettle black' to me."

"Just tell me one thing."

"What?" sighs Marisela.

"After you've made your, what, two hundred bucks? How do you sleep at night?"

"On a bed of crimson roses, misted by the dew that are the tears of joy from the women who just received them. You see, I collect those tears throughout the night, right here, in this little jar."

She reaches into her purse and pulls out the same hand—giving me the finger. I am officially in love.

"Didn't see that coming. Well played, madam, well

played. That cut-down was a little clunky, though. 'On a,' 'by the,' 'that are'—*really*?"

"Give me my keys, car boy. And just two hundred dollars? If that figure makes you feel better about yourself, then yes, I only make a whopping two hundred clams," she says, nodding dramatically.

"Give me your number," I say.

"My. Keys," she replies.

"Your. Number."

"Why on earth would I ever want *you* to call me? Oh, wait, do I get to be the chick in your acid flashback, the one where you buy me a rose?"

"Gimme your number…because I think this banter you and I constantly engage in is reminiscent of the chemistry between Tom Hanks and Meg Ryan in *You've Got Mail*. Minus the mail part. But, plus the battling professions part."

She smiles. A crack in the fortress walls.

"Wow, you're really reaching with that one," she says.

"My analogies are a bit of a tightrope walk. So what-tya say?"

"Umm…no."

"Buuuuut, you might want something that I have," I counter.

"Even if I used my imagination, I really could not possibly think of anything. What is it?"

"Leads."

"Leads? What kind of leads?" she laughs.

"Well, our company just picked up this new account. I've worked a few shifts there and, you know, cased the place. It's a hotel, at the end of Waikīkī, Diamond Head-side, with two fancy restaurants where I've seen *a lot* of middle-aged, recently divorced, upper middle-class men on first dates just *ooooozing* self-doubt and diffidence. And they'd be perfect clients for you…"

"Okay, fuck off and good-bye."

"Ah, c'mon. Marisela!" I holler. "Marisela! *No me vayas! Como me puedes hacer esto*?!"

Amid my outburst a middle-aged man flashes me a validated ticket in front of my face. "Can ya fetch my car for me, son?"

"Right away, sir, kept it nice and close for ya," I assure him, snapping into character. "You're a regular at the Sea Bird, right?" I say, greasing up this man I've never seen in my life.

"Uh, no…well, sort of? Thank you anyway, though, son. Those flower girls, huh?" he says, leering at Marisela strolling back to her car.

"Tell me about it," I mumble, shaking my head. "Sometimes I wonder why we even park them…Like, where do they get off?"

"Aw, I know why you park them," he mutters sleazily, with a tongue half out, raising his eyebrows like a perverted uncle. What a creep.

Only upshot when it comes to parking for assholes? They give you the tip *before* they realize that you just hot-boxed their car.

Flying up the exit ramp to do the loop back to the lobby, I notice Marisela waiting in her car at the top. She flags me down from the driver's seat; she's got a piece of paper in her hand. Well, look who the hell had a change of heart. She rolls down the passenger window and tosses me a creased valet ticket with a sly wink, then speeds away toward Kalākaua. I search both sides of the valet stub, but Marisela's just written three numbers.

Good form, madam, good form.

12.

Valets make good fathers?

Y ou see, one would think that the pure redundancy and mindlessness of parking cars would give a group of men a platform to think about something else. The lack of complexity or need for thought (we're literally moving vehicles from one place to another, usually, less than fifty yards away), the perfect place to ponder...I don't know, something of *worth*. That someone would step up and be that guy in those Cuban cigar factories whose job it is to read the workers rolling the cigars a novel to help the time pass in a more productive way. That, maybe, we could somehow take turns being that reader and elevate ourselves...

One would think, wouldn't they? But the reality, is that conversation among valets while working is about ten percent work, as in, the whole spectrum of job talk, from money to complaining about customers to shit-talking fellow employees to drooling over expensive cars, etc. And the other ninety percent? Sex. *Sssseeexxx.* The kind of sex where the "s" makes you drool it's so fused and basic and sloppy. Sex, sex, sex—a weird and wicked sex. Animalistic and primordial in its urges, yet totally human and vulnerable in its queries. A comical, humiliating, vicious, scratching, shaking, clawing, slurping, panting sex. Talk of fantasies and visions, dreams and recollections, of what you'd like to do to her, of what you'd like her to do to you. It's a never ending vulgar conversation, with every valet picking up where they last left off, regardless of the distance between shifts. Sacredly profane locker-room talk quoting scripture that can only be uttered among the other like-minded (extremely bored) and frenzied believers. Not to devalue the Greats of classical thinking, but perhaps it's a kind of deranged symposium. In true Socratic form, there are questions raised. Usually by Gene, who has a permanent smirk on his face like he's got a porno on loop in his head somewhere. Burning questions like:

If one girl tell you fo' blast inside her, but den she like straddle your face, and den da kine wen drip in ya mout—das not gay, yeah?

Not trick questions...but tricky.

If one chick you had from long time ago used to let you slam her in da okole hole, and all da chicks you met aftah dat, you only like do' um in da okole hole...das not gay, yeah?

This is the best we come up with. It is our anti-think-tank.

However, the sexual imagination of a valet is unparalleled. It's like that scene in *Hook* at the dinner table with Peter and his Lost Boys, but every valet shift is that scene, and instead of imaginary food, it's imaginary women, conjured into a likeness so vivid, it's just about real. Seriously, if any customer or guest truly paid attention to the valets at work, they might see what one would interpret as: (A) a brutal fight, (B) an interpretive dance, (C) copulation, or (D) all of the above. It's always D. Uniformed boy-men in high socks and tennis shoes thrusting pelvises into imaginary air-butts, grabbing the backs of air-hair and penetrating—with purpose. Expressions of ecstasy, or surprise, or Zen-like concentration, mouths drooling, forming the shape of perfect O's. Boy-men riding air-horses, whipping the air-ass of the beasts, galloping and galloping more frantically toward some imaginary climactic finish line. Boy-men humping hotel pillars and valet desks and bellmen looking the other way in plain sight. Boy-men licking air-babes, or probing air-loins, eating air-SPAM musubis and air-ice creams from air-women's rumps. Continually groping the pure nothingness in front of them.

Yet.

Yet almost *every* valet I work with has a steady partner of many years or married young, or is married and has children whom they break away to chat with on lunch breaks. Wives that actually come to work and visit them with their own mothers, parking with us while they go to the beach behind the hotel. Happy families waiting for daddy to get off (no pun intended) and relax with them. That same valet patting his children's heads still dripping from a beach day, kissing his visiting wife ever so gently on the cheek, who in between retrieving cars for hotel guests and restaurant patrons, returns to licking, prodding, and violating imaginary air-mistresses.

I personally don't know any valets with sexual assault charges attached to them, none with rape cases or anything, but Christ, do they have some oddly detailed stories about what they'd like to do to "dat chick over there." Stories that are a complete farce. A childish pissing contest encouraged and instigated by their air-humping peers. And yet, somehow, valets make good fathers?

I step into the Sands' valet office and the boy is sitting on the table by the keyring board. Palani's gifted him a bag of kakimochi, which he cradles in his arms and precedes to crunch away, every bite like a little page ripped from a spiral notebook. His legs swing, anxious and playful, off the edge. He sits with a relaxed hunch, like most little wiry kids do and his eyes scan the fluorescently lit, air-conditioned small room. He taps a row of keys on hooks and watches them swing back and forth. For spending over ten hours in a car trunk, he didn't seem especially rattled. Darwin, the overnight guy, has just arrived and is keeping a relatively cautious distance from our small visitor.

"You okay there, my man?" I ask.

He nods, still crunching with a look on his face like *why wouldn't I be?*

"What's your name, chief?"

"Not chief—*Jo-jo*," he says softly, shaking his head.

"Pleased to meet ya, Jojo," I reply, sticking out an upturned palm for a low-five, a bait he quickly bites, slapping my hand with a grin. "You're a brave dude, huh?"

His legs continue swinging, more confidently.

"Hey, D," I say, turning to Darwin, sticking out my palm again.

He offers a hand to me like someone begrudgingly giving change to a street bum. "Fine, yeah. I tink da boy make she-she, because smell...Dat your boy?" he asks.

"No, I'll explain in a second. Buddy, you thirsty?" I ask, opening the mini-fridge. "We got waaater...ice coffee... Monster energy drink, Red Bull energy drink, Rockstar energy drink, three Four Lokos, Bud Lights, a Sprite... aaaand, shit, that's it, bud."

He shakes his head, legs still swinging. "Passion-Orange?" he squeaks.

"Dis keed going have one birt-day soon?" asks Darwin, out of the blue.

"I have no idea, Darwin, we—"

"Because you know I one D.J., yeah?" He hands me a business card from his wallet. "An' I do birt-day parties, weddings, grad parties, any kine function. Saturday nights I get one show at Aiea Bowl. Dats why I never work graveyard sheef Saturday nights," he clarifies.

His business card reads *D.J. Double-D's*. (His name is Darwin Donata). Clever, and of course, always an innuendo. *Book for parties or any celebration. Call a week in advance.* In the bottom right quarter of the card is the image of a red Lamborghini, doors open and flared out like arrogant, flapping wings. Friggin' valets: always a side hustle.

While Darwin is kind of a weird dude, as far as graveyard guys go, he's actually pretty together. Most graveyard guys are fairly strange cats. Like, the way I see it, you either gotta be really desperate, on meth, or a little off to ever want to work 11:00 p.m. to seven in the morning. Darwin, however, actually does a hell of a job. A fair-skinned, fragile-bodied Filipino guy from Manila, he still carries a pretty thick accent. I can't tell if he moved here a year ago or ten. What bugs me about him, though, is how he always wears a bluetooth headset (for bookings, he'd point out), which is somehow acceptable for the graveyard guy, since he doesn't get too much contact with guests. But what *really* bugs me about him is how he always gives me one of those dead-fish handshakes whenever I arrive. You know the ones: no squeeze, just flaccid, soft cock in your palm. Downright insulting. I've even watched to see if it was just me. Watched others greet him and observe, in that split second of the hand-clap-to-shake, if he was squeezing at all with those dudes. I could never really catch it, and I never got the balls to ask any of the guys, because I know they'd all say the same thing, *Oh, yeah, always, bu. What, he nevah like shake your hand? 'Cause you one haole, das why. No can trust da haole, bu. I no blame heem, frickah going get smallpox, heem...* And then laugh their asses off.

"Sooo...Does Gene know what day da keed's birt-day ees?" asks Darwin with phone in hand, ready to log in the date and schedule a booking.

I motion for Darwin to step outside the key room with me, and I proceed to bring him up to snuff regarding our visitor's sudden arrival. He seems a little shocked by the news, but more concerned with the abandoned car than the actual small human abandoned within it. We step back inside and he looks at the board. He zeroes in on the Cadillac keys hanging off the hook and examines the time stamp.

"Ho! Dey come in at one o'clock and stay eleven

o'clock, now? Going be one big charge, ah?" he says, practically licking his lips. "I hope dey no come back and just forget da car, yeah?"

I tell Darwin that appears to be the exact situation.

The boy's legs stop swinging and he looks up at us, appalled. I shake my head and glare at Darwin.

"Oh, *heem* da kid?" he points out, gesturing to the boy with his phone. "Dey going come back, boy. You see." He offers his hand to the kid and introduces himself. "Darwin, brah, how you?"

The boy shakes the limp fillet of flesh that is Darwin's hand, and I swear I see the child frown. I *knew* it.

"Jojo, was it your mommy and daddy that brought you here in that car?" I ask the boy, as gently as possible. He looks down and his shoulders drop, his body slowly imploding. I reassure him everything's going to be fine, tussling his hair like a person pretending to be a "dad" in a game of charades. "Do you know where you live, Jojo?"

His chin begins to quiver uncontrollably, and he shakes his head, covering his face with his palms to hide his tears. His hands are dotted with chocolate Snickers residue.

Darwin, still holding the discarded Cadillac's keys, takes a look outside and down the lot's corridor. "Brah, dees car look fam-iliar…"

"I told you, it was some…" I mouth the next part, turning away from the boy, "*Junkie* couple's ride that skipped a dinner bill."

"No, brah, I swear I seen some of da Gypsies pull up in dees one before."

"Really?"

"I tink so, brah."

So, the Gypsies. Looks like one of their vehicles, but they'd never abandon kin in a car trunk. At least not the folks I know. Who are the Gypsies? Well, the first Gypsies I ever met and, I'm pretty sure became friends with, were at the Ala Moana Shore Hotel. A grandmother of one of the families rented a condo unit, and a few different families—I assume, related—would pretty much rotate in and out of the condo all year with the changing of the seasons or wind or stars or some shit. I'd let them park for a little while out front while they dropped their family off or picked up stuff from the unit. I'd talk story with them, kind of feel them out and try and figure what they were all about and into—without actually asking, like some geeky twelve-year-old, *"Are you a real, live Gypsy?"*

I dunno, I was just fascinated by them. How their people have been so romanticized and/or stigmatized through history, like Eskimos or pirates or something. Most of the valets can't stand them. For one, in a place like Hawai'i, where courtesy and respect are paramount in local culture, the Gypsies, well, they don't work that way. They're about as polite as a New York cabby with a hemorrhoid. Lotta times, just plain rude as hell. They usually slip by without dropping their keys, a big no-no among valets (we're *huge* control freaks). And if they say they'll be down in ten minutes, add on an hour to that. *"Eh, guy! You gotany spaceforme up front?! I'll be back in like fivetoten minutes, tops! Whaddya say, chief?"* And the valets will shake their heads "no-fucking-way" to me from a distance. Other valets have said Gypsies have accused them of damaging their previously dented cars or try and stiff you, even though, for the most part, they're great tippers—that surface wealth and flash, an ongoing part of Gypsy culture. Sadly, at most locations I've seen valets just flat-out tell 'em, "*Lot full*," and turn them away.

But somehow the Gypsies and I just clicked. I've been intrigued by them, by their mystique, ever since I was a little kid. That culture of nomads and horse dealers and fortune telling, despite that rep of thievery forever attached to them. Also, maybe when it came to the workplace, I felt like I was a bit of the social appendix within our valet body. And maybe the Gypsies, a little-known ingredient in Hawai'i's bubbling cultural melting pot, were treated like the world's ethnic appendix.

Whatever the case, I let 'em park. They're almost always in these big red pickup trucks—Fords and Chevys—or in old boats like Caddies and ancient Buicks. Looks-wise, they're racially ambiguous, could be Mediterranean, Middle Eastern, or Latino, which in Hawai'i allows them to blend right in, really. Most of the women, at least from the clan over here, wear these modest below the knee jean skirts with a small slit in the back and all-white Keds tennis shoes below that. It's like their dress code or something. Then they've usually got some kind of spaghetti strap top on, hoop earrings and jet-black hair. Usually pushing a stroller, in packs of two or three down Kalākaua or at the mall. And always, no matter where they're from, have that light-speed New York accent. Although one time I did hear them talking among themselves—this guy Skippy with his wife—and I couldn't begin to guess what language they were speaking. I asked him, and he told me Romany, the Gypsy language. He even taught me a few phrases and brought me down some authentic Gypsy food that the grandmother made one night. They knew I was interested and probably dug this rare, positive P.R. even though for all I knew the phrases were variations of: "I'm an idiot." They also probably wanted something. Like free parking. But I didn't care.

Career-wise, things get a little gray. Most of the men are into that mobile-dent repair biz, many accused of following prospective clients into richer neighborhoods like Kailua and Kahala and being conveniently "available" when a new client steps out of their house or a store and suddenly discovers damage on their new Range Rover. There's that biz, and then flipping used cars on Craigslist, specifically, stolen cars with scratched-off VINs that barely run, but are gussied up just enough to sell and make a quick profit. Meet ya at the DMV to switch over the title? Good friggin' luck with that. The Gypsies always seem to have their hand on the pulse of the clandestine. And c'mon, it's always somehow helpful knowing someone like that. Of course, the Gypsies are always around when you don't necessarily need to find them, and when you do—*poof*—nowhere to be seen...

13.

An odd mélange of conflicting worldviews

The first time I ever worked with Joel, one of the only other haoles in the company, was down at Pier 7. That account bit the dust once the restaurant closed, but obviously, it was down at Pier 7, at a restaurant near Aloha Tower called the Boat Room. It's where the newbies went. You park like four to seven cars a night (which is a horrible night), but since the company runs off seniority, you gotta start somewhere, right? Joel was on his way out of there, being that he'd worked there for a few months, but was initially in there because he'd shit the bed somehow. That's another thing—if you screw up, say crash a car or talk shit to the wrong guy—your punishment was working a shift at a rookie place—i.e., Pier 7. Gene, for instance, does time there quite often for transgressions involving physical threats to clients. Anyway, I was new, and despite a little bit of the customary "this company ain't big enough for two Caucasians" schtick, when he found out that I wasn't a transplant like him, we got tight fast. He was the kind of guy who'd only been in Hawai'i for a year and a half and already adopted a Pidgin English affect, a kind of repulsive habit that most perpetrators fail to see they're even doing until they've been false-cracked by a local who's not down with it. Worse yet, Joel heinously mixes this faux-local-accent with the hip-hop–inspired, ebonic dialect he showed up with. He's also got a full right arm sleeve of tattoos he shamelessly promotes, an odd mélange of conflicting world views. Like: an anthropomorphic pot plant hugging a Star of David, above a Muslim star and crescent moon above a Sanskrit Om sign, next to the band Sublime's smiling sun logo. Naturally. Regardless, Joel had some brilliant friggin' stories.

Mostly, he just freestyle rapped. That was his thing—freestyling. His rhymes were hokey as shit, as if he went through a dictionary and picked out the biggest words he could find and just crammed them into his rhymes to sound intelligent. But with Joel, it's always a pretty tongue-and-cheek affair. He had this amazing story he half-rapped to me on the first day about living in Israel and working on a kibbutz or something. How he got kicked out of the kibbutz for messing with the wrong guy's daughter and then slipped in with the wrong crowd in Tel Aviv and was deported from the country, permanently, for getting caught selling weed and Percocet. All of this in a really choppy, freestyle rap. And I mean, like, *really* shitty, but somehow he'd make every rhyme and word fit.

I like...a big...kib-BUTZ and I cannot lie!
It's Zion, untill I die!
When a yenta walks in with an iddy-bitty waist and an
Uzi in your face—
Oy vey!

Joel also showed me the ropes and introduced me to my first scam at Pier 7. He taught me a hustle (that the boss taught him) where you find out about events happening at nearby Aloha Tower. Even shit going down in Chinatown—Hoʻolauleʻa, Hawaiʻi Theatre concerts, etc. Naturally, these events are gonna require parking and will probably max out the self-parking area adjacent our valet stalls. He told me, "Dawg, people are gonna roll up, sweatin', and you know they ain't going to Pier 7, because nobody does. So you tell 'um straight up, 'You guys wanna go out but park for a while, right?' Usually they're like, 'Yeah, can we park, then?' And then you tell 'um, 'Listen, we have a few stalls left, but they're for restaurant guests only. The restaurant closes by nine and I'm usually out by nine-thirty, but what I can do is give you a stall for twenty dollars—and you can park for as long as you want, and you won't get towed because the stalls belong to our company.' If it's a car with like four to five people packed in, sometimes five dollars apiece ain't a problem. But if they're bitchin' tell 'um, 'All right, fifteen.' But never go lower than ten, because someone *will* pay twenty bucks that night. Sell dem stalls, kid..."

And so I did. And on nights like that at the reject location, I'd go home with two hundred-fifty bucks in less than five hours, wages not included. It was genius and customers were literally parking themselves and keeping their own keys.

Ten years later, he's still the same old Joel. What's more, is that all the valets call him, well, by his real name. Not "Haole Boy" or "Captain Cook." I mean, what the hell? It was rumored that for a time, maybe a stretch of two years, he was living with his dog in a ditch with a corrugated tin roof thrown on top, that he'd dug out on a friend's land he was caretaking. I'm talking way up, back in the woods of St. Louis Heights. I asked him about it a year ago, after he'd moved back into society, and he was telling me how it was his artistic hermitage. How when we'd had those rains of forty days and forty nights back in '06, he was up there in his ditch, but it got flooded. How he and his dog (his soul mate) saw God or Buddha or something.

"Dawg, the gods tried to flush me out, dawg. But I struggled. And I toiled. Dawg, I was butt naked with some Timberlands on, just digging. Making a trench to live in, 'cause the tent got soggy. And then a transformation occurred inside of me, with the cleansing of those rains, right? Like, it reestablished what it meant to be wet, reestablished my previous definitions of muddy or soaked. And after that, there really never was another rainy day. Nothing was really muddy after that. Meta-physio-forically speaking, daaaawg…"

He had a full-on transcendental experience, wrote a bunch of songs, and by the end of his hermitage created a strange visual art, slam poetry neo-jazz-band called Family Supper. I brought a few of my friends to watch them downtown one night, and we stepped into a club where he was doing a show. Joel was onstage with an ukulele and a backup band, freestyling with some other guy, trying to get an already stoned crowd to repeat some abstract hook. I stayed for about seven minutes before everyone left me behind.

When he found out that I was teaching at Punalani, he offered to come in as a special guest speaker, since he'd invented this new form of visual-audio art called a "Verbal Collage Vortex." How it would be great for the kids in imagery exercises for their writing. He also claimed to be a Big Brother for a stint, out on the Westside somewhere, and thus had previous experience with kids. I told him that I teach high schoolers, and that he'd probably have to fill out some paperwork before he came. That if there was any kind of background check needed, due to his priors (arrest/deportation from Israel and a few misdemeanor drug charges), it'd probably be a no-go. Needless to say, it didn't work out, which was a bummer because he's definitely a lot more interesting than me for four hours a day. Anyway, he has some pretty hilarious stuff posted on YouTube: music videos mostly, with hit songs including, "Step Inside the Outside," "Don't Get Too Hype," and "No Ack." All of which have all the other valets I work with in stitches. I'm not jealous or anything…I just don't get it sometimes.

Since then, the last time I saw Joel was passing the 'Ohana Beach Hotel off Kalākaua to pick up a paycheck and, per usual, he was freestyling with one of the employees from Foot Locker on a smoke break. Joel's mid-pop-n-lock, spots me, and does "the worm" over to me, an impressive twenty yards away.

"When you gon' let me be keynote, *daaawg*," he says, jumping to his feet and tilting his head in the sassiest of postures.

"Sorry, Joel, just picking up my paycheck—gotta be back at the Sands in ten minutes!" I say, trying to dodge his game.

"You get that record expunged and you're in, playah!"

He drops his head and kicks the concrete, throwing a faux tantrum. "I show you the tricks of the trade and you gon' do me like this, dawg!?" he shouts as I take the escalator up.

The thing about Joel is that he's seriously created a caricature of himself. And he never breaks character, but sometimes break dances. His depth and composition is actually pretty amazing, too. Plus, he's nearly forty, so hanging out with him makes me feel just a little bit better about still being a valet at thirty-two. Only thing is, that while I might be miserable, he couldn't be happier. He might still sell drugs on the side for studio time on his various E.P.s, though. It's hard to say. Joel, however, is another guy—in the same vein of the Gypsies—that always seems to have his ear to the ground. Which can be a useful tool if you can sit through the bullshit.

14.

Fucking Rumi

s this a date? I feel like this is a date. I mean, it's just the two of us. We're eating together. At the same table. I'm wearing a collared shirt. And, I'm reading you poetry."

"A—definitely *not* a date. B—this is not a table; it's a rollaway valet booth. C—your company polo is not suitable dinner attire. Actually…maybe for Hawai'i it is."

She's right about that one. I've definitely seen dudes taking their dates out to dinner in their neon yellow, long-sleeve construction work shirts. Tucked into Wranglers, mind you, to bump up the class.

"D—that prose is pretty expository to be poetic, car boy. And, what's your beef with strippers? Was your mother a dancer and didn't hold you enough as an infant? Do you even *know* a stripper, or is this all conjecture?"

Another Morton's Steakhouse shift and it's raining mongooses and mynah birds. So much so that Marisela is more or less trapped beneath the restaurant's drop off car awning with me unless she's willing to get totally soaked running back to her car by Neiman Marcus. It's also midway between the six p.m. "in" and nine p.m. "out" rush, but with this rain and the fact that it's a Tuesday, hardly anyone's in the restaurant anyway. So, a total wash tips-wise but with Mari obviously lingering, not to mention Morton's provides the valets a meal here every shift that we appear to be sharing…I'm chalking this one up as a date, trap or not. Plus, a subtle soundtrack of rain and thunder, and did I mention she made me read her some of my work? This is my happy place.

"I don't know many strippers *personally*, but I do know a lot of co-workers that seem to exclusively bang them," I say, slowly floating a fork of premium filet mignon to Marisela's lips.

"Nope." She shakes her head. "Not doing that. Can't reduce myself any further, car boy."

"Toots, this chow is like ten clams an ounce. Feast or frenzy, *mamacita*."

"I am not sure what the dollar-to-clam exchange rate is currently, but what the hell." She sighs, closes her eyes, and opens up wide, her tongue glistening like a pink slug beneath the fluorescent mall lights—then grabs my wrist and turns the fork of steak into my eye. She hands me a napkin, mercifully.

"Fair play, madam, fair play," I say, wiping away the peppery juice from my brow. "Well, I showed you mine, now you show me yours. What are *you* working on?"

"Ya know what, the papers are in the car." She shrugs, motioning to her station wagon across the lot, hidden by the relentless torrent. Perhaps, like a peace offering, she pokes a broccoli floret and lifts the fork to my face. I close my eyes and lean into the bait as she slowly pulls it away.

This is freakin' fun.

This is definitely a date.

"*Rumi*! *Rumi*, is that you?" shouts a voice, echoing from the elevator.

Startled, I look up from the booth, trying to register the guy with a wife and two kids in tow, walking toward us. I haven't heard that nickname in many moons.

"Graham?" I make out, feeling like a dog looking up, mid-sip, from the toilet bowl.

"Dude!" he says, pulling me in for a bear hug, "How long's it been, man? Eight...ten years?"

He looks at Mari, then pushes a cheek toward her. "Graham, and this is my wife, Jen," he says. "And that's Miles, and that's Olive." The two shy toddlers cling to their mother's legs, burying their faces in her jeans.

"I knew this scoundrel from our UH days," he clarifies, arm around my shoulder. He smells of expensive steak and Speedstick Musk.

"You called him Rumi?" Mari reminds us all, now wearing a shit-eating grin the size of a sixty-four-ounce Porterhouse. "Do tell, Graham. Do tell."

Graham throws his head back and laughs deeply.

"Gawd, was it because of the hat, or the graffiti?" he asks me rhetorically.

"Both, probably," I say, trying hard to brush this chapter of my past beneath the rug.

"This fucking hopeless romantic—*oops*, sorry, Jen, earmuffs—would wear this dope hat around campus all the time that read: *Listen to Jelaluddin Rumi.* I mean, where'd you even *buy* that? You just had it made, right?"

"Yeah, Lids. Windward Mall. It's not a big deal, like a dollar a letter—"

"*That's* dope?" squeaks Mari.

"And then he'd tag the men's rooms in Kuykendall and Hamilton—shit, I saw them around Sinclair, too— with just the most heart-wrenching passages from Rumi poems. Anti-graffiti, right? And, like, right in the stalls next to 'Call so-and-so for a blowjob.' I mean, who does that?!"

"Give blowjobs?" asks Mari. Jen chuckles, but Graham is shipwrecked on Nostalgia Island and can't find his way off.

"This guy could write, too, *gawd*, could he write. At least it seemed that way in English 460…wait, weren't you writing a novel or something before we graduated? Where can I read that puppy? Shit, how many have you written since then?"

The elephant named "I'm still valet parking" is so large, its ass is hanging halfway out of the room.

"Well, one is right here," says Marisela, reaching into the booth for the pages I read her. Bless her goddamned heart.

"Nah, kinda put it on the back burner," I mumble. "Started teaching at Punalani—"

"*What*?! Get out of here, dude! Put it on the back burner? Didn't you win that undergrad award or a contest or something?"

I did. It was the Patsy Sumie Saiki Award for Fiction. Received a $1,000 oversized-check for my efforts, too.

"What about you, Graham?" Marisela salvages, probably noticing me squirming. "Clearly you have a gorgeous family—you guys live around here?"

"Ah, my parents still live in Kaimukī, Jen's are in Aina Haina, but we live in New York. Just back here visiting the fam and showing the kids what a beach is supposed to look like for a couple weeks. Taking a look at schools in case something pulls us home. Gawd, every time we come back, though, I don't know why we left. Seriously, why does anyone leave?"

"You've been saying that the last three years, Graham," his wife chides, rolling her eyes at us playfully.

"It's just so expensive to *own* here, though, right?" he says to us, as if he's not looking at a parking attendant and flower girl sharing a slab of meat like hyenas at a valet booth.

"So expensive," parrots Marisela. "What do you do over there, Graham?"

"Ah, publishing. I work for Conde Nast. Shit, I figured you would've beat me to the City, Rums."

I chuckle and hide a blush by looking into the booth's cabinet for keys.

"You guys park with us, Graham?"

"Nah, we're around the corner by Macy's. How do you get any business here, when there's literally five thousand spots twenty feet away?"

"*Shhhh*, don't tell anyone!" I whisper.

The rain is finally letting up and his kids seem anxious to go, so he hands me a business card and they bid us adieu, strolling back toward their vehicle, both kids riding on their shoulders like a Banana Republic ad.

A silence coming to the end of its third trimester hangs between Mari and I while I rearrange the three keys hanging on the booth's door.

"Awk-*warddd*," says Marisela, piercing the amniotic sac.

I swallow hard and fake a smile.

"Who the fuck gets a job straight out of college these days?" she says.

"People that know people," I offer.

"People that kiss asses," she affirms.

"People that take chances, move away from here, and work really, really hard—"

"Yeah, no good, filthy, *hard* workers!"

"Ambitious, driven, scum."

"*Publishers*," she hisses, contorting her face like she's about to hurl. "*Woof.*"

"Book nerds that can't write, ay?"

"Well, I feel better now, don't you, Rumi?"

Christ. I'd nearly forgotten.

"Holy crap. You know what they call a twenty-year-old male scrawling quotes from a fired-up, mystical Sufi Muslim these days?"

"Number one on the local no-fly list?"

"Yes. Exactly that, you adorable psychopathic idealist, you..."

"Don't you just hate that fake-humble line locals who move to New York or L.A. give you about just *aching* to come home... 'if only they could?' It's like, just move home then! Don't tell me you hate a place that you're killing it in for my pity, bitch!"

"Ooooo, jealousy does *not* go well with those cargo shorts, Rumi."

"Fuck...off."

"Graham sure seemed to hold you in high regard, though."

"Ah, he's always had a penchant for hyperbole."

We finish the rest of the meal and continue the repartee, me a little less enthused, trying hard not to measure myself against the "made man" who I once, apparently, inspired. Marisela arranges her bouquet, says goodbye, and takes the elevator up to scope out any possible marks. I pull out Graham's business card and flip it in my fingers, noticing he'd written something on the back.

If you resent the cure, you stay sick... —Rumi / Call me, let's talk. —Graham

Fucking Rumi.

I clean up the booth's tabletop, stab the last morsel of meat left on the plate—now cooled by conversation—and chew on it all. I put the dish into the booth's cabinet and see a valet stub sticking out of the mashed potatoes. I pull it out and written on the ticket are the next four digits to her number. Good form, Mari, good form.

PART II

RAISED BY WOLVES

15.

Good for morale

Valet parking is kind of like stripping. Sure, you can get good at the job, but who really aspires to become a good stripper? And life is never kind to old strippers. Inevitably, after a certain age, you're gonna have to get off that pole. Valet's the same way. The average age of a valet is around eighteen to thirty years old. Older than that, you better be a manager in some kind of admin position within the company. By forty-something, you just can't be running up and down a concrete ramp every three minutes for eight hours at a time. I've seen the guys who try to do it. They look like old strippers—bow-legged and clumsy. Not a pretty picture.

Because, first to go are your joints—your hips, specifically. You start limping around all the time, sitting in the key room with the walkie-talkie, and when they call the number down from the bell desk and another guy walks in to hang one on the key hooks, he asks you, *"Brah, you like get dis one fo' me fas kine, my knee stay killing me. Tanks ah?!"* Just pitiful. You start wearing knee braces and ankle straps, looking like you're part android or tin man, all of the sudden. You can't clomp down the ramp like you used to and gotta take that decline all gingerly, like trying to jog on a wet street without slipping. You start delegating the not-to-be-delegated system of valet (an already straightforward chain of events), just to save yourself from having to run more. You're telling one guy to park the incoming cars, another guy to pull out the ones leaving— and you? You'll keep the front under control so the lobby doesn't get clogged. Some bullshit like that. Oh, I've seen it happen. Young men walking like old geezers from this redundant, unnatural act of fetching vehicles. That's not even mentioning the respiratory damages from working in a carbon monoxide, dusty fume-filled garage for eight hours at a time.

You do this shit for too long and start getting bitter and eggy. You develop what I call "valet-itis," a minor form of schizophrenia. You start beginning conversations about what ballpoint pen for work writes the best under pressure. Generally taking the job way too seriously. You start forgetting that they're just dumb customers and start taking everything personally. I guess it's like that with any tip job, I suppose. I see it happen all the time. No tip— and you leave that car door *wiiide* open. Like, *you can close it yourself, pal.* Guys start obsessing over that stuff, writing little messages in code on the hotel guest's key tag like NT for "No Tip" so that the next dude knows not to rush with it. Make 'em wait, you know? Some guys who see those messages will even fart in the cars with the windows rolled up. Who knows what else. But then again, some guys flip that energy and try and give the best service. Reverse the karma. Because maybe, just maybe, they might be the ones to break the cycle.

Mostly, though, the valets just get desperate. And inquisitive. And creepy. In a "let's form a coalition against this enemy" kind of way. You'll pull up some car of a guy or guest who may not have tipped in the past, and after it's left, a valet'll come up to you like some fiending crack head all, *"So did he tip you? Dat fakah nevah tip you, ah? Yeah! Fahking guy, ah? You know those fakahs stay talking about us behind our backs, ah?"* Just trying to rile you up. Trying to make you feel their rage. Trying to instigate and infuriate. But if there's one thing I learned: you can't take it personal. Sometimes dudes just don't have any cash on them. That simple. But when it comes down to it, screw elephants; a *valet* never forgets. About the bad stuff or the good.

And then Jojo came along and cleared history. The kid broke *our* cycle.

Initially, some of us didn't know what to do with the boy (me), and then some of us knew exactly what to do with the kid. A lot of the valets I work with have children—or father illegitimate ones from their latest girlfriends—and are surprisingly paternal. You know, for grown men that invest in metallic decals for their cars that read: *Panty Soakahz.* Madero wouldn't let us call the cops. He claimed that with no parents in the picture or an actual physical address, the cops would just send the kid straight to child services and Madero just didn't want that. Long story short, he grew up on Maui in a foster home, and his experience—not to totally write off every foster home—was traumatic, to say the least. Like cigarette burns and belt buckle scars type shit. A cousin of his that I worked with at the Sands one summer hinted at some pretty horrendous sexual abuse from some of the older kids in the house that were [illegally] bunking with him in the same room. Apparently, Madero was finally yanked from the foster home when a teacher at school noticed some dog collar-type marks around his neck. He was removed and then eventually sent to board at Kamehameha Schools on Oʻahu through high school.

But Madero insisted we keep Jojo for as long as we could, or until we could locate some family. I guess in his eyes, it's like we were saving him from his past or something. Besides advising us not to give him up, though, he wanted little to do with the boy.

"I no like relive da past," he told me. "I jes like forget." And that was that.

Whatever it was, we were all on board. I mean, what the hell else did we have going on?

There's a few extra rooms in the hotel reserved solely for employees that have less than eight-hour breaks between their shifts. It's actually a state law, and since some of us will work three to eleven, and then six to two the following morning, it's a practical option. Those few sleeping rooms are usually vacant too, because most guys wanna get the hell out of there after their shift, even if it's a measly six hours. So for the last couple of weeks, the kid has hung with us underground during the day, and in one of the employee rooms overnight.

Regardless, the couple of weeks that he's been camped out in the Sands have been without a doubt, the most money we've ever made. The spike definitely has to do with morale. You can't *not* look forward to coming to work when there's a smiley-ass, earnest kid like Jojo there waiting for you. Bad vibe storm clouds that come into work quickly dissipate under his ultra-violet smile. All the valets are suddenly grinning and laughing more, and inversely, bitching less about the guests. The kid is just this mood neutralizer, or *enhancer* or something. He's a surprisingly happy little fella, too, for being abandoned in a car trunk by presumably godawful parents. Or, maybe I'm just surprised by the infinite resiliency in children. In their incredible ability to adapt and thrive in any given situation. And shit, I guess even this situation—our stinky-ass, concrete skid-marked underground parking lot—looks a lot better than the inside of a car trunk, when you put it in perspective.

For fun, we take him for spins in the rental cars down in the lot. Gene, Palani, or Kainoa will be burning out, peeling rubber, and he'll be wiggling in his seat, howling at the top of his lungs. He'll even get the key, hand it to the valet, and run with them to the car, just for that thir-ty-second ride. Then jump out before the exit ramp, and wait to do it again. It's like a never-ending amusement ride for him. And he wants to do *everything*. He'll get in shotgun and already have his hand on the transmission stick to put her in drive or reverse. We teach him how to rub the scratches out from hitting the pillars with Goof

Off, and which way to connect the jumper cables when the batteries die from a light we left on. Everyone jokes about nominating him for employee of the quarter. Our company still actually has that, believe it or not. The winner gets a free meal with the other location winners, paid for by the boss at, usually, a pretty epic local restaurant. Palani actually made Jojo a name tag from the backs of restaurant valet tickets folded and stapled with a safety pin taped to the back so he could wear it. It reads "Jojo Boy" and he wears that thing like a medal of honor. Like, religiously. All of us keep our name tags in this one basket down in the key room; we just leave them there after the shift so we won't forget them at home or something. Naturally, Jojo does too.

Maybe it's his way of earning his keep so one of us will choose him. Like some puppy pressing its nose up against the glass in a pet shop. I get the feeling he's never been chosen much. But what else can I say, he just likes to help, and every young boy wants to impress a big kid, or in our case, big kid-men. Really, he's made work a lot easier, our operation more efficient, even. During the morning "outs" we'll leave a walkie-talkie down there in the key room, and call out numbers. He'll go grab the keys for us, and all we'll have to do is run down the ramp and he'll hand them off from the key room door, a big shit-eating grin on his face, like somewhere in that mind of his he feels like he's doing something productive, hell, progressive even, for a human of his size. Ironically, he is. With this extra little hand, we've been bringing up cars so fast that it's blowing all the guests' minds. Just stunned by our proficiency. Tips are ballooning, like, three-fold.

Sure, his numbers aren't always one hundred percent—he gets his sixes and nines mixed up—so we've discovered quickly that we gotta double-check, just in case.

In the two weeks that he's stayed at the Sands, he'll come down in the morning with sleep still in his eyes, a lot of times at six or seven, not even because he had to, but just because that's when we arrive. Then he'll grab his name tag from the basket, and all business-like, go to a car's side mirror and pin his name tag on. It'll take him, like, five friggin' minutes sometimes with his stubby little fingers. Believe me, we've tried to help him before, and he'd wriggle away, all pissed off with that I-CAN-DO-IT-MYSELF look in his eyes. The guys'll put up their hands, all fake shamed like, "Ho, sorry, Jojo. No get mad at me, ah…I sorry."

We've even worked it out where every guy will take twenty minutes off a shift to take the kid down to the beach behind the Sands. Just to watch him while he swims or body-surfs the shore break. He absolutely loves it and comes back with sand bits in bizarre places like the corners of his mouth or dripping out of his nose. Then he'll take a shower by the pool, dry off with a hotel towel, and then diligently put his dry clothes back on, name tag and all, of course. He's a goddamned classic.

All the valets just eat it up and humor him, too. It's pretty cute, to tell you the truth. They'll split a shift box on our weekly schedule posted to the bulletin board and pencil in "Jojo Boy" alongside someone else, and then nudge him and point at it all encouragingly, like: "Look-it, boy, you get shifts already, guy! You one workah, ah you?! *Chee!*" Just fully psyche him up. And he'll be grinning, just trying not to show his teeth—taking the compliments like a man—but he can't help from blushing.

It's like the kid just popped into our lives and flipped the switch. I mean, sure valet shifts aren't Auschwitz or anything, but instead of joking about creatively named sex moves (See: Dirty Sanchez) or the receptionist's new boob job, we've started thinking about *him*. What Jojo just did, or said, or was laughing about. About stuff that'd make the boy happy, or ways we could somehow involve him. I'm not saying we've all gained some newfound purpose in life because of him…but Kainoa's definitely air-humping less pillars. And Gene's learning to quell his temper. And Palani's brought Jojo spare clothes from his own sons' closet. I can feel it all happening so quickly—his effect on us.

Of course, all good things must come to an end, and we had to move the kid out of the overnight hotel rooms once a hotel G.M. who was walking to his car saw Jojo Boy on Gene's lap in a guest's rental. Jojo was behind the wheel with a crazed smile on his face as Gene pushed the pedals beneath him. Maybe Gene thought the next logical step in Jojo's short-lived valet career, after handing out keys, was actually operating a motor vehicle? Indeed, the boy had gone from cargo to cockpit much too quickly for his own good. You can always count on a valet to screw up a good thing. The G.M. reported Gene to our location manager, and he was suspended for a week. He also told us that all the guys on the shift would be fired if he ever saw the kid underground in the lot again. Something about liability if one of us, or a delivery guy, somehow ran the boy over in an accident. Which is right around the time when we switched over to a schedule with the boy.

16.

We regret to inform you...

I promise to make you more alive than you've ever been
For the first time you'll see your pores opening
like the gills of fish and you'll hear
the noise of blood in galleries
and feel light gliding on your corneas
like the dragging of a dress across the floor...

What could she be getting at?" I ask the class, reading to a room full of sixteen-year-olds in my most erudite and wistful story-time voice. As I read, the blur of Marisela's face sharpens in my mind. The curve of her nose and the corner of her mouth when she smiles. Somewhere in the room, I hear the sound of her cackling laugh.

"Yes, Michelle?"

"You're, like, becoming more aware? Like, you notice

your pores opening, and hearing these, like, supersonic noises? It's like, your feelings or your, like, consciousness...has been magnified?"

"That's it. Very insightful, Michelle."

For the first time, you'll note gravity's prick
like a thorn in your heel
and your shoulder blades will hurt from the imperative
of wings...

"Yes, David?"

"Like, you wanna fly? But what does *imperative* mean, again?"

"Class, anyone?" Code for: I'm not exactly sure, so why don't one of you little pricks look it up, while you're on Snapchat anyways.

Sighs and keyboard clicks from their school-issued MacBooks.

"*A mandatory, compulsory urge, unavoidable, insistent...*"

"An urge, hmm?" I encourage the Socratic method of finding answers through questions—mostly to save myself from giving any answers disprovable by a teenager. I continue, and Jojo's form materializes, in my mind, thrashing in the shore pound on our lunch break, doing cartwheels down the beach, smiling like a happy Labrador retriever in the summer sun.

I promise to make you so alive that
the fall of dust on furniture will deafen you
and you'll feel your eyebrows like two wounds forming
and your memories will seem to begin

with the creation of the world.

"'Ordeal,' by Nina Cassian," I announce. "Yeah, Jeff..."

"It's like some kind of magnified, heightened sensation of being. Like all your senses are elevated. Like you're *super* human?" asks Jeff.

"And the 'eyebrows' part?" I ask.

"Well, your brow raises or lowers depending on your mood—either from joy or sadness, so..."

"And your memories will seem to begin, with the creation of the world," I repeat.

"Like, you become god-like. All-knowing, or...more knowing?" he adds.

Although I have everyone's attention, only three out of the eighteen actually seem interested. Regardless, you take your wins where you can in summer school. I mean, seriously, who the hell wants to be in school in the summer?

"But the title—'Ordeal.' What is an *ordeal?*"

"A very difficult or harrowing experience, especially one lasting a long time," someone reads.

"So. Essentially an ordeal seems kind of negative. Harmful, difficult—miserable, even. And is it safe to say that, inferred through the title, the qualities of 'being alive' are achieved within this ordeal?"

Blank stares. Some nods. A few, to more than a few, looks of utter boredom and indifference.

"What might the speaker in the poem actually be talking about?" I prod. "Yes, Jeff," I nod.

"I think she's talking about being high. Like that's what the drug, or whatever you're on, does to you," he says, not necessarily to me, but to the class, grinning for affirmation. I was probably asking for that one.

"Maybe it's about *sex*," adds a bolder girl, the X hanging in the air like a smoky hiss.

"Okay, so we got drugs, sex, what's next?" I ask. "But why is this considered an *ordeal*? Wouldn't one view the sensations triggered by these things more as joyful, and euphoric, than problematic?"

"Maybe it's about death. Like, ironically, you feel all these extrasensorial feelings as you're dying, but like, right before the lights go out..."

Charles. The only goth kid in the class. He *would* say that. "Well, how 'bout this: what makes you feel alive? C'mon, anything else?"

Ralph raises his hand, like a silent little sage. He's laid off me lately, but I'm still wondering about his play. I nod to him like, *take 'em to church*.

"Maybe 'the ordeal' is falling in love. Like, it can feel so good and take you to such heights, but inevitably, somehow—like an ordeal—it's harmful and dooming. Maybe man can't really handle such aliveness? At least not for too long."

Ralph is my co-pilot. Ralph is my prophet.

"But, without seeing the title, these kind of superhuman sensory experiences all seem appealing. Wouldn't we all love to be 'that alive' whether high, or sexually, or while in love?" I ask.

Nods across the room.

"Even if we find out that being this alive is an ordeal, possibly harmful or ultimately dooming?" I probe.

"One of those 'better to have loved and lost' things, right?" adds a random girl whose name I can never remember.

"Despite the 'ordeal' factor, regular-alive just doesn't seem as powerful or meaningful as Cassian's alive, does it?" I ask.

"Yeah, kinda numb-er, or more average than hers," says Jeff.

"Yeah, I think it's appealing,, because most people realize that normal living is just too *normal*, that to step outside of your box, even though it may be unsafe, or to take a chance is more exciting and fulfilling than doing nothing at all," adds David.

I glance at Ralph, and he smiles demonically. He licks his lips and says, "Does this poem, by chance, have something to do with those stories about that boy that you've had us editing?"

"Yeah, what's up with that?" shouts Kaito from the back row. "What happens to that shit when we're done with it? You haven't even turned it back in to us for a grade."

Keep it together, remain in control. "Cool it, guys. These are two separate exercises," I say, turning to the white board to hide my poker face and write...write *what*? "Those stories are meant to hone your copyediting skills, and this poem, well, this poem is just amazing. We're in creative writing; you read poems like this one, you edit prose—it's creative."

"Is there really a boy?" shoots Ralph.

"Huh? What do you mean?" I ask.

"In these stories, is the boy real?" asks Ralph. "Or is

this boy just a figment of the speaker's imagination? Like his *id?*"

"The trapped, little boy inside of himself," adds Jeff.

"His inner boy," smirks Ralph.

"Listen, I don't want to say you're reading between the lines too much, but—"

"When do we get to watch *Resevoir Dogs?*" Kawika cuts in.

"Aha! I knew I was forgetting something I'd promised you today. Good call, Ka-veeks." I scurry over to the projector and tell Michelle to hit the lights.

Not more than three minutes into the film, I notice Derek's goofy-ass face looking through the wire glass window of the classroom door. "*Knock, knoo-oock,*" he mouths. Christ. I motion for him to come on in.

He walks over to my desk and drops off an envelope. "This came for ya today, amigo. *Hasta luego,*" he says before merrily sneaking out of the room.

I look at the return address and it's from the *Santa Monica Review*. Interesting... Not long after Ralph confronted me, I figured that despite him wanting the story taken down and opting for "residuals" instead, I could be in his corner and submit to some bigger literary journals. Under *his* name, of course. Because...well, he deserves it. And I really do want him to succeed. I mean, I'm not a total sleaze bag...

...Thank you kindly for your submission. Though initially we were thrilled by Mr. Saito's story, our editors did their obligatory plagerism-search and discovered that this piece was already published two years ago by a Mr. Ronald Saito in

UCLA's Westwind Journal of the Arts. The byline under your submission, however, reads: Ralph *Saito. Regardless, we regret to inform you that we cannot run previously published works by submitting authors...*

I reread the letter once more and slip away from the classroom, speed-walking toward Derek's office for no apparent reason other than that age-old adage: No Running in the Halls.

"Knock, knoo-oock, amigo!" I holler, mimicking his absurdity. "*Pregunta*: Who's Ronald Saito?"

"Oh, that's your student Ralph's older brother. Graduated here a few years ago, full-ride to UCLA. *Amazing* writer. I should email you some of his work—"

"You know what? I think I've already found some, Derek. But *gracias!*" I grin, darting back to the classroom.

17.

He stopped to smell the roses

Where are you taking me?"

"Somewhere special."

She sighs into the window and mutters, "Gawd..."

"What, do you not trust me, still? Dinner was nice, wasn't it?"

"Yeah, really nice...and cheap."

"Jesus! I'm a valet, not a friggin' neurologist. Siam Chef is quality eats, toots. I saw you clean your Styrofoam plate, so don't gimme that 'cheap' bullshit—"

"I'm kidding, I'm kidding. Jeez, you're too easy."

A strange awkwardness balloons between us.

"It's just..."

"Just what?"

"I know all the flower girls...and, I know you've hit on

like, lemme see—Jessica. Marie. Umm, Regina. It's like, how am I not just another one?"

"Lion's gotta roar, babe. I won't deny that. Wait, is Regina that short little hapa-haole chick?"

"Yeah."

"Ha! Tell her don't flatter herself. I actually *did* want to know what time it was."

"And how her blouse looked 'steamy?'"

"That's flirting, these days? I guess I gotta recalibrate or something...Because apparently I've been 'flirting' a whole lot with my own mother lately."

She laughs, a silly kind of cackle. The pressure drops in the Hyundai Accent.

"So, we're going to Hawai'i Kai," she says.

"Looks like it."

"Gawd, don't tell me we're going to the cliffs at Port-lock for a romantic moon gaze," she says, the last few words in an ersatz Antonio Banderas accent.

"One: No. What am I, like, twenty-one years old, trying to impress...some HPU sophomore from Boulder? And two: what if that's where we were actually going? That would've made me feel horrible. Just sit there and think about that Little Miss Nostradamus. Save the seven-day forecast for Guy Hagi, 'kay? Un-be-LIEVE-able."

More cackling. A crack in the fortress walls.

"Just enjoy the damn ride, chica."

We drive eastward along the south shore to the end of Sandy Beach where the southern coast corners with the Eastside. We park on the side of the road by the golf course in a vacant dirt lot and I say, "Take off your clothes...and change into your swimsuit."

"Can you say *anything* without sounding like a total creep, Mr. Weinstein?"

We cross the highway, listless this time of night, hop over the guardrails, and follow a random sand trail toward the southeast point. Occasionally, from inside the cracks of ancient lava rocks, young shearwater chicks cry out with startlingly human-like whines. Spooked, Marisela grabs my arm, as if momentarily believing that there were wailing infants trapped in the rocks. It is the first time she's touched me in any way, shape, or form, and the first time anyone you're completely infatuated with touches you...I dunno, it's like time stands still just for you two. We walk on beneath a full moon flickering in the sky like a waning light bulb with every passing cloud. Not far ahead a huge chair-like lava rock called Pele's Throne sits on the point, keeping watch over the crashing waves. Visible from a few miles away, if you walk right up to it, beneath the throne is a gorgeous natural salt water swimming cove, forged from ancient lava rock and sea. And I don't know how it got there, but there's this huge, old-ass telephone pole, so sea weathered that the wood looks furry and sentient, jutting out of the rocks at a perfect ninety-degree angle. It looks like a pirate plank or something that you can jump from and into the cove. Even though it's only a ten-foot drop, at night everything seems a little more dramatic.

Marisela jumps off the end of the telephone pole and into the shimmering, moonlit sea, a gesture somehow both sensual and childish. Childish, because as sexy as she looks in a Brazilian bikini bottom, out of pure thrill, she kinda tweaks to the side when she jumps, like the lion clicking his heels to a song in *The Wizard of Oz*. Something like that. I run after her, as much as one could on a foot-wide wooden pole, and jump in. I open my eyes underwater, and the moon is so bright that I can make out the the ivory sand shifting on the bottom with the surge of every swell. Or an occasional trigger fish darting in front of me curiously, then quickly fleeing into the hazy distance. And her. Marisela is motionless underwater, holding her breath as I swim up to her. I stare at her, as best as one could with blurry underwater eyes, but hers are closed. That goddamn hair of hers. Black strands slithering in a cloud above her head and in front of her face. A mass of eels in a frantic orgy. An undulating mess of cephalopodan tentacles. My underwater Medusa, beautiful, I tell you. She opens her eyes, sees me watching her, pushes off the bottom, and swims right past me. *Through* me, practically, her hair trailing behind her like squid arms accelerating. She slips out of the water and climbs nimbly up the lava rock. And I follow.

"Why are we still nothing?" she asks, perched on the pirate plank, legs dangling.
"Whattyou mean?" I say.
"You know what I mean."
"Are you really worried you're nothing?"
She shrugs, her head shrinking into her neck.
"I dunno, kinda?"
"Well, this ain't L.A., Marisela. Any nightclub will

let you in with swim trunks and slippers, babe...I think that's a metaphor."

"Really?" she asks cynically.

"Yeah. No one cares. That's the cool thing about Hawai'i. It's not San Fran or New York, or Paris. It's not about what you do or what you've done. It's about who you are. Like, the *kind* of person. I mean, I know you've got dreams and you're in school, and that's fine. But if you think you're nothing in Hawai'i and that bothers you, you're in the wrong place. No one gives a shit about 'how far you've come' here. The place transcends it."

I am trying to convince her. Trying to convince myself.

"That's the most profound thing I've ever heard an off-duty valet say."

I shrug. I'll take it.

"What's with this 'nothing' talk? You're further along in the process than I am. Practically there, right?"

"I lied," she says.

"About what."

"About Random House and Penguin. About an agent. About...most of it."

Sickeningly, I feel a little relieved by her failures.

"You don't have an agent?"

"Well, I'm communicating with one. But I don't really believe that she's actually read the book. Let alone shopped it to any publishers."

"It's a book of short stories about flower girl experiences?"

"No. I lied about that, too."

"Why?" I laugh.

"It's not a book of short stories. It's actually a young

adult novel about a high school flower girl that lies about her age to get the job, but she's a psychopathic killer. No…more like a femme fatale."

"Wait, whaaaa? A teenager killer?"

"No, a femme fatale, but, like, a heroine, too, because she was molested as a child and has this conviction to find the scum and pedophiles and rapists out at the clubs and bars. Somehow she obtains this microscopic mite that breeds in African roses—her specialty flower."

"Wait, obtains some obscure mite?" I ask.

"Oh yeah, her stepdad—a good guy—is a famous entomologist. Like he's got this lab that she finds the mites bottled up in. Anyways, the mites, if ingested, or inhaled or whatever, will infect your respiratory system. Like, just feed off the tissue and lung matter, and then you die, suddenly, like four hours after ingestion."

This. Woman.

"So, she researches rapists and molesters in the area—has this, like, vendetta for them that she's out to complete. Pay back for all the molested, raped, sexually abused young girls, as she once was, so she plants the mites deep inside the rose's stamen. She goes to the bars or clubs or restaurants or whatever where those guys are at, on dates, or prowling—of course she's stunning and sexy—and walks up to them. She goes, 'Wanna buy some roses? At least just take a sniff…even if you don't buy, it's free to smell right?' So they do. And then they die. The book is called *Basket Case*. But I'm almost wondering if I can turn it into a series. A *Basket Case* series, with the first one titled *He Stopped to Smell the Roses*."

"Marisela, that's fucking genius. Why would you lie to me about that?"

"I dunno. Maybe just ashamed that it was just another YA novel. It's not like anyone reads those things who isn't fifteen, let alone gets published by a *Tin House* or *Ploughshares*, or something."

"You still read *Ploughshares?*"

"Religiously…on the toilet."

"Right, right, you guys take a seat for number one and two, irregardless, huh."

"What's stopping you, stud, too macho to sit peeing down *while* reading *Granta?*"

I lean over the fallen telephone pole, grab her cheeks with two palms, and kiss her. Something in between a long-awaited urge and consolation. Her mouth tastes just like the air smells, of sea salt and wind funneling through deep and ancient lava tubes. Our tongues search each other's anxiously and our lips try to fit together like awkward puzzle pieces. The breath from her nose is feverish against the side of my cheek and sounds like the roaring inside of a seashell.

We turn and look down the cove, a narrow lagoon stretching inland to a small sandy beach. And toward the sea, the other way where the cove empties, a reef submerges like a rocky picket fence, guarding the mouth. Beyond this inlet, the surf sweeps sideways past the opening with some of the swells refracting in, sending small waves rolling down the length of the cove toward that small, sandy shore. Like those green lines rolling across an EKG screen mimicking our heart rates. We were very much alive, indeed.

"I just…feel like I'm not doing anything of substance," she says.

"Look around! Look where we are?! Some people save up their whole lives to come here and see the type of shit we call 'just another Thursday.' You better watch your back with that blasphemous talk, or the Nightmarchers are gonna steal you away."

She giggles into a sigh.

"I mean with my *life*, I'm nearly thirty—what are we doing?" she asks. Which comes out like a plea.

"We? I feel like I'm doing fine…or at least have lived life well, so far," I answer. Which comes out like a question.

"I think you're not trying hard enough either."

I laugh nervously like *I got it all under control…*

"Geez. I feel like you're doing that reverse-psych thing that my dad did to me back in Little League, where he'd tell me, 'I don't think you *really* want to win. At least that's what you're playing like right now,' which inversely made me go, 'What?! I wanna win, motherfuckah!' and put that fire in my pants to get reckless and put my body in front of groundballs."

"And did it work?"

What looks like a dark fin slices smooth zigzag tracks through the water's surface, glistening in the moonlight. The fin moves with such profound fluidity that it seems not a part of a body or a whole, but rather its own limb, dancing on the water's surface like a figure skater's glide.

Marisela climbs onto the wooden telephone pole and, just as she would at work with a basket in hand, saunters chicken-skinned and nearly nude to the end. She doesn't jump in playfully this time but dives, gloriously, with the precision of a missile falling toward a bridge. Of a falcon swooping prey. I don't really know what she's trying to prove, or if she failed to see that fin, but she swims under-water for a few moments. Just in case, I fling a fist full of rocks at the small shark in the distance. Startled, the fin thrashes for a split second and speeds away, out of the mouth of the cove. Shortly after, she surfaces and floats upon her back.

Maybe it was like, "Look at me—this is how you take a chance." Or, "Follow my lead." Or, "Fear not, the shark is our protector." Whatever it was, I jump in and float on my back beside her. No more flirty banter from my end. She could have this battle; it seems to mean a lot to her. Plus, pride aside, she looks so goddamn gorgeous in the water beneath that moon.

18.

If no fit, try spit

Basically, we worked out a system where, unless you wanted Jojo for longer than a day, or if he requests it, he's dropped off to the next guy at the end of his night shift, at ten or eleven o'clock, or whenever he gets off. Then Jojo crashes at that guy's place, and he has the following day with the boy to look after him. Rinse, repeat with the next valet the next night. Clearly, there are some guys you feel better about taking care of him than others. I mean, I'm no father, so what the hell do I know, but I do know Gene lives a notoriously dangerous lifestyle. At work with shades on? Not a hangover. That means he's hiding a black eye from a fistfight, and Gene pretty much has a shades-on-day once a week.

Gene, however, just dropped off Jojo on his most recent night "on duty" (we were desperate), and I can see that the kid has endured a life-altering experience.

Clocking out, I hear Gene and the boy arriving. You can hear Gene's muffler a few blocks away, a modification both the result of making the scooter faster, and at the same time, to create a sound intended to annoy the living shit out of you. Like those douche bags on Harleys who think their artificial "rolling thunder" makes them feel like more of a man. But the sound of an accelerating muffler-less moped is like a more pathetic version of that. Anyways, that's them around the corner, the throttle echoing through every hotel lobby from Kalākaua to the Sands. I realize now that he's been pulling the throttle every two seconds, traveling for three blocks on the rear tire in a continuous wheelie. Jojo has Gene's shades on, standing on Gene's lap, wind in his hair, like he's the king of the goddamn world in *Titanic*. As they pull into the taxi stand, Gene grabs Jojo with one arm while letting the front tire drop down with the other. I shake my head at him like, *Not cool, dude.*

"Relax, bu, I been popping wheelies since hanna-battah days," snaps Gene. Jojo hops off and he appears... also modified.

For one, he's walking differently. Like, with his chest popped out a little, and strutting, sort of flat-footed. Like Gene walks. He also appears to be hiding his right arm behind his back for some reason, perhaps for some kind of thug effect, like he's continually reaching for his piece. Gene's also outfitted him in some new garb, more or less made over his whole persona. He has one of those shirts on in a kid's size—that I didn't even know they still made—with some cheesy-ass design on the front over the heart that reads: *Ikaika, Hawaiian Legends, The Warrior.*

And on the back, a full-color drawing of a dark, shredded Polynesian man, veins bursting from a steroid-induced neck, biceps, forearms, and chest. Body-building thighs exploding from a primitive kapa loincloth. Hawaiian war helmet on—the makaki'i—with bulging, bloodshot eyes staring from the mask. One arm raised holding a lightning bolt, and in the other, a Hawaiian battle axe—a medieval weapon laden with gleaming razor-like shark's teeth. He also dons a hat that reads If No Fit, Try Spit. And new shorts, swim trunks actually, that fit at the waist, but nearly end at his ankles. Brand-new Locals slippers on with neon blue straps, too. Cherry on top of the look: a camouflage-print fanny pack, buckled and fitted right above his waist, the two side straps hanging down past the backs of his knees, fluttering while he walks.

"Seriously, Gene?"

"Meeean ah, dis fakah now?!" he exclaims.

I yank off Jojo's bucket hat and see that Gene gave him a haircut too. It's a buzz cut. Well, kind of a buzz cut. Like, a bowled buzz cut on top above the ears, and then skin-no-fade below that.

"Geeeene..."

I notice something hiding, tucked beneath the collar of his new t-shirt. It's a rat-tail. A few strands of brown hairs, about four inches long, curling like a pig's tail from the top of his spinal cord.

"Jojo!" snaps Gene. "Show uncle what I taught you, Hawaiian."

Jojo lunges low at my ankles, wrapping his arms around my lower calves, leaning his measly body weight through his shoulders into my legs. Had he been maybe twenty pounds heavier, he'd have knocked me down. Kid's quick, though, I'll give him that.

"Ho! Almos', boy! We goin' train soon, start kicking da bag lai dat."

"And is that...*blood* on his shirt, Gene?" I ask. "What the hell?"

"Das from da cock fights. Not his blood, bu," he says, squinting his eyes and examining Jojo's shirt.

"Ho, Jojo!" Gene shouts, still looking down at his outfit. "You still get da license plates, coz!?"

The boy looks down at his slippers, at the golden stickers that read size six, stuck to the back of each rubber heel.

"Remove da tags, bu. Slippahs gotta ride unmarked."

Like a soldier under orders, Jojo quickly peels off the golden tabs.

"Gene...what did you guys do for the last twenty-four hours?"

"Ho, bruddah, one au-ten-tic cultural experience. O'ahu undah-ground, haole...Chee!"

Gene starts bouncing on the balls of his feet, bobbing, weaving, sparring with the air. His neck and chin glide left to right as he glares at me, dukes up, quick jabs inches within my face. He may or may not be on cocaine.

"Solid parenting, dude."

"Brah. What nevah kill us goin' make us strongah, haole. Boy, attack!" shouts Gene, crouching low, holding up two thick paws like punching pads while Jojo strikes with one-two jab-hook combos. As Jojo bobs and weaves, the fanny pack slips from his waist.

I pick it up and unzip the main compartment. Two Just Scrap MMA Blaisdell ticket stubs from a fight, only hours ago. A lighter. Three twenty-dollar bills. A candy bar wrapper. Dice. Chopsticks. A McDonald's receipt. T&C surf shop receipt. A soft pack of Camel Lights.

"Oh, some a dat stuff is mines, bu!" Gene hollers, still blocking punches. "Like da smokes! And get my cell phone in-dea?"

"No...but there's a lighter in here—"

"Get da island chain on da side?"

"No, a purple dolphin jumping over a sunset."

"Oh. Nah, das not mines, den."

"I'm gonna give it to you anyways, Gene. Jesus... Bud, you have fun with Uncle Gene?"

"YEEEAAAHH!" he roars, turning to face me, "*Sooo fun!!*" Half of his rattail hangs out of the corner of his mouth from swinging his head around. He spits it out, after three sloppy tries.

"Ho, some-body even try fo' get wise wit Uncle, too" says Gene, shaking his head. "Boy almos got to view one street fight free of charge, yea, boy?"

"But he said he was sorry," he giggles, cupping his hands to his mouth, as if recounting something apparently hilarious.

"Gene. What happened?"

They got an early start and left his cousin Troy's pad (another valet) by dawn and headed up to the North Shore in a lowered Nissan pickup truck, buzzing like a giant cell phone on silent from the subwoofers. Two Yamaha 400 dirt bikes stood strapped in the flatbed. He assures me they stopped in Wahiawa en route for a McDonald's hotcake breakfast for Jojo, like, *Don't worry, we fed the kid.* They got up to the motocross trails in

Kahuku by eight, smoked a bowl, and watched the roaring surf below illuminate and sharpen with the sun rising slowly behind them. According to Gene, Jojo just sat and stared for a while, mouth open, practically drooling in awe at the better riders, yanking the throttle, launching from one dirt ramp to the other, clicking their heels, or twisting their waists like break dancers above their handlebars, nearly disconnected from the bike, ten feet in midair. Pretty much a personal live extreme sports show playing out before his very eyes. After a couple hours of riding, they took him to the kiddie track, where Gene's friend let him test out his son's little 50cc. Which is like a two-foot-tall moped—no clutch or gears—that can still go speeds in excess of thirty mph. Gene swears they taught Jojo which was brake and gas, but apparently, lost in the euphoria of gas, he froze up, couldn't locate the brake, and went head over handle bars into an ironwood tree. He assures me that before the crash he had a blast.

Gene said they left by eleven in order to keep their "full itinerary" that day. They headed back to town on the H-2 south and stopped off in Wahiawa again, but this time for what Gene referred to as "Da Game Rooms."

Now, if you've ever been to Diamond Head Video back in the day, like when it used to be on Kapahulu Ave, you'd know a few things about that establishment. It was independently owned, pretty ghetto, had a kick-ass indie and foreign film selection, and some pretty weird employees. What you may or may not have known about the joint was that the whole storefront was just a ruse for their giant adult section. That while the video shop looked to be about thirty square feet, once you passed through the back black curtain, it opened up into a hidden room three times as big as the front, filled to the brim with porn. Like, movies, toys, costumes, etc. It was like passing through the closet in *The Lion, the Witch, and the Wardrobe* and stepping into Smut-Narnia.

Anyway, the place where Gene, Troy, and Jojo stopped in Wahiawa on the way back to town, Frankie's Korean BBQ, is like the Diamond Head Video of illegal gambling. Obviously, the front room is as advertised, a small Korean BBQ restaurant mostly for takeout orders, and has about four tables with attached chairs. To the left of the counter is an ubiquitous hall, one of those sleazy not-up-to-health-regs third world–type hallways you see in every Korean BBQ place that leads to the bathroom. At the end of the bathroom hall is a door, and on the other side of that door is a large room with a few long cafeteria-style tables and attached chairs. Those cafeteria tables at Frankie's are occupied by nerds, anywhere from twelve to forty-some-thing-year olds rolling twelve-sided die, playing Dungeons and Dragons and high-stakes Magic: The Gathering RPG. Apparently, these games get pretty serious and there's big betting going on, despite all the Dungeon Master talk and Velcro-shoed ComiCon types. That room also has a bathroom in the corner, and at the end of that hall, yet another door opens up into, well, some heavy-ass shit. There's a Tongan bouncer at the door with a metal detec-tor, and scattered about the room are various high-stake card games—Five-figure Pipito, Texas Hold 'Em, Black-jack, Pai Gau, Roulette, Balut, Craps, etc. Even large Scrabble boards where all the two-letter bitch words like "qi" or "to" are prohibited. And in the back half of that room, in two different corners, are cockfights and I.S.F.

The cockfights are pretty much what you'd picture, men and women, huddled and shouting, money in fists, arms waving, necks straining beneath a haze of cigarette smoke and crimson wings flapping in explosive fits. The razors are real. There is much blood spatter; it's fight to kill.

But in the other corner of the large back-back-room at Frankie's BBQ in Wahiawa is the I.S.F. pit. I.S.F. was something new to me, too. Inter-Species Fighting. This is, like, mongoose-on-two-cocks action, mongoose-on-mounted-chihuahuas, cock-mongoose-Chihuahua cage matches. It's a fascinating new wave of pit fighting, born right here in the islands, Gene explains, as if we're on the forefront of something truly groundbreaking. I won't get into the gory details, nor where they found their shady ass on-site veterinarian for emergency opps, but let's say you pit two cocks on a mongoose. The cocks, of course, have spurs on, and the mongoose has a small leather face mask with no mouth guard (so that it can bite). But the mongoose's guard is down most when it stands on its hind legs. The mounted Chihuahua is a new addition to the fights, mounted being a one-inch sharpened aluminum saber strapped to the dog's head. Kinda like a rhino horn. The Chihuahuas can't really be trained to lunge with that horn, like a bull or something, but at least when they go in to bite, the horn leads.

Gene assured me that Jojo saw none of the intra-species fights, only a glimpse of the gamecock ring, before Troy led him back to the Balut table, where they waited for Gene to finish. They left by two o'clock-ish, and Gene was $476 richer. They got back to Troy's house, switched vehicles, and drove up Tantalus to give Jojo a proper view of the south shore…which actually meant that they drove to the top so they could drift down. Clearly, Gene is a Jack of Black Trades, the art of drifting or sliding down lanes sideways in a lightweight rear-wheel sedan, another one of his favorite hobbies. Gene's even won a few drifting competitions out at Barber's Point since they've legalized a few events on a controlled track. He assured me that Troy and the boy rode ahead in the pickup to block cars and watch for cops, while he drifted down in a friend's Subaru Impreza, whom he'd met at the top.

And then, of course, hours before Gene dropped off Jojo, they went to the fights at the Blaisdell. Also not the greatest place for a young child, being that a crowd of a few thousand men drinking and watching other men fight makes everyone, well, punchy.

"Gene, haven't you told me about, like, three different fights you've gotten into at the Blaisdell parking lot on M.M.A. night? Why the hell'd you have to drag Jojo to something like that for?"

"Brah, Holloway." Somehow this explains everything.

Suddenly, Jojo jumps on my back and wraps his little arms around my neck, straining to lock his fingers.

"Boy! Uncle nevah taught you how fo' do one rear naked arm bar lai-dat, bu…" Gene exclaims, shaking his head.

"Lock dat fahkah, Hawaiian…"

"Gene, in a matter of twelve hours, you've managed to create a mini-moke."

"You know what, Captain Cook. I find dat term offensive. Easy fo jes sit on one soapbox and call one strong

Hawaiian male one moke because his hobbies stay different from yours, ah? Sucking haole-privilege, you! I just gave Boy one edu-cation dat Punalani could nevah give. And free of charge—no tuition, no moa scholah-ship, no moa' notting."

"Fine. Thanks, Gene. Take your lighter and cigarettes. I'll see you at work tomorrow."

"Kay den, haole," he says to me, then looks down at Jojo, "Kay den, Hawaiian." They reach to shake hands and simultaneously grab each others' forearms gladiator-style, then pound their chests with the side of their fists. "Boy! If you need new shawts, get one sale da-enna-da month at T.J. Maxx on Ward Ave." He speeds off onto Kalākaua, cutting a tourist off in the process, eyeing the guy out, mid-turn.

"Vamanos, Jojo!" I say. He grabs my hand and holds it as we walk, a tender break in the persona Gene had built while we walk back to my car.

"Wanna snip that tail, or you wanna keep it, bud?"

"Will Uncle be mad?" he asks sheepishly.

"No, Uncle Gene won't even notice."

"Yeah. Thinp it, den," he decides, his tongue poking through two vacant teeth like a lizard. I definitely didn't recall the kid losing any teeth yet.

19.

Wholesome-ass mentor-shit

I find Joel reading a *Star Advertiser* during his normal Wednesday afternoon shift at the 'Ohana Beach Hotel. Naturally, he looks up and dives straight into character. I really try not to indulge him when he gets like this; you could get stuck in this trap for hours with him. Which is exactly what he wants—someone to run lines with or someone he can try his shtick out on.

"Hey Joel, watsup, my man!" I say, sticking out a palm to shake his. He slips his wrist through my grasp, grabbing my forearm, pulling us chest to chest, actually, more nose to nose for the Polynesian exchange of breath, greeting. Which is probably equal to white-guy dreadlocks on the scale of cultural appropriation.

We are almost touching lips when he starts his whisper-rap verse. I try my hardest not to lose it, but here we friggin' go again.

Boy, this ain't no secret
You know I love you deep-let
Hold me close like a brotha
From anotha mothah...

He bumps the volume up with each line, nearly yelling now.

Let the world know we kin!
Love ain't out, nah, nah—IT'S IN!!

"Um, yeah, Joel, so I assume you're keeping with
your 'Year of the Rhyme' vow that I've heard the guys
talking about..."

I'm like the high priest of rappin', CELIBATE from
un-rhyme
But I don't fuck wit choir boys—I spit my verses on time!

He looks genuinely pleased at his process, beaming at
his own impromptu show.
"Kay, Joel. I came here because—"

Dra-dra-dra-Droppin' lyric-BOMBS on soulless cities
Jus' to make um hear sum-thin'
This is the YEAR of the rhyme, I don't STRAY from the rap
I swore an OATH in January, Joel keep his PROMISES in tact!

"Joel, I really gotta..."

Even on the IN-side I keep rappin'
The soul is a nail—you gotta keep on tappin'!

"Right... Joel... focus. I have to ask you something."

The soul is a nail...you gotta keep on tappin, the soul is a nail...you gotta keep on tappin'...

He's whispering now, repeating the hook over and over again, and between each line he mimes pounding a nail, beating his fist on his chest.

The soul is a nail...you gotta keep on tappin'...the soul is a nail... you gotta keep on tappin'...

And then suddenly, like yanking a heart out of his own chest, he passes the rhyme to me in his palms, like, *Now, your turn.*

Begrudgingly I repeat it, knowing there's only one way out of this game, "The soul is a nail...you gotta keep on tappin'" Sigh. "'The soul is a nail...you gotta keep on tappin'...'"

Yeeee-uuuuh, Boy-eeee, you caught the hook,
Now what kinda problem you got; let Dr. Rhymes take a look!

This is far more painful than I thought it'd be. He'll go off on a tangent like this for as long as you let him, and, the more frustrated and fed up you get, the more he revels in the charade. With Joel, the joke is always on you.

"Okay, so you told me you did some volunteer work as

a Big Brother for the Boys and Girls Club of Hawai'i, right? But did you ever work with any homeless or foster kids out there? Seriously, Joel, just chill—I'm being for real."

So I offer you my services, at the beginning of the summer,
But you never called me back, jus' cause my record was
a bummer?

He grins mischievously. God, I knew this would come. "Joel, I'm sorry, man, I was super busy. I nev—"

So you're a business man, coulda' sworn you was a—

"JOEL! Just cut the shit for *one* second. I'm serious, dude."

He looks at me, cocking his head, stifling a smile.

"Were you or were you *not* a Big Brother to some kid out on the Westside?" I ask.

Joel pinches the bridge of his nose and makes a show of looking up, over and around me both ways, so no one catches him breaking "his vow." "Yeah, dawg, I was," he says. "Like, last year I started seeing this chick that was a Big Sister, so I signed up, too...pretty much to impress her."

The shit you do to get laid, huh?

"And you were out on the Westside?"

"Yeah, she'd worked in the program for a long time— she might've even been a Little Sister at one time, dawg— but she linked me up with a kid that lived near Makaha. Pretty much every Wednesday for a couple months when their school got out, me and her would drive out there, pick up that kid and she'd pick up hers, and we'd hang out at the beach or go for a hike. Wholesome-ass mentor shit, playah. But *her* girl, daaawg…she got a tough little mini *tita* that lived in the tents out by Kea'au beach park. That little girl would fuck up my Little Brother whenever they'd play togther," he laughs. "Kind of felt bad for my boy. Why, what's up?"

"Okay, well how about this, did you ever see this little guy around?" I scroll through my phone and show him a picture of Jojo. Joel leans over, takes a good look, and starts glowing. He shrugs.

"What, Joel?"

"Yo, what if I've seen this lil playah, an' what if I haven't?" he grins.

"What are you…are you trying to negotiate this?"

He looks back at me blankly.

"Whattaya want, Joel?" I say through my teeth.

"I want some time in the ring, dawg."

"I'm not following."

"I want a day with you at Punalani, playah. Guest speaker mutha-fuckaaah!"

"Joel, with your record—this isn't public school rules—"

The soul is a nail…you gotta keep on tappin'…the soul is a nail…you gotta keep on tappin'… he chants, winding back up into character.

"Fine," I surrender. "You got it, Joel. You'll come with me for a day."

He pumps his fist like *Yesssss!* and grabs my head, kissing my forehead.

"*That*," he says, pointing at the boy on the phone, "is my dawg Jo-Squared, kid. That boy's got it rough, dawg. Lives out in the bush *past* Kea'aus. And we never ever saw his parents, the kid just ran wild around there. My girl said his parents, or *whoever* looked after him, were all tweaked on ice or smack or something. Always gone, lookin' for more. I think they shared a tent with some old lady, though. We'd stop by now and then and give him our leftovers or fresh malasadas. I'd play him some uke tunes. Jo's a sweet fuckin' kid, always had a gecko or chameleon in his paws. Probably was lonely as shit, man. Dawg, is Jojo straight? He ain't hurt or anything, is he? What's going on?"

"No, Jojo's fine. He's been with us…over at the Sands."

Joel frowns, confused. "The…Sands? With *ya'll?*"

"Listen, everything's fine. We're just trying to get some papers for him and put him in school this fall. You don't know anything else about his parents do you?"

"Uh-uh. Never seen 'em, just heard they're dirtbags."

A line of cars was beginning to clog up the valet lobby, snaking out onto Kalākaua Ave. I look at the traffic and then look at Joel, like, *You gonna get that?* He doesn't seem concerned one bit.

"Hey…what happened with the—you're not a Big Brother anymore?" I ask him.

"Nah, kid. Things went downhill with that chick, plus my vehicle…doesn't exist, so there went my ride to the Westside. Yo, how soundproof are the walls in the class-rooms at Punalani, dawg? And what's the dress code? You got a washer/dryer at your pad? Mine is like my vehicle…"

"Laundry service wasn't part of the bargain, dude. See ya next Wednesday," I say, crossing the street from the hotel, not believing for a second that Joel would show up.

20.

Den he started pal-pa-tay-shens

As a valet in a hotel, you always work around or near, but never really *with* bellmen. Working "bell" is where careers go to die. I know... "says the valet," but anyway, a "doorman" is just a glorified bellman. Doormen or "Door," as it's called, don't have to take the bags all the way up to the rooms; they just "control the front" or greet people, pre-check them in, and make sure the flow of vehicle traffic is, well, flowing in the front of the hotel. Many of these guys were once valets. Like, over twenty years ago. I'm guessing they got too old to run, or blew out their knees and moved on to other things. Ideally, we're all supposed to work together, but these guys can get fairly lecherous. Their tricks and schemes are finely tuned, polished, and all out in the open, masked with an old-timer's charm. They receive bribes and illegal commissions off various taxis, driving services, and tour guides. That's one of their main hustles: Taxis, which are going to and from the airport (a generous fare) *want* to be around when the hotel guests are ready to go. So the doormen control the lobby and let a group of cabbies park in our lot all day—for a price. They charge at least twenty dollars for each cabby to park in our zone and we don't see a cent. The doormen will literally track those cabbies down like mobsters demanding their package if they don't get their cut promptly.

They also piggyback cars we bring up to the guests, insisting on lifting bags for them (which should be our job), and then take or expect half the tip for lifting one bag. That's a five-second gesture versus our two-minute run to the guest's car, and they want half of that? Shit just ain't right. And the bad part is that we can't say anything, because we're a contracted company working for the hotel, while the doormen and bellmen are hotel employees. Thus seniority and preference goes to these bastards.

Some of these saps who've been doing this for over twenty years have developed lucrative, long-lasting "relationships" with guests. Obviously something that as valets, we could and should be doing, but Christ, we're too busy running to fetch their car. And so while we pull up their rental, the door/bellmen schmooze the living shit out of them. I mean, these guys keep books on these guests. I'm serious, they literally have mini pocket pads that they'll mark all the intricate details about, say, the Henderson family. *Haole dad, Colombian wife. Two kids— Brian, Jasmine. Accountant from Fresno, housewife. First visit: Summer of '07. Brian—going to college soon. Occasionally, grandmother accompanies (how is she doing?).* Et cetera, et cetera. Until the doormen have officially become their "Guy in Hawai'i." Off-the-beaten-path tourist sites, restaurant recommendations, private(ish) beaches, B&B beachfront rentals (with commission!), the list goes on. Until they're happily receiving a big fat tip at the end of their stay or five-spots as frequent as alohas. These families, maybe hundreds of them, have become their valued, cherished, perennially returning clients. Extended friggin' family. At the same time, you can't knock the hustle; that's some long game right there. Ten years in development. Respect.

Everyone knows that there's undeniably something special about Jojo. The valets, the guests, *anyone*, immediately sees his insatiable appetite for life. That pure, wide-eyed gusto for every minute of the day—and they're changed by it somehow. Softened, even for a moment. Even the doormen notice, who, like I said, as valets we have a relationship with comparable to, say, the U.S. and Pakistan. Allies on paper, but we suspect the doormen might be harboring Taliban. Whatever—even those cretins see it.

Anyway, lately we've noticed Jojo has a new pet: a gecko. A gecko he refers to as Chuck (short for Chucky Cheese). I was unaware, however, how Jojo tamed Chuck until Wade—a particularly devious doorman—gave me the scoop. Lately, Chuck just chills on Jojo's little shoulder, and Jojo just walks around and comes up to us, pretending like he "just happened to be around at the time," but is totally fishing for compliments. I was halfway through a grueling three-eleven shift the first time I saw the two of them. Jojo walks up to me in the key room, looks over his left shoulder, and shifts his right one to me with the hapless reptile clinging to his t-shirt. Clearly, my cue.

"Woow, Jojo boy. Where'd you find your new bud?" I ask.

"Saved 'um," he replies, nonchalantly.

"Saved him, eh?" I encourage.

"No *fo' reals*, brah—he wen save dat gecko, coz," exclaims Wade, eyes wide, nodding solemnly. He appears to be lingering, out of camera view down here in the garage, on a smoke break. He takes a drag. "Brah, I seen 'um happen last week, coz," he begins. "Jojo boy was hanging out by da kine wit us, da valet desk in da lobby, yeah? An' was supah busy, so was me handing out da valet tickets while da boys was running fo' cars. (This means he was handing out tickets, so that the driver gives *him* a tip, mistaking him as the valet. The dirty scum…) So, I pull out one ticket from da ticket box an had one gecko attach to 'um! But I nevah knew what da ting was, and da ting wen scare me, ah? So I wen *fling* da ticket," Wade pantomimes the gesture, arms flying limply, nearly hitting Gene, who's jogging to a car.

"'Chout, Wade!" shouts Gene.

"Ho, no need get mad, Hawaiian. I sorry," says Wade, continuing. "So I wen fling da ting dat way, yeah? An it wen arc ovah two guests dat stay waiting for da car, and I tink da ticket was stuck to da gecko's paws, yeah?" He pats his palms together for emphasis, eyes still saucers. "Anyways, it wen hit da fountain seat, bounce off, and fall on da floah. Jus' *make*-die, I tought. But maybe …was *playing* dead," he says, pointing his index finger skyward, reasoning aloud. "Fahk, I dunno, but Jojo boy seen da whole *event*, and wen rush ovah to da gecko, spock 'um on da floah, and he wen pick up da gecko's body."

Jojo nods solemnly as the doorman recounts the tale.

"Anyways, I tought da ting stay dead, or, maybe jus' playing da kine, but Jojo pick da ting up—an he staht *respirating* 'um! Like, mout-to-mout kine stuff, bu. I no shit you, brah! I couldn't believe 'um. Musta seen 'um on TV or some-ting. He had da gecko in his palms and da ting was all..."

Wade makes a lifeless pose like that of Jesus in his mother's arms after the crucifixion in Michelangelo's *La Pieta*.

"So den he started pal-pa-tay-shens. Jus' two thumbs lai-dat, going: one...two...tree... And den he wen blow into da gecko's little mout, but I was like, 'Jojo, no do dat, brah—*pilau*, da gecko's mout,' but he no like listen, just kept working, fo like two, tree moa minutes...And den da gecko *kick*! So Jojo open up his palm and da ting staht squirming, like *stree-eetching* back to life."

Wade arcs his back and cranes his neck like the small creature.

"So Jojo put 'um down, took one step back, an da gecko wen run up to Jojo, den up his leg and onto his chest. Was so heavy, I almos' tear up. Fahking nay-cha, yeah?" he shakes his head in reverence. "And now da ting stay riding Jojo's shouldah, lookit," he says, pointing to Jojo. Jojo nods an affirmative like, *Yup*.

"Sucking ting is like Jojo's pet now. My wife can make origami and can make da kine aloha shirts outta dollah bills. Would be classic if we made 'um one origami aloha shirt, ah?" says Wade.

Jojo looks up and nods. "Chuck needs a shirt."

"We'll get him a shirt, bud," I assure him. "What's... that around your neck, Jo?" I ask, noticing a sparsely clustered puka shell necklace beneath his collar.

"Gene made 'um for me—it's teeth!" He pulls the string around his neck, and they are not puka shells, but six or seven lost baby teeth with small drill holes in each of them, thread together by twine.

"*Gene!*" I holler down the hallway of the lot. Gene's hanging out by the trunk of his Subaru, talking shit with Darwin, who just arrived. He flicks his chin, *Wat!*

"Why is Jojo wearing a necklace of human teeth like some kind of AWOL psychopath?"

"Brah, you told me fo' cool it wit him on da high action—so we had one arts-n-craffs-kine day, last week, coz!" he says. "Most of dem is my niece teeth, brah! *Mean*, ah?"

21.

Tūtū Raymond, the last of Honolulu's formidable Flower Madams

Take a seat, bitches, take a seat! Don't *make* me late for my evening zumba class, mutha fuckahs."

Five women, somewhere between nineteen and thirty-five, plus Marisela and I, settle into lawn chairs of varying heights facing two collapsible plastic catering tables. Somewhere around 10th Street in the heart of Kaimukī, we've gathered in a large single home garage, awaiting orders from the boss. On one table are stacks of leftover *Star Advertisers* (the garage doubling as a regional paper route home base) and on the other table, bundles of roses, tulips, carnations, lilies, daffodils and more, separated into brilliant bouquets and floral arrangements. Sitting on the edge of the plastic table, sagging from her weight, is Tūtū Raymond, the last of Honolulu's formidable Flower Madams. Formerly a he, and some hours of surgery away from a she, Tūtū Raymond is an imposing figure. Wig off, she is completely bald, donning smoky eyeliner and thick, clumping mascara. She wears cherry-red lipstick, a loose blouse open at the third button (exposing an ample, albeit artificial bosom), skin-tight denim leggings over platform slippers, giving her six-two-ish frame a couple more inches of fuck-off. With the way she sits, heels planted and legs spread, leaning up against the edge of the table, an unmistakable lump of sex protrudes from her left inner-thigh.

"Here comes the pep talk," whispers Marisela through the corner of her mouth.

"Ya'll here, ladies?" says Tūtū, scanning the small crowd. "Ooo, and a plus-one—*dame la gasolina*, Mari!"

She looks me up and down quickly and winks. Two fit and handsome local men in matching silver dress vests—who I just now realize have been behind her the whole time arranging flowers—look around both sides of her at me and nod, "Mmm-hmm."

"Now, I've said it once, and I'll say it every mutha-fuckin' time..."

"*Every* time," mouths Marisela to me.

"...Tūtū Raymond didn't come to run the flower game on this here island by *sharing*, queens...Tūtū fuckin' TOOK it. Now, some of ya'll know my story and some of ya'll don't..."

"Literally, *everyone* knows her story," Mari whispers to me.

Tūtū snaps her fingers and one of the young men clicks play on a small iPod speaker. Beyonce's "Love on Top" begins, a soundtrack to accompany her subsequent monologue.

It's not some wild *X-Men Origins* story, or anything. A pretty standard last-man-standing-tale, really. Fifty-seven-year-old Raymond Kahoʻai was born and raised right here in this very home where we sit. Graduating from Kaimuki High School and unable to afford college, she became a bouncer at Waikīkī nightclubs through most of the '70s. Before coming-out in '82, she'd frequent the drag shows at Hulas and Bar 7, where she came across her first flower girls. Right around that time, the Hawaiʻi economy was booming and in a rapid upswing, the Japanese yen strengthening rapidly. There were multiple flower ladies with respective routes and crews patrolling, if not battling, around town—an era known as the Flower Wars. Raymond decided to quit bouncing and start his own flower girl company. After nearly a decade of building a small team and buying product from an unnamed and exclusive local florist, Tūtū Raymond bought the game.

According to Marisela, based on a rumor that's endured decades, Tūtū Raymond crushed the competition with an unusual added ingredient: cocaine. It was the ʻ80s and her eldest brother Roger was a well-known dealer. Until Roger was caught (who would go on to serve time for six years before returning home and starting a paper route), Raymond would steal a few grams of blow from him here and there and sprinkle it in some of her flower's petals. Then she'd urge her flower girls to have prospective customers take a sniff—most of which already had a taste for coke—and very quickly the flower sales tipped in Tūtū's favor. Her signature seller was known among the public as Rose Bumps. But before her brother went away, thus terminating Tūtū's secret ingredient, she'd done too much damage to the other companies. Today, she's the only one left.

"And why is Tūtū Raymond still around today in this increasingly artificial world, queens?" she quizzes, one hand to her ear, call-and-response style.

"Coo-cainnnne," sighs the crowd sarcastically.

"No, bitches! Through sustainable, locally grown, and responsibly farmed flora!" A few girls chime in with her toward the end. "Yes, queens. You get it." Her boys behind her nod affirmatively, *Mm-hmm*, and separate the bouquets for their respective brokers.

"All right then, *wahines*, ya'll got your Square Readers, yes? No drinking on the job, no matter who's buyin,' and last but not least: *Push the lilies.*"

"Tūtū, people ain't feeling the lilies this summer—"

"Queen, I don't necessarily *feel* that tube top you rockin' but another man might, if you sellin' it right, baby. *Learn* the customer. *Push* the lilies, bitches! Tūtū's only three grand away from flippin' this thing inside out," she says, grabbing the denim bulge between her legs, "and it's you babies that are gonna transform me! Now come and receive your routes, queens."

I have the night off and decided to accompany Marisela on her beat, and with no warning given, showed up to this.

"So, I think it's safe to say that your employer officially wins 'World's Most Fabulous Boss.' Are you *kidding* me?" I hiss at Marisela, "This is amazing. Why on earth would you ever wanna be a self-employed author? Tūtū Raymond is better than *any* agent you could ask for!"

"Tūtū Raymond can't get me published," she says, walking up to the table to get her basket.

"Horse shit," I counter.

"Now, it's a Friday, queens, so if ya'll gotta re-up mid-shift, text Perry," says Tūtū, motioning to one of the boys behind her. "*Not* me, okay?" Perry shakes his head and mouths, *Not her.* "And don't be afraid to touch up the carnations, dolls. A lil Krylon spray paint keeps those petals *vivid.*"

I watch the other flowergirls get in line, and they roust each other, slapping each others' asses crudely and hamming it up. When Tūtū Raymond has her back to the girls, one of the flower girls grabs a tulip and holds it like an erect cock, thusting it into Tūtū's butt, showing off to her friend. Her friend laughs and holds two fingers to her mouth, wiggling her tongue through the "V." Their behavior was oddly familiar. These flower girls are a lot like...*my* guys.

"So, this is the male suitor," says Tūtū Raymond to Marisela, sizing me up. "Woulda thought Mari had already chewed you up and spat you out, *flaco.*" Her two backup boys giggle hysterically at her flank. "Push the lilies, lovebirds," she tells us and clomps away on her gigantic heels.

Marisela approaches the table and Perry hands her a basket and a spreadsheet. "You get mauka side of Kalā kaua and Kuhio, all of Kapahulu and Kapiʻolani up to Piʻikoi today, honey. Need any protection?" he asks, pointing at an open tray with pepper spray, switchblades, and personal attack alarms.

"I'm good, Perry. Thanks," says Marisela. "Got my key chain mace and my bodyguard right here." Perry looks at me, rolls his eyes, and scoffs.

"Has it ever come to that?" I ask her, a little shocked. "Not with me, but apparently it has with a couple flower girls in the past. But Tūtū and the boys found the dudes both times and kicked the living shit out of them. Like, sent them to friggin' Queen's Hospital. No pun intended."

"Well, goddamn."

We roll down Kalākaua toward the heart of Waikīkī, and Marisela explains how she hits the early diners this cycle where it's a bit slower, before the late night action. Late night is the strip clubs, dance clubs, dive bars, and after-hour joints listed on her Excel spreadsheet that Tūtū scheduled. There are so few employees most girls don't cross paths, and as we dip into restaurant after restaurant I witness a lot of no's, which don't particularly seem to phase Marisela one bit.

"You can have an okay night selling a flower here, or a flower there, but what you're really trying to score —and it *does* happen—is to get some schmuck to buy the whole basket," says Marisela, pulling into the Royal Hawaiian, also one of our valet accounts.

"Who the hell does a guy buy an entire basket for?"

"Honestly...*us*."

"What!?"

"So, you let him flirt with you, maybe hint at how amazing it would be to find a guy so generous that he'd buy the whole shebang, maybe hang a lei around his neck, and if he feels like wasting his money—ya let him. Then you stick around a few more minutes after he's bought you a drink and then slip the hell out as fast as you can before he feels like you're obliged to reciprocate."

"You go girl. Hashtag Me-Tu..tu."

"Tūtū taught us well."

"Mari, I've been meaning to ask," I say, rubbing my chin, "But...why do they call her *Tūtū* Raymond?"

"Oh, Tūtū knocked up some girl in high school when they were both seventeen, and then her kid knocked up a girl when he was seventeen, too, sooo...she's been a grandma for about five years now."

Compared to most of the hotels us valets work at, Mari's night is relatively tame. But there is something very freeing about her constant mobility. Sure, her income depends on hitting as many venues as she can, but that steady movement makes the night go *sooo* much faster than in the confines of a garage. Between bar stops, we talk shop, share tricky scenes that we've been working on, and flesh them out aloud together. We come up with a couple new characters and bounce concepts off one another. We trade Jojo stories and imagine what he'll grow up to become in ten years' time. She gets a few bites at some of the restaurants on Kapahulu, and when we swing by Femme Nu, she actually makes a big sale in the line before she even steps through the door. Two local guys jog up to her from across the street, and both buy arrangements for their girlfriends dancing inside. According to Mari, most of her sales are at strip clubs, and I find that pretty adorable.

Tailing Marisela into the club to deliver their flowers, two men slink out past me, half-drunk, one with a very familiar face. I notice those red lips on his neck and realize it's one of the Gypsies—Steve—Skippy's younger brother.

"Steve! How are ya, bud?" I greet him.

He glances up and smiles, glassy-eyed, "Eh, bro!" but keeps moving.

"Steve...Steve! Can I get a sec?"

"Can't right now, bro..." he says, jumping into a Chevy Blazer, his wife at the wheel. "Catch me another time!" And the truck skids away. I was getting the sneaking suspicion that they were avoiding me.

"Haole, you goin' come in o' wat?" asks a burly bouncer in a pressed suit.

"Is there a cover if I'm with her?" I ask, pointing toward Marisela, who's dissapeared down the red carpet, more of a faded, pale pink these days from foot traffic.

"Pay to play, you fakah!" he laughs and holds out an open palm.

Amen to that.

22.

Break out the good shit

'm as quick as a cricket...I'm as slow as a snail...I'm as small as an ant...I'm as large as a whale...

"I love you, Jojo," whispers Marisela, leaning over his olive face and softly kissing his forehead. He's just showered and smells like a goddamned Irish Spring soap factory.

Jojo's face implodes ecstatically. Like he just saw the Promised Land. Like a kitten getting scratched in that spot behind the ears. He literally purrs.

Quick as a Cricket is Jojo's fav and whenever we get to, *I'm as wild as a chimp*, Jojo tickles his underarms and grunts, "Ooo-oooo-ooooo!" like a monkey.

"Wait a sec!" I spurt.

"What, Uncle?" asks Jojo quizzically. The two of them stare at me for a moment.

"That's a coincidink, because...I love you, *too!*" I say, burying my nose into his ear and sniffing rapidly like a curious dog. It's kinda our thing. He giggles, tickled by the sniffing, and flips his head to Marisela, who meets him with another quick peck to the cheek.

It's my night for Jojo watch and he lies between us on Marisela's sofa bed, back in Palolo Valley, where we've tucked him in with a bedtime story. I suppose it's *our* night, really. We both crave his affection, both yearn to see his eyes flutter from the kisses. Right beneath our noses, it went from *having* to take care of Jojo—to *getting* to. What a power play. What a friggin' hustler.

Jojo pauses from giggling, looks up toward no one in particular—at the ceiling, really—and exclaims, "I love you." It comes out almost like a question, and he starts laughing by the end of "you," but regardless, Marisela and I both melt. I think the phrase startled him even more than us. *I...love...you...* As loud as a whisper. Like a careful secret to himself. I wonder if he's saying how he honestly felt. Or if he's saying what he knew Marisela and I felt about each other. If so, I appreciate the assist.

We hear one of those summer showers rustling the tī leaf and plumeria trees just outside her studio window. We hear the trade winds sweeping by, carrying the rain through the valley, from the mountains toward the sea. It splatters softly against the roof with each gust.

Jojo pulls the covers higher to his neck and yawns an impossibly wide gulp, something that reminds me of a hyena I'd seen one time on *Animal Planet*.

He's never once called us Mom or Dad. He knows the score.

"Tell me a storrrrryyyyyy," he says to the both of us.

I look over at Marisela, and she grins back, shrugging.

But she begins, her voice so clear and soothing, "There once was a young boy named Flo-jo, and he was raised by a large pack of wolves..."

"Flojo!" cries Jojo. "Das almos' like *my* name!"

"Yes, it is," she continues politely, "And coincidentally, Flojo looked a little bit like you as well..."

"Auntie Mari, are there any wolves around here?"

"Not on this island," I say, "But Flojo was playing too close to the shore on a certain North Shore beach when, before he knew it, a huge shore-break wave grabbed him from the shoreline and washed him out to sea, and *aaallll* the way to a forgotten, outlying Hawaiian island..."

"And on this island—what's the name of that island?" asks Marisela.

"Loco Moco," I reply.

"Right, and on Loco Moco island, there are no humans, just animals. And of these animals, a *lot* of wolves..."

"But the wolves aren't vicious or mean," I say.

"No, not at all," she adds.

"I mean, yeah, they're feral and wild, but maybe more...misunderstood, right?"

"Well, what do da wolfs do there, Uncle?" asks Jojo, lazily now, between yawns, quickly fading.

"They run. All day they run. On the golden sands of beaches that surround the entire island."

"And on trails through the mountains that *reeeeach* into the sky," says Marisela.

"Through the tall grass in the meadows at the foot of the valleys," I continue.

"Through the puddles in the swamps that splash with every swift step," she whispers.

"Until the pack has run itself worn and gathers in a place in a corner of the meadow."

"Where they fall asleep together, huddled in a pack of plush fur, on a bed of spongy, soft moss."

Jojo's eyelids do their last dance before falling to their knees.

"And snore a song in the night sky…"

We kiss him on the temples simultaneously, and he grins a very subtle grin, nearly asleep.

We slip off the couch like fleeing sloths and move to the kitchen to listen to the valley. Outside, Palolo's song is a brilliant symphony of weather. Marisela works open the cork of a half-empty bottle of Costco merlot.

"Breaking out the good shit, huh?" I say.

"Kirkland's finest."

"Kirkland is that region of France where the soil's enriched with blood of fallen soldiers from the Napoleanic Wars, no?"

"*Oui, oui*!"

"We make a pretty hot dream team, huh?"

"Whoa, daddy—don't know if I'm quite ready to squirt out chillin's for ya yet," she says.

"I meant with the improv story," I laugh. "We kinda killed it. I mean, you were definitely the Pippen to my Jordan…but you held your own."

"Oh, riiight. *Sure* that's what you meant," nods Marisela.

Apart from various nights with Jojo, as of late, we'd been sharing work with each other. Having passes on one another's chapters, editing revisions and rewrites.

It was something more intimate than the sex, I think. I helped her polish her query letter and had even felt more inspired at Punalani. As in, well...*teaching*, more than using my students as unauthorized underlings. I hadn't told Marisela about the Ralph predicament, or really any of my sketchy misdoings in there. Maybe I just care more now. About something. About someone.

"You hear back from any agents, lately?' I ask.

"Mmm, sort of. A friend of mine who did a year at UH represents a few YA authors out in New York, and she claims she's reading it...Sooo, hopefully her intern gives it a fair shake," she laughs. "You?"

"Aw, a 'Top Ten Coffee Shops on O'ahu' here, a 'Discovering Honolulu's Historic Chinatown' there... Thirty cents a word, and worth every penny!"

"Any new info since you talked to Joel about Jojo's folks?" she asks.

"Nada. But most of the valets unanimously claim they've seen that car with the Gypsies before the couple. Of course, they're nowhere to be found. I thought I had some cell numbers, but none of them work."

"Well...more Jojo for us then, huh?"

"Yep. We gotta get him enrolled somewhere after summer, though," I say, finishing the last of my glass. "And we need some papers for that."

23.

Rink rats

The Ice Palace indoor ice skating rink in the blue-collar community of Salt Lake is already a bizarre socioeconomic slice of O'ahu's pie, but when Jojo stepped through the tinted doors and saw his breath for the first time, it was as if the clocks stood still. Sure, seeing your breath for the first time is old hat for anyone on the Mainland, but for a local boy who's never ventured off-island, watching that air condense and vaporize—that's goddamn sorcery.

Indeed, Marisela and I watched Jojo get his mind blown for a full five minutes, trying to grab the smoke in his hands, or see if the same phenomenon would occur through his nostrils…basically, the kid nearly hyperventilated before he could even get his ice skates on. But I say "bizarre" as far as the scene goes mostly because of the demographic. It's just all over the spectrum, from extended families in polar-level parkas celebrating birthdays to off-duty marines in t-shirts and cargo shorts welcoming the cold they left somewhere behind to awkward teenagers faking their ineptitude so they can cling to their dates more closely to mini figure skaters in tutus attempting double axels under their mothers' hawkish supervision to rink rats spraying unsuspecting patrons with aggressive hockey stops.

And that's just the scene on ice. Upstairs, behind the plexiglass are the reserved party tables where parents mix brutal cocktails with the liquor smuggled in their coolers hidden below the fried noodle entrees. The zit-faced concessions kid will turn a blind eye on the boozing with some minor baksheesh. Then there's the DJ booth, where a middle-aged man calls out birthday shout-outs and "Baby, take me back's" like a hip hop hype man, all the while spinning the latest tracks from 2003. You know, because Hawai'i.

And all of this following that loaded question that comes after payment and sizing that may or may not reveal something about your sexuality: figure or hockey? Ice skates, that is. Because even if a young boy wanted to go with figure skates, or a young girl with hockey, they'd never hear the end of it from their cohorts. Because even Hawai'i has some work left to do with social constructs. Go figure.

Anyhow, try as he may, you could probably get a good idea of how well a kid that's never seen his breath in his life fares on ice skates. Picture the classic man-steps-on-banana-peel cartoon trope and that's pretty much every slippery step with Jojo. We've been holding his hands between us, steadily making our way around the rink with him, Jojo kicking his skates up chest-high frontways and backwards, uncontrollably...the stubborn S.O.B. That, or he doesn't want to look like a complete nerd in front of the other kids, thus casting us away to work the steel training walker on his lonesome. Which we've respected, keeping a close distance behind the centerline rink opening.

Watching from the players seats, Mari's gaze never leaves the boy, like a watchful mama bear. She even had the front desk plug in that it was his birthday, and every time his name flashed on the electric scoreboard, she'd holler at him, "*Yeahhhh, Jojo!*" and Jojo would try to stifle a smile, looking away from us to hide his blush. It's been nearly half an hour of him behind the walker with little improvement (we're thinking he's more of a water man than ice guy) when a small gang of rink rats discover Jojo, his back to us at the moment, barely within earshot. But the three small ruffians greet him like a long-lost brother.

I can feel Mari's instincts kick in as she tenses, perhaps to move toward the boy and interject. Rink rats, a breed of lawless *keiki*, akin to the surf rats on the North Shore, the skate rats at Keolu or the Wall rats in Waikīkī, are a rascally brand of local boy and girl that reek havoc on Palace patrons deserving of an ice-laced hockey stop. Or, hockey check if need be.

These rascals, however, appear to know Jojo, welcoming him with open arms and a series of complex handshakes, a relationship from years in and out of shelters. Mari relaxes her posture and offers to grab us a pizza from concessions.

"Promise me you'll keep an eye on him?" she asks, leaving the bench.

I nod profusely and while waiting for her to return, play with my phone and pretend like I'm not eavesdropping on the boys' curious conversation...

"Bruddah, you not adopted yet?" exclaims the alpha boy, a hoarse preteen wearing a giant Supreme hoodie and backward Tap Out cap nesting so lightly on his hair one could blow it off his head with a strong puff. "Jojo, you gotta get on board, bu, da train stay leaving da station."

"All *aboardddd*," echoes a smaller boy that appears to hang on every word of the alpha's.

"Choo-choooo," affirms a third of similar stature.

"Coz, adoption? Game changah, Hawaiian," says the alpha, dabbing after each statement like a physical punctuation mark.

"Changes da game," chirps number two.

"All bets off, brah," solidifies number three.

"You outta da sheltahs, yeah?" says alpha.

Jojo nods. "I'm wit dem now, up there," he says, motioning to us. "Usually..." which comes out more like a question.

"Brah, one adoption house like one Hilton compared to one fostah home, let alone one transitional."

"Like one Marriott, Jojo."

"Sucking Disney's Aulanis, bu."

"All you guys adopted?" asks Jojo, struggling to keep upright, even with the metal walker.

The two smaller boys shake their heads, but the alpha answers for them regardless, "Not yet. But dey getting there. Das your fostah parents, dem?" he asks, flicking his eyebrows at us behind the low wall.

Jojo nods his head.

"He get one record?" asks the alpha.

"He get one job?" asks number two.

"He get one house?" asks number three.

"Jojo, you gotta start da process, Hawaiian. Get one case workah, da home study goin' take, like, tree months for make 'um legal, bu."

"Get in gear," adds number two.

"Apply pressure," adds number three.

"Jojo, my new parents? I get *any-ting* I like, bu. You just gotta learn how fo' work 'um. If I like one PlayStation and dey tell me no can...I '*regress*,'" he says with air quotes.

"PS4," confirms number two.

"GameStop, Kahala," says number three.

"It's all about da triggers, Jojo," says the alpha.

"Milk da triggers," says number two.

The third boy pantomimes milking a cow, pulling the udder carefully, with two hands.

"If dey say no, but try fo reach out fo hug you: flinch, like taught was goin' hit you. One time I wen curl up in one ball and fake like was crying, like one flashback-kine ting. By enna da week: sucking iPad Pro," says the alpha, throwing both arms to the left, chest-high, burying his forehead into the crux of his elbow, a formidably long dab.

"*Cherryyy* apps," nods number two.

"Apple stock," says number three.

Christ, these kids were crafty. Feigning like I wasn't spying on this nefarious reunion, I holler out to Jojo before shit got too real.

"Jojo! You hungry, my man? Got some hot pepperoni coming, bud..."

The three rink rats look at me like they've just been

busted shoplifting, dab to Jojo farewell, and skate away, kicking up ice with each lunge. Jojo just barely makes his way back to the centerline gate ten feet away, then clunks toward me, the blades on his skates bending outward awkwardly, like a toddler walking in high heels. Nearly at the bench, he snags an edge on someone's hockey bag and trips forward onto his face, two steps from my arms. I jump over to inspect the damage and he's pretty much fine, save a couple scratches on his palms.

Arriving with the pizza and fountain drinks, Mari must've seen the fall and mouths to me worriedly, "*I thought I told you to watch him. This is what I was SAYING...*"

I shrug, like, *I thought I was!,* and we tear into the stringy, hot mess of mozzarella in silence.

"Are you guys gonna adopt me?" asks Jojo, slicing through the bullshit.

Mari, sipping her Diet Coke, almost does a spit-take.

"Also, I like join the HHL youth hockey league."

"Well, which one is it gonna be?" I ask. "You know you gotta get off the trainer to be in the league, right?"

Mari slugs me in the shoulder while Jojo looks out at the ice to think about his options.

"I can join da league after I get adopted, yeah?" he says charmingly, batting his eyes with a grin.

"Yes," I answer. Which kind of slips out of my mouth accidentally like a belch.

The boy looks at me for a split second, dead in the eyes, searching for any glimmer of truth in the bullshit. That kind of look you never forget, big brown eyes carrying his entire human experience, every pain and let-down and car trunk (and, oh, there wasn't just one trunk) orbiting those pupils, blazing a hole right through my core.

His gaze breaks. He reaches into the box and scarfs down almost three slices of pizza without breathing.

"I'm gonna practice hockey stops now," he decides, and clomps toward the ice, grabbing a walker again with hands shiny from the pizza grease.

Together, Mari and I watch the boy slip and slide in place, involuntarily gliding forward, struggling to stand.

"Were you serious about that adoption stuff?" asks Mari, eyes locked on Jojo.

"Yeah. At least, I think I am. We gotta figure out something for him, better than Palani's house or a foster home, right? I mean...why not?"

Mari's head drops onto my shoulder tenderly.

"It's really hard to picture you as a dad."

"Aw, thanks for the support."

"But I could help you...if you want?"

I nestle my head into hers while we watch Jojo make his way toward the rink rats. Graciously, they encircle him, and the alpha pulls Jojo's walker while skating backward. Jojo hangs on for dear life, and I can see the whites of his eyes from here while the two smaller boys flanking him diligently push forward. I can't figure out if Mari likes me for me, or me as a wannabe dad, or if there's even any light between the two anymore. But I can slide into that role if that's what it takes not to screw this up.

24.
Rome wasn't built in a day

Nobody really knows Jojo's exact birth date, but we're thinking seven or eight...ish. Somehow, he doesn't really know his exact age or date, either. Sweet parenting, huh? Anyways, Palani kindly shared one of his sons' birthday parties with Jojo's. His son is turning nine, so their interests are pretty damn similar, and Palani's boy is such a champ that he's even splitting his presents with Jojo. I mean, who does that? I know I wouldn't have, but at that age I was probably a spoiled little brat. The kicker is, Palani's sister is married to the guy that owns the leading bouncy castle company on the island—Hale Nui Inflatables. So, yeah, bouncy castle game strong. Eight of them strong. Palani told me that he had once seen the guy while parking cars, walking out of the Sea Bird with a hooker. He told me that while it wasn't a full-blown affair, there was a mutual unsaid agreement that his brother-in-law owed him at least one favor. Who knows how long Palani might've held this piece of info above the guy's head, but shit, Palani does have three kids, and bouncy castles are a valuable commodity. At any age, really.

Anyway, the party is way up the eastside in Hau'ula at that big-ass beach park, right before the Polynesian Cultural Center. It's one of those cool Kona weather days, not a cloud in the damn sky, just a low mist blown in from the surf, dissipating before your eyes while the sun rises above the horizon. We're driving through Kaha-lu'u, and the Ko'olaus look like green fingers of the gods reaching down from the heavens—or maybe up from the earth—I dunno which one. But chickens are running across the road, bah-gawking, and we're stuck behind The Bus, so we're driving extra slow and Jojo is tripping out because the wandering horses are chewing right up against the fence at Kualoa Ranch. To the right, the sea is a horizonless, glassy mirror, and some fishermen are already throwing their nets at the sun. Jojo asks, "Where is everybody out here?" because it's his first taste of real country. We are trying to find him the Crouching Lion in the rock before Kahana Bay, and though we haven't found it yet, he's going, "I thee it, I thee it!!" All wide-eyed and spitting through his vacant front teeth. "I thee da grouchy lionnn!" I can't stop laughing, nearly swerving off the road, and Marisela is psyching him up like, "YEAH, Jojo, you did it!!" hollering with him like a little kid. She's friggin' amazing, I tell you.

We see the signs a half-mile before arriving to the party, going, *Get Ready to Jump!!* And *Almost Here!!!* Until a bush erupting metallic balloons next to the Kokololiho Beach Park sign frames another sign that says, in that grade school, multicolor puffy font: *Hau'oli La Hanau Ka'iwi and Jojo Boy!!* Jojo crashed at my house last night, so I was the one who drove him in, along with Marisela, who's pretty much been at my pad for the last five mights. I know, right? Marisela keeps reading every marker sign in this silly-ass Elmo voice. That, or in a horrendous pidgin accent, to Jojo in the back. I can see him wiggling in his seat, like, literally lunging against the seat belt so it'll catch and repel him backward. He's making odd noises like he's going to hyperventilate. Like he knows something huge is awaiting him, but at the same time can't really wrap his mind around exactly what it is. So it's just these spasms and bestial little grunts and squeals coming from the backseat. I don't know how else to explain it. He's friggin' *amping.*

We hit the final two signs and Marisela reads out his name, pointing, "Look, Jojo, your NAME!!," I look in the rearview mirror, and Jojo has this flushed look on his face like he's having an aneurysm.

"Uuuuuhh-IIII-gottago SHE-SHE!!!" he yells, and I slam on the brakes while Marisela scrambles to help him out of his seat belt. He jumps out and just lifts up the left leg of his shorts and pisses all over the side of my car, right then and there. Pretty damn gangster, really.

It's a little past nine and Palani already has a sweating Heineken bottle in his hand, directing the bouncy castle crew, tugging on the beer with one hand and pointing with the other. Instead of scattering the castles around the park—again, he has eight of them—he opts to set them up in a sort of circular octagon formation. Like a bouncy castle multiplex, or what that Church of Jesus Christ of Latter Day Saints temple looks like in Lāie a mile away. I walk over to Palani to give him his son's gift and he looks at me, really serious, takes a quick swig and says, "Bruddah. Dis goin' be one *nuts* party, bu."

Then he stares at me, but sort of looks through me as if seeing a vision beyond my form in front of him. A twenty-yard-stare like he's remembering some battle from ages past.

"Oh, yeah?" I laugh.

"Jus' goin' be plenty kids, brah. Das all I going say. Tings could get ugly. When you get one keiki pahty, you no can jus' invite immediate friends, ah? Have to invite da whole class. An' guaranteed dey all come if one bouncy castle pahty. Das why I booked eight," he says pointing at the colorful ring of rubber mounds, "and still going be hectic."

Rome wasn't built in a day, but the bouncy castle empire arises within minutes, a *Dora the Explorer* slide palace swelling next to a Hello Kitty chateau beside a *Toy Story 3* multi-bounce vis-à-vis a deluxe *Disney's Frozen* dry-slide combo bouncer, with more and more people filing into the beach park. As the morning blooms, slanted rays shine through the ironwood trees and cover the park grass in shards of broken sunlight.

Shit, when I was a kid, you know how many times you could get into a bouncy castle? Maybe twice a year. Once at the Hawai'i State Fair at Aloha Stadium and the other at the Punalani Carnival. That was it. Back then you had to be *rich* to rent one of those suckers. And at the carnival you had to wait half an hour in line, get maybe ten minutes to jump with some hawk-eyed prick watching you to make sure you weren't doing backflips or tackling your friend (the only two things a bouncy castle is designed for in a ten-year-old's mind).

But by noon, Palani has orchestrated a small carnival. Of course, there is the gift table, and beside that quite a few long tables for the adults to eat, drink, smoke, and talk shit. There are a few half-drunk uncles manning hibachis, flipping burgers, and grilling hotdogs, plus the usual potluck set up: plates and platters bulging with sticky rice, fried rice, squid luau, pipikaula, spam musubi, huli huli chicken, mochiko chicken, lau lau, mac salad, poi, manapua, malasadas (Leonard's of course), haupia, limu poke, ahi poke, tako poke, and so on and so forth.

There are no assholes watching the doors to the castle gates. The entry is EU style, a free-crossing Schengen Area, and the adults, including myself, are getting increasingly more tanked as two o'clock stumbles around. Increasingly *less* vigilant of our young. We watch a massive migration from sand castle construction, tunnel digging, and boogieboarding at the beach move back to the castle complex. Half the kids, like fifty of them, rush straight from the sea and head sopping wet into the complex. The other half move for cake and ice cream seconds. Somehow, I catch the party's tipping point.

Somewhere in between Jojo stuffing handfuls of ice cream into his face (there's been a hard deficit of plastic cutlery), he and half the others eating dessert suddenly notice how much fun the kids in the bouncy castles are having. Since everybody in the castles are straight from the beach or park shower, they're virtually slipping and sliding all around in them, bumping the whole experience up a whole new level, really. Since the castles are all situated in a kind of inward-facing octagon, the kids start jumping from the entrance of one castle to another, or, at least attempting to. Most are colliding with one another in midair, face planting, cracking heads and giving each other bloody noses and the parents still haven't noticed the chaos yet. Two uncles who have been at the beach and were designated to watch the kids at that location have not moved from their poles or beach chairs and are both one Bud away from blackout. Definitely not catching any fish. I'm beginning to believe they'd only been chosen for the job because they were just there already fishing, and for all I know, of no relation to anyone at the party. Just fishermen who were like, *Yeah, yeah, yeah, we'll keep an eye on them.*

Palani's son Ka'iwi makes the call from the dessert table. I watch him look at the rest of the kids with sticky hands and red plastic plates and yell, like some Guevarran revolutionary: *"FOOD FIIIIGHT!!!!"* And thirty kids charge into the castle complex with plates of cake and malasadas and ice cream and Safeway cupcakes and Costco muffins in hand. *Tings going get nutz*, predicted Palani earlier in morning, and his words echo through my head. And so they have. I watch Ka'iwi ambush the other kids and storm the rooms with Foremost vanilla cups and malasadas hemorrhaging haupia crème. They smear the faces of the enemy with fists of haupia crème and malasadas savagely. The enemy, shocked by this unconventionally filthy sneak attack, screams primordially in delight.

Engaged, they pick up the shrapnel of cupcakes and splattered birthday cake and launch it back at their aggressors. The frosting, icing, Hershey's sundae sauces and caramel, now an added component of slip-and-slide to the previous no-gravity zone. Cake and icing and Bavarian crème coats the walls, ceilings, gutters, and floors of each castle like blood spatter. The parents finally notice the shit hit the fan when they see a couple of kids dragging garden hoses over from the bed of a pickup truck. Originally brought to wash off sea kayaks, the kids are hooking them up to two faucets at the park showers and shooting streams into the castles.

"Shet." Palani sees the cupcakes, water, and other debris vomiting from the rubber edifices. "Gene, try tell Ka'iwi dem no chrow food. Tanks, ah!"

Gene and a skinny valet named Peanut march over to the fortress, barking orders to cut the shit and calm it down. They are met with hose fire and cookie shards. Gene jumps into the war zone to capture Jojo, but starts jumping, feels that euphoric momentary weightlessness, that nostalgic thrill of flight, and immediately forgets all sense of mission. Peanut steps in too, and is instantly reborn. Gene grasps Peanut through the legs, and body slams him over the shoulder into the rubber castle floor. Jojo and three kids lunge onto Gene's back, one of them slapping icing into Gene's eye sockets, quickly blinding him. Gene reaches for the kids and throws them one-armed, into the castle walls. Battle cries and hoarse shrieks ricochet through the fortress. Kainoa and Madero head over to help, followed by a few more drunk uncles and random dads. Cage matches ensue. Generational battles play out. I even jump in with Marisela, because—how could you *not*—and once again feel that magic of the bounce. Hopping around in one of the two story chalets, out of nowhere, a boy jumps from the inflatable balcony and drop-kicks me in the side of the head.

Gene's just tapped out four adult contenders with various jiu jitsu submission holds, and the inside of every room looks like an edible Jackson Pollock, smeared with cake frosting, dried or dripping ice cream film, chocolate chips, hair, sand, grass, vomit, and a little bit of DNA. CSI Hau'ula, awaiting the forensic investigator. It's almost dusk, and the company just pulled up to deflate and remove the castles. Gene has a cigarette in his mouth with nail marks on his neck, trying to spray out the rubber rooms with one of the hoses when the crew walks up. He looks at the castle guys and flicks his chin, " '*Sup, bu.*" They stare back, appalled.

Palani, somehow not entirely wasted after drinking since eight, directs the clean-up. Most of the kids just dance around the park showers and take turns washing dessert out of their hair. Aunties and uncles fill up trash bags with used cutlery. Tūtūs arrange take-home leftovers capped in tin foil for anyone who wants them. They walk over to the homeless and others camping out and offer them some, and they accept with warm hugs and smiles. Like a circus moving towns, the party, tents, and tarps collapse and are packed into the caravan of lifted Silverados, Tundras, F-150s, and Tacomas. Everything vanishes but the fishermen in their beach chairs, still pounding beers, still patiently awaiting the ring of bells hanging from their forty-pound lines. The castle complex lies deflated in the park, pathetic mounds of primary colors: the remains of a fallen empire. Palani rolls by us as we get into the car. He's co-pilot, his wife at the wheel, Jojo and his three sons crammed in the back, tearing open a few leftover gifts.

His elbow hangs out of the door and he says, matter-of-factly, "Told you was goin' get nuts."

"I'm sorry, I can't hear from this ear. Ka'iwi punctured my eardrum an hour ago."

"Good boy, Ka'iwi. Jojo, you get some cracks in, too?" he says into the rearview mirror.

The following night at the Sands, I find Palani, messing around on his iPhone, and ask him about Jojo. "Did our man have a good birthday yesterday, or what?"

He looks up from his screen and starts laughing. "Frick yeah, he did."

"Thanks for that, Palani. For the castles and sharing your boy's birthday with him, that was big. Probably the best day of his life, maybe."

"Nah. Everybody like Jojo. Brah, dat frickah was so pumped yestah-day. My wife wen tuck him in. She told me dat he come out da showah an his eyes stay all red. Was crying lai dat. My wife said, Jojo Boy, whas wrong, honey? Jojo Boy was having one flash back or some-ting, still crying and was all 'Auntie, I was *flyyyying. Flyyyying.*' Hannabuttah all dripping out his mout', all, 'I *fliiiiiied...*'"

"I love it. So, who's on schedule next, Gene or Kainoa?"

Palani pauses and clicks his phone off, rolling his tongue around in his mouth and patting his flat top down to tame it—all visual cues as if to say, *So, how can I break this to you...*

"Yeah, I actually wen trade days wit Gene, and my wife an me goin' take care Jojo again. Moa easy, I tink dat way."

"Okay, yeah, I guess..." I frown, wondering how that's any easier. "So, what's that mean, we all pick up two days in return or—"

"We can trade off and take care of him for you, too."

"Wait, why would I need that? Did I miss something, Palani? I'm confused."

"Listen," he says, fixing his metal name tag. "You know dis not one part-time kine job, yeah?"

"No, I think I'm basically full-time here. I mean, I get benefits—"

"No, bu—*faddah*-hood. You tink Jojo like pack up his life every day fo one new uncle?"

"Yeah, I get that, but why don't I just split Jojo-days with you, then? Mari and I are basically living together and her pad is pretty spacious..."

"You know what, coz...my wife wen tell me...dat Jojo ex-press dat he like stay moa time our place, brah."

"Which wife? First one...second one...?"

It's below the belt, but whatever. I'm feeling patronized. "Did Jojo *really* say that?"

"Brah, I just telling you what she said. I mean, I already get, like, tree keiki at da condo, so I not trying fo steal one moa, coz."

"Why have you never liked me, Palani?"

"Brah, I no like most people. You not special," he

chuckles. "I nevah said I no like you. I tink you stay, da kine, *projeck-ting*, coz. Take it easy, bu. Dis not personal."

"Well, what's the deal? Clearly, you don't trust me as a dad. What makes you, or your '*wife*,'" I frame with air quotes, "doubt my competence?"

"It's like...you don't have to be here, brah. But 'chu hea anyway. You wen graduate university, you get one foot in da door at Punalani—but you stay futting around wit us...*hakam*? 'Coz get good health care and cash on hand? I *have* to be here, brah. Dis just one comfy option fo you. I *have* to be one faddah 'cause all da keeds is mines. If I was you, I would take my wife's offer."

I swallow hard and can feel my face reddening, but I can't tell if it's from anger or shame. "Well, I appreciate the offer, but I'm just gonna go ahead and keep my days with Jojo," I say, leaving Palani at a speed a few miles per hour shy of "storming away."

"*Et tu, Brute?*" smirks Kainoa, materializing from behind a parked car, enveloped in a cloud of e-cigarette vapor like a movie villain. No idea he'd been eavesdropping.

"Lemme guess, you did some Shakespeare in high school?" I ask.

"Nah, bu. Actually doing 'um *now*, at community theater."

"Good form," I say, pounding his fist with mine.

"You really like moa days wit Jojo? Or, you jes shame fo geev him up to Palani dem?"

"I'm all in, man. I wanna give that kid a home. More than anything. Between Marisela and I, if I switch to morning shifts when summer school's out, we'd take him every day if we could."

Kainoa takes a drag, his gaze locked on mine, as if to test my sincerity. "You need to talk wit Monty, den, brah. Fakah geev good council, bu."

I've heard conflicting reviews on that.

25.

Funyun dust

I have never seen Monty Goo without food or a beverage in hand, and I don't believe anybody else has either. A valet that solely works the Elks Lodge lot, parking the high-functioning drunks coming in and out of the Clipper Bar, Monty's who you see when you need legal council, as he is a self-proclaimed expert in the law, having taken the bar exam a whopping seven times with no success. Yet. Equally slovenly as he is persnickety, Monty's helped quite a few valets navigate sticky alimony cases, complex insurance claims, DNA tests, DUIs and TROs for a nominal fee.

Maintaining the persona of know-it-all-jovial-slob, Monty's got a perpetual glaze to his face from a digestive system locked in overdrive and short, expressive alligator-like arms hovering over formidable thighs. *Homo hippopotamus* man. The kind of guy that hops in a car and immediately slides the seat back in front of the customer with no intention of correcting the alteration upon return. The kind of guy with faded amber Kikkoman shoyu stains on his company uniform shirt that he's clearly given up on bleaching out.

But if you dress for the job, as they say, I can see why he's no lawyer.

"So you need my council," he makes out between grotesque smacks. As advertised, one hand clutches a half-eaten Five Dollar Foot-long sub, while the other's wrapped around some heinous Monster energy drink flavor called Ultra Violet Taurine Assault. At least he's trying, with the Subway.

"I'd like your friendly advice, as you're not *technically* a practicing attorney yet."

Monty snorts and tips the Monster back, his consecutive gulps painstakingly audible. He gasps in a breath of air like coming up from a long free dive and wipes his oily brow with a shirt sleeve by craning his neck awkwardly to the side, as both hands are plainly occupied.

"Yet," he confirms, which comes out like a correction.

"So…did Palani fill you in?"

He stuffs the rest of the cold-cut combo into his mouth, chews twice, and through half-masticated bread wads murmurs, "Yeah, he did. You don't want to adopt."

"Really? Why?"

"Adoption's messy, brah. And it can be tough to take a kid away from its birth mom."

"'Don't know if there's even a birth mom in the pic."

"Doesn't matter. Adoption, which technically terminates the rights of the kid's parents, is a long-ass process.

It's also permanent. Not to mention, the biological parent will no longer be obligated to pay child support."

He swallows hard and winces, pounding his chest with a newly freed fist. I am suddenly not sure whether he's choking or in cardiac arrest.

"Monty...you good, man?"

He raises an index finger like, *gimme a sec*, slurps on the battery acid again, washing down whatever's lodged in his gullet, and continues.

"What you want is legal guardianship, brah. *Wayyyy* less paperwork. Custody with less strings attached, bu."

"Hmm. I like the sound of that..."

"It's like, get the guardianship, see how it goes, and if you're really trying to ice out the biologicals, you can try and adopt down the line."

Monty reaches a hand into the valet booth cupboard, but instead of extracting a set of keys or vehicle ticket, presents a bag of Funyuns, ripping it open with his teeth, the other paw still clutching the sixteen-ounce can.

"Want one?" he offers, yellow Funyun particles leaping from his mouth onto his chest.

"Sure," I say, humoring him. "So what are my next steps?"

"Well, first you file a petition stating your interest in obtaining guardianship. I actually printed out the docs and can file them for you the next time I'm at the courthouse...wait, maybe you have to go in person. Whatever, I'll check on it," he says unconvincingly, pulling out a few forms from the booth with fingers caked in Funyun dust. "Sign here."

He hands me a pen and, go figure: it's sticky.

"You think you can get a letter of consent somehow from the kid's parent? Because you're gonna wanna file that too."

"I think we could get a letter signed somehow," I grin, picturing Gene's unorthodox methods of persuasion.

"Right. Well, after the petition's filed, you'll go to a hearing at family court downtown. We can also try and expedite the hearing, because usually that can take months to schedule. Probably helps your case if the parent doesn't show, let alone can't be found. Shit, if you can get some photos of the boy's living conditions, that'd be a game changer."

"Amazing. Thank you so much, Monty," I say, bracing for the blow. "So…what do I owe ya?"

"Mmm," he says, cracking open a new, ungodly flavor of Monster. "You know that one flower girl? The one with those legs and that hair?"

Those two things that most women have?

"I want you to try and get me a date with the chick."

"Monty, she—"

"I'm just fucking with you, brah!" he shouts. "I know that's your chick. Gimme, like, two hundred bucks, that'll cover the fees and I'll get it started and file them for ya."

"Can I pay you in Subway gift cards instead?"

He bursts into laughter and Funyun particles spray onto my shirt like buckshot.

"But seriously, does she have a sister?"

26.

"I might just have to steal yo job, dawg."

My God, are we going to be like our parents?
Not me…Ever.
It's unavoidable. It just happens.
What happens?
When you grow up…your heart dies.

Solemnly, I mouth each word at the screen, hidden in the dark beneath the dusty beam of the classroom projector. We have finally come to that special day in the course where we watch *The Breakfast Club*, my quintessential movie pick for dialogue-writing exercises—which will follow in the second half of class. The whole room's eyes are glued to the screen. Thirty-odd years later, and the scene's just as relevant as ever.

Joel was supposed to come and have his "time in the ring" today too, but appears to be a no-show. Typical.

Hell, I specifically told him to come in on this day when I was showing a movie, it being a sort of safety net for him if shit got too real. He had his chance, though. Not my fault if he can't be punctual.

I'm thinking I'm gonna get some tears today, too. The B-Club does it every time, I swear. And right when these little suckers thought I didn't have any more tricks up my sleeve...

"What is that?" asks Emma, craning her neck toward the door.

"Yeah, you hear that?" says Kawika, perking his ears.

There does seem to be some sort of commotion outside. I get up from my desk, pause the movie, and move to the door. "Express Yourself" is blaring somewhere outside in the hall, and not the original by Charles Wright, but the sampled version by NWA. I open up the door to see what's happening and Joel, standing right outside, walks in with a gigantic ghetto blaster on his shoulder and a phonebook-sized manuscript under his other arm, playing that very song full-blast. He pushes past me, puts the boom box and book on the floor, hits the lights, and throws his hands up, side-to-side, hip-hop-hooray-style to the rhythm.

How the hell did he know where the lights are?

"Joel...*Joel*!" I holler. "You wanna turn that down a little, dude?"

Joel turns and looks at me, drops to his knees, clicks a button, and the next track, Dizzy Rascal's "Fix Up, Look Sharp," begins, the bass of the boom box literally shaking the retractable projector screen like the cup in *Jurassic Park*.

Joel continues to dance to the beat with his hands in the air, looking…whatever you call that look between homeless and beachy. His tennis shoes are tattered and blackened, surely the same ones he valets in and probably the only pair he owns. He's in floral surf trunks, a loose tank top revealing a sleeve of tattoos on one arm, and a backwards baseball cap, tilted at an angle. He looks at me and bops his head side to side to the beat, stomping and lunging his chest toward me aggressively. He looks at the class, grimacing, waving his hands around to hype up the room, pop-n-locking, then morphing into a full-blown krump dance. Krumping, by the way, which looks like a combination between a hip hop break dance, an African tribal ceremony, and an epileptic seizure. I look back at the class, and everyone's jaws are on the floor, eyes-wide, glued completely on Joel.

"BUP! BUP!" he shouts, turning down the volume. "Welcome to the Verbal Collage Vortex, young earthlings, I am Jo— nope, I am that I AM! That's who I am. And you are,who YOU are," he says, breaking into verse. *"And ain't nothin' gonna breaka my stride—nobody gonna hoooold me dooo-wn,"* he sings, pointing at me. The classroom erupts into laughter, a few kids clapping, even. *"Oh-NO, I got to keep on moo-oovin'!"*

He keeps on krumping, dropping to the floor occasionally to break dance, then explodes to his feet and torques his body backward in slo-mo like *The Matrix*. The song ends and he composes himself, dripping wet with perspiration.

"Yeah, dawg, it's all about the chest pop, dawg!" he says. "You feel it, right? You feel it, and you find that *sentence*, right? And then you just pop the chest and

STOMP, right? It's like an affirmation gesture, dawg, like, 'Yeah, Universe, here I am. I am cosmic and I am being!' There's nothing more affirming then the chest pop and a stomp."

Screw it, I think to myself. The next two hours are his. Guess we'll just finish *The Breakfast Club* another day.

"Now, some of you earthlings are probably askin' what I got in store for ya'll?"

The kids look around and at each other, nodding in accordance, like, *Yeah, I'm pretty goddamned curious...*

"One thing," says Joel, picking up a random Sharpie marker and walking to the white board. "Reprogram DNA," he writes in all caps.

"Joel, that's not a dry-erase pen..." I offer uselessly.

Kaito raises a hand sheepishly from the back row. And, he *never* raises his hand! Joel points at Kaito.

"How...do you reprogram your DNA?"

"Through vibration, tension, imagination, and..." Joel pauses, like he's searching for the last one, "*intuition!* Embrace your infinity, follow your blissipline, and be liberated by randomness, earthlings."

Ikaika raises a hand. "Are we still gonna get to watch a movie?"

Joel drops his head in disappointment, his posture softens and he slowly melts downward...then looks up with an enormous and insane smile, pops upright into a b-boy stance with his arms crossed at his chest, cocks his head, and says, "Ya'll ever seen *RIZE?*"

Everyone shakes their head. He hooks up someone's laptop to the projector and proceeds to play the film in its entirety over four pirated YouTube segments. And, over the course of the next hour, what can I say—the class is unequivocally captivated. I mean, showing a prep school classroom of high schoolers a fascinating documentary about a young, marginalized subculture in South Central L.A. that most of them have never heard of? Well played, Joel, well played. When the movie finishes, he has everyone pull their desks back to clear a space for a big circle. Then he clicks on E-40 and simulates an in-class krump battle. Which they absolutely eat up, bopping and dancing and chuckling. And not laughing at me, for once! Seriously, who gets eighteen sixteen-year-olds to *dance* in a classroom that isn't…well, a goddamned DJ?

After each kid has had a turn, he busts out the Verbal Collage Vortex—that huge black marble composition notebook that he'd walked in with. He opens it up, and it's about a hundred pages of collages that he's created from magazine cutouts, pasted into the book. Random images, photos, and textures that he's blended together to create motifs and themes evoking anything from indigenous rights to terrorism, to homelessness to politics. Certainly nothing that would pass as fine art—pretty rudimentary, really—but it's his method that is the kicker. He passes the book around the circle, has a student flip to a random page, and then he beat-boxes a little rhythm while the speaker attempts to freestyle rap, slam, or spoken-word about what they see or feel before them. The wilder and more random, the better, he encourages.

This also proves an absolute hit, as every single student wants a turn in "The Vortex." As the clock strikes noon, not a soul notices the time, or has their bags packed. I literally have to announce the hour, an unprecedented event, really. Even Ralph is so preoccupied that he forgets to grill me on the status of our submissions...or for more royaties, for that matter. I motion for him to hang back, though; those terms will have to be renegotiated since my recent findings.

The rest file out of the room, buzzing, tickled, and grinning. Joel gives each and every one a fist bump for the road. Over the past two summers, with sporadic sub days in between, I'd never seen the kids this psyched leaving the room. I guess I just figured their indifference was... normal. A defense mechanism, as not to show me their hand. I mean, it couldn't ever have been because I was a shitty teacher or something...

"And don't forget, earthlings," hollers Joel. "If you can remember one thing from today: GET BUCK! Also my jam band Family Supper gigs at Next Door Saturday night at nine, CDs and merch available by the bar!"

"No one's twenty-one, Joel," I tell him. "Epic class, by the way. You're...kinda made for this shit, huh?"

He nods and smiles, putting two palms together, bowing namaste-style. Then he wipes the sweat from his brow and pulls me in for a bear hug. He whispers in my ear, "I might just have to steal yo job, dawg," and laughs demonically.

He lugs his boombox and notebook out of the classroom, and this time it's me approaching Ralph.

"Ralph, you happen to have a summer job—delivering papers, bagging groceries, Zippy's or something? Because this cash cow has dried up if you're still saving for that iPhone X," I smirk, aiming two thumbs at my chest.

"It's done when I say it's—"

"How's your brother, Ralph? Ronald, right? The hotshot with the full ride to UCLA?"

The life in Ralph's face evacuates, taking the stairwell to his gut. He gulps and I can hear the lump in his throat slowing clawing its way down.

"Ralph, I know you stole his story," I say.

His eyes are welling up. He blinks nervously. "It's like... it was all so fucking ease—ease—easy for him," he stutters.

Well, now I just feel like an asshole. I really figured he'd go out with a fight. I suppose he is a sixteen-year-old.

"Ralph, take it easy, bud. I'm not flipping this on you," I say, running a hand through my hair uneasily. "Square?" I offer him a hand, he nods, and shakes it.

"You don't happen to have a twenty-spot on you, though, do ya? The food truck outside only takes cash and I need some lunch," I say. "And I'm tapped at the moment."

Ralph frowns, wipes his face with the back of his wrist, and reaches into his backpack for his wallet.

27.

"You could've just called the class Novel Mechanics..."

About a week later, Joel stole my job.

"You're letting me go?" I say, pinching the bridge of my nose, signifying my utter disbelief. Not like I didn't see this day as a possibility, but playing out like this? Yeah, I'm a little shocked.

"Well, we're not 'letting you go,'" says Derek, curling both index and middle fingers for air quotes. "We've just got someone else lined up for the last three-week course of the summer. Not to mention, you weren't under contract or anything, so you're not getting terminated."

I sigh and look around his small office, processing the blow. The wall behind him is covered in an oversized poster of the 1991 Montreux Jazz Festival. The shelves are equally as cluttered with vinyl records and CDs as they are with novels. An old brass trumpet, green from time, leans against a bookcase. Quite the music nut.

"Isn't verbal agreement and a handshake legally binding, or something?" I offer, grasping for straws.

"Do you really wanna go there?" he asks, tilting his head and smirking curiously.

"Joel?" I blurt, with my palms up. "It's him, isn't it?"

"We really don't discuss these matters with—"

"Joel doesn't have a college degree, Derek. I'm not even convinced he graduated from high school!"

"The students *love* Joel, and he does have a diploma."

"*Pfft*," I scoff. "I brought Joel into the classroom for some comic relief, to lighten the mood a little, and now you're offering him a job?"

"He contacted me and let me know he was interested, and the kids can't stop talking about him. I had him come back this week on Monday and Wednesday to sub a music theater course, and he killed. Listen, bottom line: Joel breaks a sweat when he teaches. You pop on *The Royal Tenenbaums* and sit back."

"Derek, he doesn't make lesson plans or anything. The guy just shows up spitting some stream of consciousness hip-hop-cosmo-dogma in an Ali G voice with, like, dance steps...is that what you really want?"

"Joel taught the entire class on Monday by ukulele. Half the class he taught freestyle rapping with an *ipu* gourd. One of the students filmed it on her iPhone, and it's gone viral on YouTube with over 70,000 views and counting. This is the type of guy who rounds out our program and builds interest. This is the type of guy who secures *my job*. Joel's already talking about spearheading a Krav Maga Israeli martial arts course for us next spring. Joel makes *me* look good. I mean—"

"Do you even know why Joel left Israel? Derek..." I say, on the verge of pleading, "I can bring a tambourine to class and jump around reciting Ginsberg if that's what you want, man."

"What I *want* you to do is finish your book," he says. "Then give us a call, and we'll see if there's room."

I shake my head and lean back in the plush leather seat facing him. "He tries to hock his band's CDs in class, for Christ's sake."

"Listen, I didn't want to get into this, since none of the accusations have actually been proven, but...do you really want to call out Joel on his ethics?"

I squint my eyes and shrug at the director like, "Come again?"

He leans forward and locks his fingers on the desk. "After a field trip a couple weeks ago, some of your students are under the impression that they've been editing...well, your *life*."

"*Whaaa?*" I say, shaking my head dismissively, in a voice high on helium.

Field trip, field trip, field trip... The Museum of Art. Sonofabitch. The Museum.

"A few of your creative writing students were on a field trip to the Honolulu Museum of Art for their Buddhist Philosophy and the Game of Go course, and you were spotted at your *other* job."

Ah, the Museum. They use our company to valet for their shnazzy new café a few hours each day and by God, there *was* that Friday when they called a few of us over from the Sands to sub for some guys who got double-scheduled.

★　★　★

"Bruddah, wat kine lotion you use fo' jack off?" asks Gene.

"Um, like, whatever's around, I guess…" I say, looking down Kinau St. at possible clients turning in for the lunch rush.

"Coz—you gotta be careful! You cannot use jus any kine stuffs, bah."

"God, I was totally unaware of that, Gene. Thanks—"

"Like, bah-rah! Neutrogena lotion, fo' da face and hands—dat shet is fo' getting rid of wrinkles, brah. It *shrinks* and *tightens* the skin, bu…You goin' shrink your *boto!*"

He seems really concerned with my personal well-being, so I've learned to humor him. It's the only way to get him off your case. But c'mon, who am I kidding? I love it, too.

"Well, shit, what do I do, then?"

"Brah, da safest way fo' wack 'um is your own spit. Bottom line, haole," says Gene.

Jensen, a younger valet that recently graduated from Pier 8, interjects, "Ho, brah! You know what I do? I drink one Coke fo' get da spit all slimy, yea? Den dat way, da ting stay like one organic lubrication."

"Cheee, brah! Jensen know how. *Akamai*, ah you?" agrees Gene, nodding encouragingly, slapping Jensen's hand.

"Welcome to the Café at the Honolulu Museum of Art, ladies," says Gene, all smiles, helping a woman out from the passenger side, "Do be sure to try the chicken fettucine and ginger lemonade, folks: *to die for.* Just ask the server for parking validation on the way out."

"There's a rare Gauguin in the Diamond Head room facing the courtyard," Jensen whispers to the other woman charmingly as he slides into the driver's seat.

"Wait, wait, wait…so you goons are telling me that the safest way to keep your penis healthy and prevent it from shrinking while masturbating is to (A) use only saliva, a natural liquid scientifically proven to break down and shrink food while chewing, and (B) supplement that with Coke, a carbonated chemical-beverage proven to break down and deteriorate a goddamned copper penny and other metals? *Really?*" I ask them.

I park the car around the block in our private coned-off valet zone—it's literally thirty seconds away—and jog back to the boys. Gene approaches me with a particularly mischievous look on his face again.

"So wat, 'coz, you still banging dat flower girl?"

"Roger that, Gene."

"Ho…*nah!*"

He is salivating now, which means he's gearing up for the play-by-play. Because even if all that's needed to be said has been said, he wants to, from what I've learned, become a part of the experience. What is the place between vicarious and actual called?

"So wat, she *mean* naked?"

"Yeah, she's hot."

"Like, how big her su-sus?" His brow furrows, like he's calculating, or measuring some estimate in his mind. He lifts up his open palms and mimics a small handful, a medium-sized one, and finally one extending all fingers, his eyebrows raised as if to signal "not enough for one hand" sized breasts. I give him the medium-sized ones.

"Ho, pretty good, pretty good," he affirms, turning to a customer holding out their valet ticket. "Well, good afternoon, Mr. Robinson. Puh-*lease* tell me you went with the mahi salad—so *ono*, yeah?"

I grab the ticket and find the keys, sprinting to retrieve the car, but Gene follows. We're clearly not finished yet.

"And da cho-cho. How was?"

"It was good, dude. Delicious, well-kept, the whole shebang."

"*Aaaaah...*" His eyes sink back into his head, like a giant vagina is right there in front of him.

"An wat, you wen lick 'um?" he asks.

"'Course, man. Why wouldn't I?"

"I KNOW, RIGHT?"

He's grabbing his crotch now, oozing excitement, jumping up and down a little.

"An wat, she come?"

I mean, I couldn't just tell him no, right? "Of course."

"An wat kine face she make...? Show me."

I'm already caught in his web, so what the hell. "Her face was kinda like...do you know that famous painting by Edvard Munch, *The Scream*?"

He shakes his head, losing the image. He jumps into the customer's Benz with me for a ride back.

"You folks have a good Aloha Friday," I say, helping an elderly couple into the Benz. "Try Young Street if King and Kapiʻolani are jammed."

"So *that's* Gene...and that over there must be Kainoa... or..." says a familiar voice from behind me. I turn around, and Kaito and Ikaika from class are standing right in front of me, arms crossed, sporting matching shit-eating grins you can practically smell.

"Uh...hi, guys," I make out, as if they'd just caught me naked in the shower.

"Aloha, gentlemen, you guys have your valet ticket?" coos Gene.

"Oh no, we took the school bus," smirks Ikaika, pointing back toward Beretania Street.

"Say, Kaito, when's the last time you had deja vu?" says Ikaika, looking me dead in the eyes.

A school bus honks in the distance and they turn around to trot back. "See ya on Monday, Teach," hollers Ikaika, the two laughing maniacally to each other while they run. "Or, not!"

★ ★ ★

"Ikaika..." I murmur in a daze.

"Now, I didn't say that name...but students have been known to petition causes before, some of which have had little basis, which is why I'm just letting you go and not investigating the matter."

"*Petitioned?*"

"Listen, bud," he says, removing his glasses cinematically, huffing a hot breath of fog into the lens and clearing them with a thumb in his polo shirt. "I actually ran into an old friend of yours a couple days ago in admissions. Graham was in there inquiring about enrolling his daughter, and I overheard him mentioning your name, essentially serenading your praises. I introduced myself and told him that you reported to me, and the guy just went on and on about you from college days. How talented you are. Guy practically begged me to fire you so you'd start writing again."

"How do you know I'm *not* writing, Derek?"

"Yeah, well, I don't doubt you're writing..." he says, oddly. "It's just that your personal work shouldn't be a 'group effort,' if you catch my drift."

I feel my neck retracting.

"There have been murmurs. But it's like, we're pretty open here. You could've just called the class Novel Mechanics or Long Form Fiction, had them read some books and helped you write this out in the open, and not undercover. Hell, what if you wrote a draft as a whole class in one course? Could've been a useful marketing tool for the book..."

Shit, that is a stellar idea.

"Listen, that's neither here nor there. Just hit me up in the fall. You don't have Joel's mailing address, do you?"

I sigh. "I don't think Joel has one, Derek."

28.

Children are not rental cars

How often does shit hit the fan in these lots? Often. Enough to make you uncomfortable. You back a car into a stall and/or put a water pipe through the back dash weekly. You clip a side mirror on a concrete pillar every other day. The way some of us valets drive, let alone reverse, there've been wrecks within the hotel garages—verified by security cameras—of valets t-boning each other at speeds exceeding forty-five mph. They'll literally find the drivers' shattered iPhones ten feet away from the crash like the shoes of some poor schmuck hit by a train, crossing the tracks. But that's what the accident report forms are for. That, and the company's multimillion-dollar insurance policy.

Hell, I remember a few Christmases ago at Morton's Steakhouse, I heard about a valet working the booth there. Crazy thing was, *I* was supposed to be working that night, but I switched with the kid to go work some private party near Diamond Head ('tis the season for giving twenties). Anyway, we usually do this thing with cars that are double-parked. It's pretty much procedure that when you park one car in front of the other—and perpendicular to it—you don't hang the keys at the booth. Reason being that just in case the double-parked car gets called out first, you have be able to move the one in front of it quickly— even if you're just shuffling it. So we just put the key on top of the front right tire, or whatever tire is *not* facing people walking by. Anyway, I guess the kid was slammed, and at Morton's you usually have about twelve of your own private stalls up front, twelve more between there and Neiman Marcus, and then you start "doubling" the cars up front if you still have people coming in.

It was one of those nights, and the idiot on shift doubled-parked a brand-new Porsche 911. And you *never* leave the keys on the tire of a new Porsche. Camrys and Accords, sure, but a Porsche? C'mon! Someone must have been spying on his operation, which for a thief is ridiculously easy when it comes to us, as the key stand is almost always unlocked. Anyway, the dude must've watched him place the Porsche keys on the front tire, and as soon as he got into another car to park it, the guy hopped into the Porsche and took off. Now you see 'em, now you don't. The kid freaks, jumps out of the car, and starts running toward the sound of that thundering four hundred horsepower, galloping to the exit on the Pi'ikoi Street ramp. Ironically, mid-stride, mall security pulls around a corner to block him, thinking that *he'd* just committed a crime. Shoplifting, probably—I mean, the kid looked disheveled and sweaty and was desperately running away or *toward* something. Not to mention our company has a lot of employees with neck tats, so the profiling probably wasn't too far off the mark. Out of breath, the kid's trying to explain the carjacking, and by that time the 911's long gone, so the valet jogs back to a snaking line of pissed-off customers waiting with tickets in hand...with the Porsche owner at the front of the line, tapping his foot. Apparently, the kid crumpled to the floor and started weeping. That, or barfed in a planter—depending on whose version you hear it from.

But sure, valets are accused of damaging cars *all* the time. Some accusations founded, others not. You'd be surprised how often people try and pass shit off on us. But Valet Law across the friggin' board is Shaggy 101: It wasn't me. Deny by any means necessary. Some of the guests' bullshit is just obvious, too. Like, a guest will come back from wherever tourists go—Pearl Harbor, Hanauma Bay, WalMart—and have some big green paint mark scarred into their bumper. They say, *You need to take a look at this*, as if we're going to just fold on the spot from the guilt we've been harboring. Politely we'll assure them, *You know, I don't think that happened in our lot. Our walls are white, and the pillars are yellow. There's no green paint in our lot. You can go down and see for yourself.* So then we gotta kindly walk a guest through the garage and show them that, indeed, there are no red or green pillars or poles in the entirety of the space. It's impossible, unfeasible. *We have security cameras. Do you want to see a tape?* Of course when you take 'em deeper into the lot toward Security, you risk seeing Gene yanking on an e-brake or drifting a rental down the hall. Sometimes they just drop it and give us that *Well, try and be more careful* bit. We'll even do our own detailing for them, whether it was our fault or not. That's a guaranteed ten spot for five minutes of work. And then, if they're adamant or have some sort of substantial proof, yadda, yadda, yadda, we just hand them over to security and they'll fill out a simple accident report sheet.

Other than that, sure, we rub car doors against corners and garage columns on a damn near daily basis. But that's what Goof Off's for—it's a lifesaver. You spray that stuff onto a car and it gets pillar paint off like they hadn't even met. You clip a side mirror off a rental—slap on some crazy glue and drive it up nice and slow. Then you close the door for them, as not to flick the mirror off. *Nice and easy.* The great thing about cars these days is everything's made of plastic, so if you back into another car or whatever, you just get horizontal, slide under that bitch, and pop the bumper dents out by hand.

But children are not rental cars. And relationships don't have corporate insurance policies. And when Mari saw Jojo after another day in the care of Uncle Gene, she'd had enough of the bullshit.

It was only a couple days earlier when, after hearing the alarming echo of Gene's souped-up moped, Jojo snuck up behind me and shot for my legs, per Uncle's orders. I noticed something rigid rubbing against my calves attached to Jojo's arm, and when I looked behind me, I could see that it was a fresh fiberglass cast.

"Gene! What the hell?"

"Relax, haole. Jes one hairline frack-cha. Had one small kine gribble on da 50cc at the Kahuku track. Good as new in what, boy—tree weeks tops, ah?"

Jojo looked down at his cast, tapped it with his left fist, then dug into his fanny pack, pulling out a Sharpie, and said adorably, "Can sign it if you like, Uncle?"

Of course Mari shows up shortly after, basket in hand, with Jojo rushing over to proudly present his new battle armor, Sharpie ready for her autograph. She signed it, gave me a look that "stink-eye" can't quite render (try: gangrenous-rotting-flesh eye) and walked away without saying hi, or bye.

After a couple days of not answering, she finally took my call. The conversation was by no means cathartic.

"You don't get it, do you?" she says.

"I guess not. Help me understand. Was this about hitting on your friend at WholeFoods?"

"Okay, so clearly you don't get it. We weren't even going out then, so, no, it's not about that."

"So *what* then? You're still pissed about Jojo breaking his arm?"

"Yes, I am. But it's like, Jojo, me, your work, your life—you aren't careful with any of it. What will you protect? Or at least care about enough *not* to break?"

"Mari," I sigh, thinking hard but not hard enough about what I'll say next.

"What."

"You're not...his mommy, and I'm not his daddy."

"Cool."

"I didn't mean it like, you're delusional or something. I mean—"

"You mean we're not obligated to him somehow. Grow...the fuck...up. Sometimes it's okay to owe someone something. It's okay to love something when that wasn't originally part of the plan. Honestly, what have you got to lose? Is giving Jojo your everything getting in the way of your complex lifestyle? According to Graham, once upon a time you gave a shit about something, right? Do we need to start calling the kid Rumi or something for some recall? You are not Peter Pan, guy. You're just a Lost Boy with no hero to follow."

"Ouch."

"Alas, he feels something. Good to know you're still alive, dick."

"Mari, I'm— Mari. Mari...?"

And since then, she hasn't responded.

29.

Double-dipping

On Kainoa's day with Jojo I'm supposed to drop him off and slip into a shift at the Sands, but it's so slow that they opt on cutting a guy, so I volunteer as that guy. Kainoa says that he has to go up to the North Shore with Jojo for the day to visit some family, so I ask if I could tag along, maybe get in the water up there and surf if there happened to be any waves, even though it's summer and there probably won't be. He says whatever, so we hop into his raised quicksand-colored Tacoma with massive F.B.I. (From Big Island) decals on the back.

Jojo is stoked because according to him—he'd been out to the North Shore before, and thus was an expert—the sand up there is "da best-est." And he's right. Compared to the powdery Lanikai dust or filthy Waikīkī shit, North Shore grains are big, pearly, and in a word—fun. Your feet nearly sink to the shins trying to run through it, and for a seven-year-old, that's as good as any reason to take a trip to the beach. What I didn't know, and really shouldn't have surpised me, was that Kainoa had ulterior motives. "Brah, we going check my properties."

"You have properties?" I ask, amazed at both the matter and its pluralization.

"Yeah...basically," he says, shrugging.

"The hell do you mean, *basically?* Do you or do you not have various properties?"

"*Basically!*" yells Jojo from the extended cab, in hysterics. I turn and look back at him. He's teary-eyed and laughing in the middle seat.

"Da fahk got into him?" says Kainoa, gazing into the rearview mirror, "Kay, so da rentals—"

So, the rentals. I've heard of people doing this, but I never really knew anyone who actually did. With Hawai'i being one of *the* most popular tourist destinations on the globe, it goes without saying there's hundreds of vacation rentals, AirBnbs, VRBOs—whether houses, mansions, rooms or goddamned closets—rented weekly, on or near, pristine beaches. So a lot of those rentals need upkeep—cleaning, light carpentry, maintenance, etc.—in between stays, especially in the off-season. If you get in with the owners, a lot of times they'll let someone they can trust stay at these rentals rent-free if they just clean up before and after the guests who come in on those one-to two-week stints. A lot of times, there's an extra room or attached studio on the property, and that's where one lucky sucker stays. It's a pretty choice gig, and because the owners never rent the place consistently for a whole year, you've got a free beachside pad, and a lot of times, you've got the property to yourself. Clearly, rent-free is a great way to save money, should you have a day job. Kainoa, however, *makes* money and does what is known as "double dipping."

The property owners usually have a pretty good idea of what the bookings will look like for the next six months or so, and the groundskeepers, or Kainoa in this case, are given the schedule. But Kainoa fills in the blanks. Most of the property owners live on the Mainland anyways, and in Kainoa's eyes, three thousand miles is a mighty long way from knowing the difference. So, Kainoa Airbnbs these properties to anyone from global vacationers to local families wanting a beach house for the weekend for a grad party. He's even worked out a deal with one of his exes (he has four kids from three different women), where he trades child support money for free rent. The single mother and child literally rotate with a suitcase between the properties that have vacancies. It can get a little complicated.

But he does okay for himself on the scam—about an extra $40,000 a year okay. I mean, his weekly rates are competitive, even a fair bit cheaper than what's usually out there, and somehow he maintains control of this risky situation and still works a few valet shifts a week to keep the medical bennies the boss gives. Hustle game strong.

We coast down Kamehameha Highway, and the entire North Shore from Ka'ena Point to Kahuku lies in front of us, tranquil and dozing. Pungent fields of pineapples carpet the earth, followed by coffee plants as we near Hale'iwa. Compared to the winter months with the masses of international surfers, fans, and surf contests, some of tourists stuck in the Waikīkī vortex don't even bother driving out this far. Nonetheless, the beaches and sea out here, for a stretch of over ten miles north and west of Haleʻiwa, is a stunning marriage of sapphire and gold.

We arrive at an old two-story, three-bedroom home overlooking Keʻiki beach, its wooden façade furring from the weather. Kainoa needs to give the place a quick once-over before some renters come in on Monday. He grabs a broom and busies himself in the kitchen, while I walk to the back porch to look at the ocean, Jojo running through the naupaka bushes and straight toward that North Shore sand, screaming the whole way down. Next to the screen door a megaphone sits on its mouth.

"What's the megaphone for, Kainoa?"

He looks up from sweeping, "Oh, das da wahine wranglah. You know how da life-guahds use 'um fo call in da kooks? I use 'um fo call in da cheeks. Try watch..."

The megaphone does seem like a fairly useful tool out here. The beaches are vast, crawling with fit, dusky Brazilians, lithe pro surfer wives, flat-tummied milfs, and resident local beauties, jogging all day long in the golden sands. It's a strange phenomenon you notice when you come up here. Kainoa scans the shoreline and points the horn toward the water. He flicks the signal alarm that blares violently through the calm. Jojo yelps, as does a girl jogging in booty shorts and a bikini top, ducking at the sound. Kainoa disconnects the mic attached by a coiled cord and presses the talk switch.

"Honey girl! No be scared, my dea. Fo ya own safety, I need you fo move away from da shore break. I no like one tsunami fo swallow da most beautiful mermaid I evah did see. *Maaaaah*-halo. Mattah-fack, try come up hea. I'm hosting one open house, and get one monthly special fo' supah-models."

I hear his banter and barf slightly in my mouth.

But the girl stops, bewildered at first, and starts laughing, pausing in the sand with arms askew, head cocked to one side in a posture screaming, *Oh yeah?* Kainoa keeps the mic to his mouth and walks down the steps to the beach toward the girl, babbling smooth, saccharine bullshit the whole way.

"Honey girl, I sorry. I nevah meant fo stun you wit da kine, was for ya own well-being. My name is Kainoa; das my place up dea. I am also head-a-da local neighborhood watch chaptah, so, clearly, you safe now. And wats your name, my deah?" he rattles, clutching the megaphone for comic effect until Kainoa is but a few feet away from her. She's blushing. Somehow, it's working.

"Uncle Noa, Uncle Noa! Check out my tunnel!" cries Jojo, peeping up from the sand like a psychotic gopher.

"Get one supah-model evacuation exit, Jojo?" asks Kainoa, gesturing to the giggling new girl. "Follow code, bruddah, follow code."

"I'm not *done* yet!" erupts Jojo, ejecting sand and spittle with a shout.

"Ho, sorry, ah? I nevah knew, Jojo, I nevah knew," says Kainoa, faux-humbled, ducking his head, feigning shame.

The girl is eating it up, her guard fully down, now comfortable with this cute kid and charming local boy. They exchange numbers, I think even make plans for the night (and Jojo would be *where?*), and the young brunette jogs away, with a little added pep in her step, through the island's best sand, toward Sunset Beach. I watch as Jojo follows Kainoa back into the beach house, Jojo now carrying the megaphone, yelling, "Honey girl! Honey girl!" into the mic, searching for the "on" switch. Kainoa struts back into the rooms to wipe salt spray off mirrors and tighten bedsheets, when suddenly I hear a desperate *"Ho, SHET!!"*

Jojo fires back playfully, "Ho, shet!!"

"You all right, Kainoa?" I holler into the back. "You spot a rat or something?"

"Bruddah! We gotta go. Get one emergency at one of da properties. *Now, bruddah, NOW!!*"

Kainoa is scrambling, explaining that he has, as he puts it, "roll-ovah-rentahs." One of which is currently unconscious. And how did this happen?

Kainoa says that with the way he books these places, between the real renters and his own bookings, there can be overlaps. That usually when this happens, he just moves one of the groups to another property—one out of the four that's possibly vacant, and beach front, and gorgeous. They usually don't know the difference. Unless they're Mormon and wanted the Malaekahana rental with its proximity to the LDS Temple—which has happened before.

Anyways, about the unconscious one. Per usual Kainoa had been shuffling around an ex-girlfriend and her kid. He told them they'd have about two months at the Malaekahana home, as bookings were slow. Anyways, she'd been seeing this guy, kind of a loser, who owed some money. Gambling debts or some shit. So that particular day his ex, their kid, and the new man were out of the house and cruising on the beach for a few hours when the ex's new boyfriend—Sean is his name —walked back to the house to go get some more beers for the cooler. He walked in through the back door, went into the kitchen, was rifling through the refrigerator when he noticed a big man lounging in the living room on the couch. The man was Mr. Mika Regas, a burly, bear-like, bald-headed restaurant owner from Philadelphia on vacation with his family. Mr. Regas and the fam had just arrived to the beach house about an hour or so after Kainoa's ex and them had left for the beach. Immediately after lugging the suitcases into the home, Mrs. Regas and her two daughters drove to the Foodland down the road in Lāʻie to stock up for the week. Good food, prepped, and cooked with their own two hands meant a lot to the Regases. He, being a chef: that was priority number one. Jet-lagged and exhausted from the ten-hour plane ride, coupled with the hour and a half it took to find Lāʻie in the rental car, Mika had quickly dozed off on the couch.

Sean, however, thought that Mr. Regas was a thug that one of the many bookies he owed money to had sent to collect, if not to torture him. Maybe kill him. I dunno, he wasn't thinking so straight. But from the kitchen he saw the huge Greek's image in the mirror of the Samsung flatscreen. He couldn't even see the couch in the reflection, just this huge, sleeping Shrek of a man. Sean ducked behind the countertop and quickly searched the drawers for a weapon. Spoons? No. Baking pans? No. Butcher knives? Mmm, maybe…if it came to that. He slid one under the side of his belt. Frying pan? Bingo. I shit you not, he got a Teflon-coated frying pan, army-crawled over to the back of the couch, rose above the great man's body and smacked the back of his head—right on the sweet spot—with the bottom of the steel pan Looney Tunes-style. He peeled the big man's eyelids back to see if they had rolled. They had; Mr. Regas was out. For a little while, at least. And then Sean noticed the four suitcases and various backpacks lying by the coffee table and got confused. He dropped the frying pan and ran back to the beach. And that's when the ex called Kainoa.

For obvious reasons, we need to get there before the man's wife and kids return from shopping. And certainly before they call the police.

Jumping in the car, we fly down Kamehameha Hwy, Kahuku bound. There's roadwork stops every few miles, so it's a pretty interrupted flight. Kainoa's in panic mode, figuring out his options. Along the way he calls his "lawyer."

"You have a lawyer?" I ask, stunned.

"Bruddah—you *don't?*" he retorts, equally as shocked.

His lawyer is Monty and Monty's legal advice is limited to dreary. Unless Kainoa can reason with the landowner, he's screwed, and so is his ex and her new beau.

"Fakah!" screams Kainoa into his phone. "Das why you no pass da bar: you not *creative!*"

A huge Samoan in an orange reflective vest holding a SLOW sign waves us through the coned, potholed, one-lane detour.

"Tank you, bruddah," nods Kainoa courteously to the man, throwing him a loose steering wheel shaka. "Fahk, bu! What I goin' do?" he continues into the windshield.

"Take him to da beach!" chirps Jojo from the backseat, helpfully.

We both laugh. Kainoa guns it down the straightaway to Kahuku, the shrimp farms, fruit stands, and windmills a blur until we get to the old sugar mill. Finally, we arrive at Malaekahana—where there are two HPD patrol cars, parked precariously on the side of the road.

"Fahk!" explodes Kainoa. And then a light bulb. A change in the weather.

We park next to the two Crown V's and Kainoa immediately makes a call.

"Calvin…eh, bah, I need your help fas kine, bu…"

Now, I'm not saying that every cop on the island graduated from St. Louis School…but chances are, one in two did. And those are stellar odds in Vegas. And classmates help out classmates. Period. It's code. Especially in Hawai'i, where nepotism is the rule. Calvin, a day-shift valet at the Sands, is actually an ex-cop, and, whattyaknow, graduated from St. Louis.

Kainoa just walks on the scene with Calvin on the line, phone in hand, and pulls one of the cops aside. He explains the situation, and Calvin pulls a few strings with the cop. Of course, some bargaining goes down too. Kainoa tosses them some free stalls for an undetermined number of months at: the Sands, Ali'i Beachside, and Waikīkī West hotels, where a few popular restaurants are located. Cops have date nights, too. And I've said it before and I'll say it again: parking is power.

Meanwhile, Sean and the ex get there to work out the situation, and Mrs. Regas and fam come back, too. It's a total shit show. She's hysterical, but luckily Mr. Regas—a proper beast—doesn't need medical help. It'd take a lot more than that to keep this Greek down. Through Mrs. Regas' hysterics, the cops downplay the situation. *An honest mistake!* Silver-tongued Kainoa introduces himself as the property manager and convinces them not to call the owner, renegotiating a free-of-charge stay. The awkward part is that Kainoa's ex and new boyfriend still need a place to stay, so they just transfer to the studio on the same property, ten yards away from the scene of the crime.

We speed away back toward Kahuku to check on one more property, the sunlight waning with the dusk. Kainoa tells Jojo and me what happened, with his usual embellishments, as we drive on.

"Kainoa, with the way you can sweet-talk your way out of a pickle, why do you even need legal council? Take the bar yourself and quit this property hustle."

"Brah. Das why I like da *stage*. Pretty much like court, but I'm making folks cry fo da right reasons, yeah?"

30.

Show, *don't tell*

Sometimes, while working at these hotels, I look around and feel sick to my stomach. I see the valets, the cabbies, the bellmen, the doormen, the limo and shuttle drivers, see them hunched over and counting like wretched little Scrooges. It's a nervous tic, this counting. Involuntary, anxious counting. Wads of grimey, oily ones and fives and tens yanked from their pockets, cradled, then flipped, rubbing out the creases, stroked continually with sweaty hands. It's sickening, that pervasive, faint, fricative sound of bills peeling off one another. And some sort of dumb hope that three minutes later, the amount might have increased...*Now let me check...* The tips, the bribes, the baksheesh passed relentlessly, and all the intricacies within the relationship of giver and given. The faux thankfulness and disparaging bows and smiles. The phony generosity. The millions of complex and subtle transactions in plain sight. The utter degradation of "the tipped one's" graciousness.

You fake a smile in this business so often, you go home with a hurt face. So many curt *Thank yous!* and fake *Welcome backs!* and other master and slave-like moments between guest and host. The lowering and cowering of heads. The squashing of dignity and biting of tongues. And still. And still some kind of deranged sense of dignity to somehow feel bothered, annoyed, *offended* even by the customer who is paying for his place of superior status and class in this scene. I constantly ask myself, ask my fellow valets and employees around me: *How does that still bother you?* All the guests' dumb questions, their clueless behavior so typically touristic, that it should be a given by now.

But sometimes, though...just sometimes, for around two hours on the morning shifts, say, from six to eight or seven to nine, you can almost love this job. No one's rushing in for brunch at that time, and the hotel guests just trickle out slowly like a drippy faucet. You get to relax and notice things. Everyone's got that look about them— the valets, the cabbies, the bellmen—like a lover's face just waking up beside you, a little sleep in their eyes, but not yet fully roused enough to be bitchy. She is awakening and, for that brief moment, is lovely. The sun slowly creeps up from behind the Koʻolaus, giving everything and everyone that angular tinge of gold. The housekeeping gals have just had that first, defining cup of coffee at the Starbucks next door and have a twinkle in their eyes while they gossip in Tagalog, scone crumbs raining on a crisp *Star-Advertiser*. The tips are pretty decent because guests grabbing their cars at this hour think it's more a chore for us than it usually is. So we play it up for them, yawn and droop our eyes like we've been here *all night*. We give them those "Can I have some porridge, sir," Oliver Twist looks and usually they're gracious. Sometimes, even a *Oh, please don't run; it's not urgent...* But we do anyway, because then that's a guaranteed a five spot.

The Vietnamese cabbies standing on their haunches—a comfort left over from the motherland—converse over black coffee and unfiltered cigarettes, the conversation, a thousand different tones. They smile, nod hello, and wait their turn for an airport or Pearl Harbor run. Half-naked surfers wearing anxious, zinc-painted expressions filter in or filter out, carrying surfboards upon their heads. The Polynesians driving the garbage trucks roll up, and one jumps out like a burly matador to wave the horns of the huge green bull into his cape. The truck groans and booms, frightening the tourists, bucking the steel containers skyward and back into itself. Japanese tourists with their young stop and point at these bulls, and their children stare awestruck and terrified at the vehicles, utterly speechless. Europeans, blistered and fiending, take long, drawn-out puffs off cigarettes on the corners with the cabbies and waitresses. They breathe smoky life back into themselves before facing this new day. The overnight security guard claps an intricate handshake with the day guard, and the overnight valet does the same with the morning guys. The dawn trade winds blow in from the mountains and kiss your face, almost makes you shiver before the sun rises a little more. The Hawaiian music mix, looped eight times a day over the lobby speakers, is somehow bearable, the lyrics somehow making sense. *Hey you, pretty wahine, I wanna know what you're all about...There ain't no doubt I wanna check you out... Girl, my heart's been so dry 'cause I've had a love drought...*

You're thankful you're not locked in an office, that you can breathe in cool trade winds, smell fresh-picked plumerias in the desk ladies' ears or hear the slush of surf behind you, and feel your whole body warm with the morning, as if the day and you are one body. You and the doorman are not suspicious of each other yet; you're practically on the same team. You realize it's a brand-new day and you're working in a place most people only dream about. And for a moment, there is no shame or suspicion, only gratitude. An awareness of this fortune. An awareness of breath and life and sound and sense and—

"Kay, kay, kay, kay..." says Gene, derailing my train of thought, bouncing up to the lobby valet booth after parking a car. "Marry, fuck, *killllll*...Melania Trump, Michelle Obama, Sherry from da front desk."

"Not in the mood, Gene," I sigh.

"Which Sherry?" asks Kainoa.

Gene spins away from us and opens a returning guest's car door, eyes wide and smiling graciously. "*Aaaaa-loha* and welcome back to the Waikīkī Sands, Mr. and Mrs. Turner! Did you folks knock off Pearl Harbor, or was it Hanauma Bay, from the bucket list?" He fake-chuckles and turns back to us, smiling devilishly, "Fakahs, you know which Sherry." Then back to the guests: "*Yes!* I was hoping you'd say Hanauma Bay—such an island treasure, that place, yeah? Terrific snorkeling, yeah? Now, will you be using your car again later tonight, Mr. Turner? I just wanna know how deep in the stable we should keep this horse…" They both laugh hysterically as if this *wasn't* Gene's first horse metaphor, then glances back to us, switching back to pidgin. I wander away and notice Kainoa following.

"Coz, hakam da flower girl no come around hea any moa? Trouble in paradise?"

"Yeah, Kainoa. Mari left me. So I guess this is what it looks like when you're being avoided."

"An wat, you wen try fo get her back?"

"Of course. She's not having it, man."

"Wat, you wen fuck around on her?"

"No."

"You wen steal some-ting from her?"

"No," I laugh.

"Den how da *fahk* you not get her back yet?"

"Geez, man," I say, tugging at my collar dramatically. "Not for lack of trying, dude…"

"There is no future, there is no past; live dis moment like your last, brah. Hang on to your love."

"Shit, Kainoa. Where the hell do you mine these gems?"

"First one was *Rent* and da oddah one was Sade from *Diamond Life*."

Well, goddamn.

"So you just goin' let da chick leave and den Palani goin' take Jojo? Easy out, ah you? You like take my shifts, too? Look like you love it here, brah. Maybe you goin' be valet captain soon, hah?"

"Yeah, yeah, man," I say, brushing him off, but bubbling from within.

"No *yeah-yeah* me, brah. You say you miss her and dat you love da boy, but fakah: *Show* me, no tell me dat shet!"

Show, don't tell…that's supposed to be *my* goddamn line.

"I *want* Jojo," I growl through clenched teeth. I can feel my vision clouding with rage. "*I need Mari!*" I say, suddenly realizing that I'm yelling right into Kainoa's face. He slaps me on the cheek with a hollow *POP*, and I can taste blood in the corner of my mouth.

"Was that necessary?"

"Teatric-ally speaking—yes. Listen, brah. You know da story about da 'ōhi'a lehua tree, ah?"

"Mmm, kinda-sorta; refresh me."

"Well, 'Ōhi'a was one handsome stud-kine guy, legs like tree trunk, back all 'V' lai dat, and probably get one *thick* boto. And Lehua, she was one smoking hot wahine, eyes like one anime chick, tits like two plump manapua and one chocho all perfeck like da kine folds in da Ko'olaus, yeah?"

"Uh-huh," I say, increasingly curious where this was going.

"Any waze, 'Ōhi'a and Lehua see each oddah and instantly fall in love. Like, inseparable-kine shet. But one day da goddess Pele wen spock 'Ōhi'a in da forest and Pele like oof heem, but 'Ōhi'a was like, cannot, I stay wit Lehua, das my numbah one. So Pele get supah infuriated, all jealous, yeah, and wen trans-form 'Ōhi'a into one crooked tree fo break dem up. Lehua was heartbroken, she wen lose her man, yeah, but the oddah gods saw what Pele did and decided dat Pele cannot break up love dat strong. So dey wen trans-form Lehua into one flower on da tree, so can nevah be apart. Hence da name: 'ōhi'a lehua. Nevah get one witout da oddah."

He presses a glowing blue button on his vape pen and sucks in deeply, exhaling a cumulonimbus cloud of vapor. His face materializes through the dissolving fog, and I'm wondering if this effect is all just performance for the punch line.

"You know what your problem is, coz?"

No, but I have the feeling he's going to tell me.

"You not hanging on to da tings dat mattah," he says, poking his ballpoint pen right into my sternum. "Maybe dis job get tree-strikes rule and always goin' be around... but Mari, Jojo? Maybe cannot get sum tings back, yeah?"

"Ummm...can one of you pull my car up, or is this, like, a bad time?" asks a customer standing behind us, ticket in hand, lord knows for how long.

"On the double, ma'am," smiles Kainoa, then turns back to me, before disappearing down the ramp, "Hang on your love, haole. And try wipe your face already, bu. Get blood still-yet."

31.

Fucking Manny

On the afternoon that Emmanuel "Manny" Dapidran Pacquiao knocked out the undefeated five-division champion of the world, Floyd Mayweather Jr., the sounds of celebration penetrated the wealthiest neighborhoods of Oʻahu. The sound crept up Hawaiʻi Loa Ridge, through Portlock even, like a piercing battle cry. It hopped over the seaside mansion gates in Lanikai, causing the elites to look up from their *Hawaiʻi Modern Luxury* magazines toward the Great Wall of Koʻolau and shudder.

There were impromptu as well as meticulously planned and extravagant parades down the streets that marched and sang and flaunted until the participants collapsed from celebration exhaustion in scattered lumps of humans, banners, and instruments, late into the night. There were victory walks through the hills of Kalihi up Nihi Street, down the dusty avenues of Waipahu, and firework stashes left over from the Fourth of July were raided and lit, peony and horsetail explosions showering towns as far off as Ewa, Wahiawa, and Waialua. This was bigger than Obama.

Grown men cried openly in bars, in crowded homes, in backrooms huddled around radios, in cars stuck in grid-locked H-1 westbound traffic, in halls of hotels, in other public and precarious places. This was not a win; this was a conquering. It was a flag on the moon, a step onto the soil of the New World. This was bigger than Obama.

Many babies were conceived that night, and the sex was brutal. Couples, co-workers, one-night stands, and spouses reenacted the fight—with their genitals. Men imagined their members to be the fists of Pacquiao and jabbed, hooked, and crossed through rounds of copulation. Lackluster lovers were, for once in their lives, *imaginative*, performing startling combinations on their opponent's nether regions. The already androit lovers shocked even themselves. They took turns being Manny— man and woman—so they could all feel what it was to be the greatest on earth. Manny was an aphrodisiac. Manny was God. And it goes without saying what every child's namesake was nine months later, like the christening effects of some maniacal dictator or worshipped deity.

On this night, and maybe as far as a week onward, the Philippines were a global superpower. A force to be reckoned with. There was talk of sovereignty, of creating an autonomous territory within the state—the island of Lāna'i perhaps—said area becoming a far-flung protectorate of the motherland. Well, it was just talk. In Waikīkī, those at work who couldn't see the match on TV at the poolside bar and grill, or even hear it by radio, received phone calls and texts from friends and family, even enemies (in momentary cease-fire) to bring them the news. They read the abbreviated text messages in Tagalog and Ilokano and Visayan and shrieked in delight. Feeling that something monumental...millennial...no, *celestial*, had just occurred, drastic measures were taken. It was natural disaster-style thinking, and men and women walked off their shifts, some exclaiming, "*I quit!*" like a precise and powerful KO uppercut supplementing Manny's victory with their own. Even though some of the men, the very next day, hungover and late to work, dehydrated and de-semen-ated, would plead and grovel to management for their jobs back. They were sorry, they had been drunk off patriotism and Manny. And Manny.

Fucking Manny.

It was on that very night, on the corner of Kalākaua and Seaside, in the midst of cheering fellow countrymen, packed bars and packed restaurants that had just shown the fight, soon overflowing into the street with wailing Pac-Man fans, that an animal was taken. A dog on a leash wrapped around a pole, waiting patiently for her master—a mid-thirties white male—to get off work and make the long haul back up St. Louis Heights. The canine was a beige American Staffordshire terrier who had two splotches of black around her eyes that connected and formed an uncanny sort of villain's mask. The man who stole the animal, as the masses' hands were in the air praising Jesus, snuck up behind it and shoved a beach towel dipped in chloroform over the dog's mouth. The dog passed out in a matter of milli-seconds, barks muffled in the terry cloth, and the man quickly rolled the dog into a large duffel bag, slung the bag over his shoulder, and trotted away without a single witness.

This dog was Joel's and her name is Ulu. Ulu-lei, actually, since most times he carries the dog around his neck—like a lei. Joel and Ulu's companionship began because Joel got robbed. (The first time.) Back then, Joel was living full-time in a tent up in the woods at the top of St. Louis Heights. Occasionally, he had visitors (usually people who he sold or bought or smoked weed with) and suspected that one of them had actually been the one who robbed him. Anyway, it was an existence that he strived to maintain. Way up there on a friend's property that he was allegedly watching, he survived various catastrophes such as the spring rains of '06 that lasted forty days and forty nights. He was up there during all that. With his dog. *Rippin' tickets... hangin' keys... settin' up tents... un-der trees...* he'd rap to me.

For two years Joel worked one Sunday brunch valet shift a week at John Dominis. He made about $150-200 cash that shift, then did two open mic nights, free-style rapping/slam poetry-ing in order to score two free dinners on top of that. With no rent to pay, he stretched the Sunday shift's tips out until the following Sunday. And so on. Occasionally he'd sleep in random women's apartments around town, had he gotten lucky that week.

One night, after the twenty-minute walk from the last bus stop on the mountain to his humble abode, he came home to a tent that'd been rummaged through. He had stashed some money in a sock, about fifty dollars, and it was gone. To someone living off less than $200 a week, that was a substantial blow. He decided he needed a dog. A guard dog. Or so he thought. So he did his research. Originally, he wanted a Rhodesian ridgeback. He obsessed over the breed. Went to the UH library faking he was a student and read everything he could on them. Read those silly *Puppies for Dummies* books, shit like that, maybe even a few "raising your newborn" books too. He was friggin' committed, is what I'm saying. It was all in preparation for the Adopt a Pet expo at the Blaisedell Arena, which was quickly approaching.

And then it came. There were dozens upon dozens of breeds, and people lined up for interviews with the breeders. Most were in line for golden retrievers, poodles, huskies—the booshie dogs most people want. Not many for the ridgebacks, and Joel beelined it for the gal in charge. But she wouldn't give one to Joel. He was nearly unemployed, kind of a musician, kind of a valet, kind of homeless. "Why would I ever entrust an animal to you?" she asked. She was kind of bitchy, he told me. Joel slunk away, defeated, but was stopped by an HPD officer on duty for the expo.

According to Joel, he was one of four African American cops on the island, and his side hustle was raising pit bulls out in Makakilo. He had a legit kennel called Hawai'i Five-O Kennels, and he told Joel that pits make *fantastic* dogs if raised with love, despite their bad rep. Said he'd give Joel a deal on a puppy. A payment plan even, which Joel, for well over a year, adhered to diligently.

He named her Ulu, but Joel says it best: "Yeeeeeahhh-Boooyeeeee, you see at first I just wanted a dog to guard my shit and pull me on a skateboard, but when I brought him up there on that mountain in the sticks…it's like…for a little while we were free. I let her run wild in nature, and I did the same, and for a week or so, the two of us were just babblin' in the wind, all caught up in the moment, in the quiver of a leaf, right? Just followin' dat blissipline, riiight? But eventually, you gotta come down off that mountain and function in the real-world lower-earth, riiiiight? So I packed Ulu into my bike basket, and we rode the wind down to reality, dawg." I swear this is how Joel talks.

They started at the bark park, over by Kapiʻolani Community College where people train their dogs to interact with other dogs. He made a deal with an instructor there, which meant he'd trade half an ounce of weed a week for three lessons. Ulu-lei had social issues, though. Maybe "rambunctious" is a kinder word. But despite all the positive reinforcement, the behavioral lessons, the rewards and treats, according to Joel, Ulu was far too vocal—far too emotional—for her canine counterparts. "Ulu, or pit bulls for that matter, are hyper-sensitive, just like me. We vibrate at higher frequencies than your average dog or human. We're emotional, manic, whatever you wanna call it, dawg. So when you disrespect the pit—she lashes out and fucks some shit up," he told me.

According to Joel, she did this thing he calls a "self-inflicted muzzle" to channel her energy constructively. Joel'd bring a tennis ball to the bark park, and Ulu would attack it. She'd keep it in her mouth and then faux attack, or *play* (depending on perspective), with the other dogs that way. She'd be bouncing off the other dogs and dog owners with her ball mouth, seemingly vicious, but never actually opening her mouth, let alone biting anyone. But her energy was intimidating, and the two were kicked out of puppy classes. And furthermore, the bark park. But the two continue. Are inseparable. Versions of themselves, as Joel puts it. Ulu is his spirit animal, his daemon if you will. His living, barking 'aumākua. And he's been good to her. Bought her a harness, even paw booties for running (pulling him on a skateboard) on asphalt. She hangs out, somewhere in the shadows, tethered to a pole while Joel works a shift. He's written songs about her. He's never clipped her ears. He lets her tail wag long and free.

The two of them remind me a lot of Henderson and the trained-bear Smolok in Saul Bellow's, *Henderson the Rain King*:

This poor, broken ruined creature and I, alone, took the high rides twice a day. And while we climbed and dipped and swooped and swerved and rose again higher and higher than the ferris wheel and fell, we held on to each other. By a common bond of despair we embraced, cheek-to-cheek, as all support seemed to leave us, and we started down that perpendicular drop. I was pressed into his long-suffering, age worn, tragic, and discolored coat as he grunted and cried to me. At times the animal would wet himself. But he was apparently aware that I was his friend, and he did not claw me...two humorists before the crowd, but brothers in our souls—I enbeared by him, and he probably humanized by me...

But one night, on an absurdly chaotic Friday evening shift at the 'Ohana Beach Hotel, on the corner of Seaside and Kalākaua, in the forty-five seconds it took to park a car, when Joel looked back at the pole next to the Foot Locker—Ulu was gone.

32.

"Sappho can't save you now..."

Where's Auntie Mari?" asks Jojo.

"She's just at her house tonight, bud," I say. "You ready for cowboy food?"

"Uh-huh."

I crack open two eggs into a frying pan, flip the bacon popping on the other, stir the beans once, and rip open a new bag of Sinaloas.

"But I like it better when we *all* eat da cowboy food. Taste better dat way, Uncle," Jojo whines.

"Listen, Jojo, Auntie Mari and I are good friends, but we don't hang out as much now."

"Are you guys divorced?" he asks.

"No, Jojo, we were never married, so we couldn't be divorced."

"I wanna call her."

So do I. Every goddamned minute. "You want

passion-orange or passion-guava?" I ask, peering into the refrigerator.

"I wanna *caaall* her."

"All right, Jojo." I pick up my phone, punch in Mari's number, and hand it over to Jojo, knowing she probably won't pick up.

"Auntie Mari!" Jojo exclaims, but stops and looks puzzled. It's her voicemail. "What do I say?" he asks.

I shrug, speechless.

"Auntie...It's me, Jojo. Come have dinner with us. Please, Auntie, I lost another *toooth*! Umm...I love you, Auntie. Miss you."

He hands the phone back, and the sound of the bacon, still crackling, is deafening.

"Will she—" and just then, the phone rings. I hand it to Jojo. "Auntie *Maaaaaaari*!" he howls, practically weak at the knees.

They talk for a few minutes while I finish our breakfast-for-supper. I'm toasting the tortillas when he taps me on the back and hands me the phone.

"Here. Auntie wanna talk wit you now."

My stomach drops. She hasn't spoken to me in over a week, "Hey..."

"Really? That's your play? Using *Jojo*?"

I can hear the lump in her throat over the receiver. She sounds as if she'd been crying. "That's not fair," she makes out.

"Mari, I've tried...Jojo just wanted to hear your voice. He misses you, too."

She exhales for what seems like ages.

"*I used to weave crowns…*" I offer. "*I talked with you in a dream…*"

"Sappho can't save you now," she says.

"Sappho? I thought that was Sade. The singer, not the—"

"Yeah," she stops me. "Listen, it breaks my heart that I don't get to see Jojo just because I don't want to see you. That's not what I wanted. If you want to drop Jojo off with me now and then, if he really wants to see me, then that's fine. But as far as you and me…I need some time."

"Mari, could you talk with me in person, at least?"

"Lemme say goodbye to Jojo, please."

The sound of forks clanking on plates echoes through the kitchen while Jojo attempts to serve us what I've cooked. "What she say?" he asks, with a mouth full of eggs.

I pass him the phone again. "Auntie wants to say goodbye, Jo."

So, things with Marisela and I are still on the rocks. Hard to say if I could pinpoint the exact issue, whether it's the passing Jojo around, him getting his arm broken with Gene, me getting canned at Punalani…take your pick, but we haven't been sharing bottles of Kirkland's finest lately. Don't get me wrong. I've tried to get her back and made a serious effort, too. Left her pathetic, desperate voicemails, reading Lorca and Neruda poems—in friggin' Spanish, mind you—to no avail. *Es tan corto al amor, y es tan largo el olvido…* She wasn't having it. Me having to pick up a few more valet shifts to make up for the Punalani layoff just made it that much more awkward, too, since I've been seeing her more often at her target spots. She'll time it perfectly, too, pulling in and rushing away *right* when I'm parking a car. It's pretty clear she wants no part of me.

But what the hell lasts forever? They say love does and as a feeling maybe that's true, but clearly its form—the person, the smell, the timbre of their laugh, the sound of their sigh in the morning—eventually fades.

Because love is a liquid, a pool of shockingly cold water that we leap into off cliffs, holding hands, bellowing "cannon ball" to the universe. Love is a liquid, a hot Jacuzzi bubbling with passion, a foamy aphrodisiac that eventually exhausts each one in the hot tub. Love is a liquid and when we hold it in the palm of our hands it always runs right through our fingers to escape. What lasts forever?

Didion said that "we tell ourselves stories in order to live," but we tell ourselves lies, too. Lies to fight that very gravity that pulls love through our fingers. We tell ourselves lies in order to live, like religion and pledges and wedding vows. We repeat that tiny forever trapped between a fragile "I" and "you" like superstitious rote. We constantly shoot for the stars, constantly resist the figures and the data and the advice of the scorned. We try to hold onto that liquid by pressing our palms more tightly together to prevent a leak. We tell ourselves lies in order to live like: "She'll never leave." Or, "Life is fair." "Good conquers evil." "I'll never lose interest."

"I'll be a great father."

But the strange truth is that no matter what you read, all those epic novels and brilliant films, the *Love in the Time of Cholera*'s and *Cinema Paradiso*'s, the shit you base your beliefs on because it hits you in the gut so squarely—they're just stories. With no guarantee of success if attempted by a mere mortal in the comfort of their home. The strange truth is that no matter how hard you love a person, how much you're willing to sacrifice, sometimes shit just doesn't work out and you can't get her back. Most times, really. Sometimes when she's made up her mind, there's just no changing it. It's done. And like I've said before, you can always count on a valet to fuck up a good thing.

Jojo can tell I've been hurting. Little kids always have that sixth sense, no matter how hard you try to hide it. They're like animals, whining and whimpering, hearing an earthquake minutes before the ground shakes. Always asking questions. I wonder how many times grown-ups have let him down in his short, chaotic lifetime. I wonder if he had any concept of what "normal" was, or if all he really knew of was this confusing suspension. Of floating like driftwood in the stormy sea of each adult's fucked-up-ness. Of mandatory resilience.

"How come everybody every time *LEAVE*?" he suddenly erupts, his face flushed with anger.

I've seen him lose his temper before, but this one seemed bottled up. Pressurized. A kind of rage that's been broiling for, maybe, his whole life.

"I'm not going anywhere, Jo-man," I assure him.

"You *lie!*" he growls through a clenched jaw. "You're just like *him*. Take me Palani's, I hate this place!"

I wince at the words.

"Just like *who*, Jojo?"

The boy buries his face into his hands and groans, tears and snot slowly seeping through his fingers. He collapses in his chair. I get up and wrap my arms around his shoulders and put my forehead on his mess of black hair.

"*Ev-ev-ev*-everyone always leaves," he sobs.

"I'm not gonna leave you, Jojo," I say, pulling him tighter. "I don't wanna go Palani's," he sniffles. "Kinda crowded over there. Here I'm...I'm da only son. *Your* son, feels like."

Took the words right out of my mouth.

"I feel the same way, Jo."

"I don't wanna go back," he says, and I know he didn't mean Palani's, but rather the "back" that he'd left when he showed up in the trunk.

"What do you want, Jojo?"

"I want you and Auntie Mari and me to live together. I just like stay somewhere—*here*."

"I'm working on it, Jojo," I say, feeling his hot face on my forearm, sopping wet from tears. "I swear I'm working on it."

I glance down at the table by his plate of half-eaten tortillas and notice the phone timer still ticking. Jojo had forgot to hang the phone up. I pick it up and listen, walking out of the kitchen.

"Hey," I make out.

"Your move now, Peter Pan," she says evenly. "Prove it." And clicks the phone off.

★ ★ ★

If you resent the cure, you stay sick.

I tuck in Jojo after he's showered and finish the dishes. I stare into the soapy water and think about the boy, what it must feel like to never really know where you'll be the next day—but that hopefully a bed or a couch comes.

I think about Mari. "There is a shredding that's really a healing, that makes you more alive," wrote Rumi. More alive. I must be more alive for them. I reach into my wallet on the counter and extract Graham's business card. *If you resent the cure, you stay sick.*

I punch in the digits and wait, tail between my legs, heart on the floor.

"Rumi. It feels late. Is it late?"

"Right. You're still on New York time…Two weeks later," I roust. "Tell me about the Big Smoke, Graham. Is the Apple as large as everyone says?"

Graham laughs. "Fair 'nuff. I'm sure I sounded pretentious asking that."

"Lil bit…Why'd you get me fired, Graham?"

"So that you'd call me now."

"You didn't have to convince Derek that I was over teaching, man."

"He didn't need much convincing, and whether you like it or not, you were on your way out. Which is great, because you're a way better writer than teacher, and I have something that'll suit you perfectly once (A) you finish your book, and (B) we move the family back to Hawai'i in August."

"I thought you couldn't leave New York."

"You can always leave New York."

"You have that written on a bumper sticker on your second car at home, huh, Graham?"

"No one drives in Brooklyn, Rumi. Listen, most of the reason why we're moving home—besides the fact that

New York totally fucking sucks—is that Conde Nast is launching a new title out of Honolulu. *Pacific Traveler.* I've scoped out an office space already. I know the landscape. I'm kama'aina—"

"Kama-*kinda*," I correct.

"Right," he laughs. "And my role is publisher, but I want you on the team as a writer or perhaps in an editor position. It'll be a nine-to-five, the pay will be shit, but maybe you'll get a free trip to Tahiti or New Zealand out of it. Oh, and you can stop parking cars. Whattya say?"

"I say, 'Yes, please.' One condition."

"What's that?"

"I bring along an intern. A former student of mine; the kid's a hotshot. Not even a senior in high school yet."

"Fine by me, man. Good night?"

"Night, Graham. And, thank you."

33.

"On da fucking edgeadeeart."

There's a pretty good chance of seeing some Gypsies on a Saturday night coming into the Sea Bird at the Waikīkī Sands for dinner. I don't know why, but they love the place, and apparently it's just a total shit show in the restaurant when they come in. Loud as all damn hell, taking their sweet, sweet time to finish up. Luckily, on a party of eight-plus over there, the waiter gets to include gratuity with the bill. Which kind of backfires, because they'll take that as an insult—as if they aren't civilized enough to know what's customary or not. Then said-backlash ends up being a crummy tip. I let the boys know they'll probably be coming in and to not turn them away—that we *need* them to identify that Caddy. And sure as hell, they come in, a goddamned band of them.

In typical fashion, they try and park themselves. This

really pisses a valet off, especially when there are signs everywhere saying, *No self-parking.* Complete control freaks, remember? Kainoa and Peanut are fuming, arms spinning like third base coaches trying to wave them back around to reenter.

"No can self-park, bruddahs. Look da signs, ah! Drive around and we goin' take you at da lobby...Fahk, you make one traffic jam, already!" The two turn and glare at me like, *This is your doing...*

The first car of Gypsy men—actually, four men crammed into a new Porsche 911 drop-top—make this mistake, then scoff at us and burn out of the valet lobby back onto Kalia Road to reenter correctly.

"Haole, you take your cousins, bumbai I going snap," utters Peanut, hands clenched, on the verge of meltdown.

"All right, all right. Take it easy. You know they usually tip well, man. I'll handle them."

Moments later, the Porsche pulls back up, with one man sitting on top of another in the passenger seat, and the fourth man somehow straddling the stick shift between the seats. They screech to a stop, pull the e-brake, and step out of the car. I look up and double-take. For one, they're all matching, each in black suits, all with huge Gucci belt buckles on, just these big-ass "G"s like subtle clues to their ethnicity. The suits look left over from a C & K concert, with lapels like massive wings about to take flight from their chests. All of them with those copper Mediterranean complexions and emerald eyes glowing in their sockets like gems. I recognize the driver from the Ala Moana Shore—Skippy, they call him. They fix their chains and bracelets, look at their watches and iPhones, and draw out their arrival, hotel guests piling up behind them. They chatter in thick New York accents blended with Romany.

An old woman with a cigarette dangling from her lips arrives in a yacht-like Lincoln, sagging with the weight of five other women and six kids. The doors fly open, and four of the kids fall out and onto the lobby floor. The women, mostly mothers and adolescent daughters, step out all dressed identically in flowing skirts hanging down modestly to their ankles. They wrangle the children brusquely, light cigarettes in our clearly marked no-smoking zone, and shout at one another in brassy voices. Their hairdos are raven waterfalls sweeping around six-inch hoop earrings. One more car pulls up, a new red Chevy pickup with no plates, carrying two other young Gypsy couples. They look at Skippy instead of us for permission to park. We ask them if they're parking for the Sea Bird, and again they look at Skippy for an answer to our queries. Skippy nods, and they hand us the key.

I jog over to Skippy before he slips away.

"Greetings, brother!" I say, grinning, with open arms.

"Eh, gadje!" he says.

Coincidentally, *gadje* is basically Gypsy for haole. Really, it just means non-Gypsy. But whatever, I'm used to it.

"Skip, my main man, I really need to talk to you if you have a moment."

He whistles through his teeth impatiently, answering in that lightning-fast New York accent, "Uh reallykindabusy now, chief. Kinda withmyfamily now, bro."

"Skip, just one hot minute..."

"Kay, kay, kay, gadje. What's this allabout, den?"

"Ok. Listen, nothing's wrong, but we just have to know if you sold someone this car," I reach into my pocket and show him a photo of the Coupe DeVille on my cell phone. Luckily, I snagged a photo of it before it got towed.

He takes a look, cocks his head, and sucks in air between his teeth dramatically, "Gadje, we flipalotta cars, bro, reallyhardta say, bro..."

"Just take a good look, because it's really important to me, man," I say, handing him the phone.

"Hmm," he says, frowning ambiguously.

"Hmmm, what? What the hell does that mean?" I goad.

"Hmm," he nods.

"Skip, c'mon man, it's a simple answer."

"Listen, gadje. Idunno what ya involving me in here. I could tellya one thing oranother, but say I did sell it; it's outtamy hands now if da car broke."

"Skippy, we don't care about the car. We're trying to find the owner because he left something in it."

"I dunno, my clients got rights, ya know? Privacy 'n shit... but if I tellya...whatsinitforme? Whadda fuck's initfume?"

I sigh deeply and flip my palms up like, *what do you want?*

"Yaboys over at Dukes...Dey always tellus da lot's full. Every fucking time werollup... I want that to not happen anymore," he says, rolling a gold bracelet around and around his wrist.

"Done, man. I've worked that spot before and know the on-site manager personally. I'll call him up and tell him that there *always* needs to be room for you and your fam, Skip."

"Anhow ya gonna prove dat to me, gadje? Ya gonna makedacall rightnow?"

"Skippy!" shouts someone in the backround. "Dafuck yadoin wegonna go in already!"

"Yeah, yeah, I'll catchup inasecond." He looks at me and puts his thumb and pinky to his ear like a telephone, so I ring up Kekolu working the Aliʻi Hotel and plead with him not to send the Gypsies away anymore.

"All right, Skip, you guys are straight. They're gonna make room for you guys from now on, any busy night—"

"Yeah, yeah, yeah. Kay, sowe solddat DeVille to dis junkie outonda Westside. Toldme hisname was…uh; Robbie, or Robert. We tried tatellum dat da ignition was all fuckedup [we sold him a lemon] but he wantedit anyway. Probably 'coz there's allottaroom inthose things. So himanhis girl or wifeor whatevah could roll around-lookin' fuh dope or whatevah and then have a place ta sleepin when they're just, like, zonked. You'd be surprised how manyguys want beaters likedat ta sleep in."

In other words, you'd be surprised how many lemons I sell to junkies.

"Okay. So Robert. He's a junkie, and did he have a wife or something? Does he live in an actual house out there?"

"I don't thinkso. Think helives indabushes…witda homeless out dere. Like, waaay out dere. Past Waiʻanae. Onda fucking edgeadeeart."

"Edgidy-ert?"

"Yeah, daedge, ud-dee-eart." Earth, he means.

"All right. Okay," I nod, processing.

"Da fuckdoyouwant wit his car anyways? Datting can't berunning still."

"He parked here a couple months ago and left something in it...valuable."

Skippy turns to walk down the lobby, then quickly turns around again, facing me and fiddling with his necklace.

"Oh yeah," he says, snapping his fingers. "Was out dere a few days ago. You know deygotchaboy's dog out dere, too. Whattyoucallit—Ulu?"

"Wait...What? How do you know Ulu?"

"I buy weed from Joel. Da one wit da Zoro mask, right? Anyway, I was out dere visiting a client when I saw it. I calleditsname...and it came...but it's chained up."

"Jesus, how'd it get out there?"

"People livin out dere buy 'um for guard dogs. Somebody musta stoleit and soldittoum. I dunno. I gottago, gadje."

"Listen, Skip. I'll guarantee you free parking at *every* one of our locations if you do something for me."

"Gah-head. What?"

34.
Game plan

ene gets to the meeting forty-five minutes late, huffing and puffing, just a sweaty yard sale of a human. Which is a little inconvenient, as I'd planned it fifteen minutes before our shift at the Sands starts, but I watch him jog down the ramp as Palani pulls a car up. Palani yanks the e-brake right as he passes, the violent shriek his twisted greeting. The window's down and Palani's fleshy elbow hangs out like a shark fin.

"Fakah, you late!" he shouts. "Where's your 4-Runner, Hawaiian? Break-down?"

"Yups," nods Gene, hurrying into the valet office.

He trudges in and flicks his chin, hello, to us. He also looks a little rattled—girl problems, I assume. For such a deviant, he sure wears his heart on his sleeve. His ongoing and bizarre long-distance relationship with a newly divorced mother of two in Vegas doesn't help his fragile disposition either.

"Watsup, Gene, you look a little shook. Your car that messed up?" I ask.

"Nah, minahs. Jus' getting hundred-K checkup at da kine off Beretania. Nobody could take me work, so I wen catch da bus," he says.

"Why do you look like you just fell into a swimming pool? Don't, like, ten different buses roll down Kalākaua?"

"Yeah...but had one accident on da Bus—"

"Eh!" shouts Palani, swinging open the office door to hang a pair of guest keys.

"Den I had to run Macy's fo' buy one new pair shorts," Gene continues.

"Wait, wait. What *kind* of accident happened on the bus?" I ask. Gene's usually quite forthcoming; vagueness isn't a common valet trait. Unless, of course, if the topic is tips.

"Kay, so I stay waiting at the bus stop by Jack 'n a Box, Pi'ikoi. I get on Numbah 19. We cruise down Pensacola till da road end, den take one left, den one right fo' get on Ala Moana. But I get in one *new* bus, yeah? Da kine wit WiFi, and cherry new seats, new graphics on da side; not like da old kine, all orange-yellow-doo-doo, yeah? An' buh-*lasting* AC. Had all kine roadwork on Ala Moana, and traffic was jus' stand-still, yeah? An' wit da AC, I jus' wen conk-out, yeah? Straight *moe moe*. An den I jus' started fo' dream about dis one chick I knew...and...and had one accident. I wake up to da drivah asking me if going get off already. Den I realize I wen splooge all ovah my work shorts!"

"Ho, how's dat pun!" says Kainoa.

"You had a wet dream on TheBus?" I clarify.

"One meeeeeann wet dream, brah," he corrects, grinning.

"Happens, dawg," shrugs Joel.

"Anyways, had to run from da zoo all da way to Macy's, find one sale rack, an' buy new shorts. So hum-bug, yeah?"

"Tell me about it," I mumble, taking a head count. "Okay, so everyone's here, right?"

Gene nods, Palani and Joel throw up middle fingers, and Palani sighs, "Yeah, haole, we hea."

"So thanks to my longstanding relationship with the Gypsies and my crackpot P.I. work, we've discovered where Jojo's parents—if that's what they are—reside. Oh, and interestingly enough, where Joel's stolen dog, Ulu, ended up as well."

"Somebody wen take Ulu?!" exclaims Kainoa, flabbergasted.

"Yeah, last week during the Pacquiao fight. So, Skippy, the Gypsy who sold the Deville to Jojo's dad, or whoever the guy is, is gonna drive us out to Jojo's place on the Westside, and we're going to try and find any papers for Jojo. A birth certificate, immunization records, that kind of thing. We'll also get him to sign a letter of consent to grant me and Marisela legal guardianship."

"Ho, you get da flowah girl back?" snaps Gene.

"Working on it," I say, quickly brushing off the subject. "So, who's coming? It's me, Skip, Joel, and we need two more for backup. We'll leave Saturday at noon."

"My youngest daughter get one soccer game dat day," says Palani.

"Can," says Kainoa, raising a shaka.

"Fantastic. Gene, you in?" I ask, pointing at him. "*Ua mau kau kauuu...*"

"*Ae!*" he shouts. "And don't ever say that again, haole. That's *our* word."

"Are you even Hawaiian?" I frown.

"Half-Korean, quartah Samoan, so...more den you!"

We break and the boys file out into the garage, Joel rapping about our upcoming journey to the Westside in the key of the *Indiana Jones* theme song. Palani, however, hangs back and tips his head at me to do the same.

"Fakah, you stepping up already, ah?" he says, looking me dead in the eye.

I shrug ambivalently, pretending to check my phone for an incoming text. "What do you care?"

"C'mon, bu. I care. Listen...You know my wife nevah said dat about you, yeah? Was just trying fo get you to *man up*, brah. And you did." He offers a palm and we shake on it, bumping shoulders.

Well, fuck me.

"You sly fox, you..." I grin.

"Fakah, das reverse psychology, brah—you susceptible! Woulda been one psych-majah at Wyoming if nevah had my firstborn."

"I bet you would, Palani."

He steps out of the office, and all that I'm left with is the familiar drone of the rickety A.C. unit, the sound an overwhelming bestial groan. I grab a Sharpie marker from the drawer and, remembering something in particular from bygone days, write a message on the beige door frame. *Be a clear and rational lunatic.*

Just then Kainoa blasts into the room to hang some

keys, practically nailing me with the doorknob. He follows me out into the garage and spots the quote above the door.

"Ho, Rumi in da house, ah?"

I look back at him perplexed like, *how the hell'd you know that one?*

Kainoa backhands me in the shoulder before jogging away and says, "Seen dat same quote couple months back on Sherry's desk calendah."

"Japanee-Sherry, or *hāpai*-Sherry?" asks Gene, trotting down the ramp.

And so for a time, the boy was raised by wolves. By con artists and hustlers, gamblers and brawlers, poets and actors—*valets*—who loved him like their own. In dark parking lots below the earth, and in high-rise hotels, reaching toward the sky. In households and apartments of other wolves with their own families, who nurtured him like their own pup, if even for a couple of days a week. By wives and girlfriends and mistresses and fuck buddies that melted at his smile and hugged him desperately, like a tragic wish.

And he moved. Constantly. A small nomad, bathed in wind. They kept bits and pieces of his essence at each place, so he didn't have to lug his whole life around every single time. So he could feel as if any one of those places were his home. Always shifting, shuffled continually, in the seat of a stranger's car.

But the boy had done something to us. Since opening up that trunk, we wanted more for him and, for some reason, ourselves. We were no longer floating through this life in a valet's numb limbo, nor accepting the status of has-been-ness any more. Since the boy, we were *being*. He tamed us like his animals.

We've even been giving up shifts to newbies in the company, slowly parking less and less. Shit, since the boy, Kainoa tried out for Kumu Kahua Theatre and got casted for a performance next spring. Palani's coaching his oldest son's Pop Warner football team, vicariously back in the game again. Gene and another valet named Bubu found (threatened) an investor and are spearheading a kind of Cross Fit-mixed martial arts fusion workout for morbidly obese toddlers called Child Soljahz. Joel...well, Joel's teaching the last couple weeks of a summer course at one of the state's most prestigious private schools. And I am writing, furiously. Between the dinner in and out at Morton's. Before shifts at the Sands. Finally finishing what I started, mowing through pages, breaking lead, before Graham gets here with the new gig. Pecking away late into the night after Jojo's hit the sack. Trying to patch things up with Marisela. Sure, maybe this is just what happens when you get fired from one of your jobs, but I like to think that it's the boy. And we can do better for Jojo. We can be better.

PART III

JOURNEY TO THE EDGE OF THE EARTH

35.

Farrington Hwy, Westbound

Veering onto the H-1 westbound where the freeway splits with the H-2 north, a woman in a copper late-80's lowered Corolla hatchback passes us from the right lane. She sits so reclined she's nearly in the backseat, wearing oversized, blacked-out wraparound shades, long hair braided tightly behind her head, shaved bald an inch above her ears up to the braid. On the back of the hatchback window is a decal that reads: *If You're Gonna Ride My Ass, At Least Pull My Hair.* She sticks her burly left arm out of the window and throws us a shaka before peeling away.

The deeper you drive down the Westside, the more offensive the bumper stickers get. Or maybe it's the more hilarious they get, depending on perspective, I suppose. Before Nānākuli, around the water park on Farrington Highway, they're cute, if not benign. It's a lot of, *Have you hugged your keiki lately?* memos that eventually turn into, *Have you hugged your kumu lately?* Some references and language that maybe someone from the more insulated, affluent parts of town might not even get, like Kahala or Lanikai. Last names are always trending—*Keaulana, Kealoha,* etc. Then the farther you get into Wai'anae, the more militant and edgy they become. The more audacious the humor. Many, just common phrases or place names advertised on the back windshields that more or less reflect the sentiment of the driver, like Facebook mood messages. An array of metallic laminates over illegal five-percent tint and countless two-toned, snarling pit bulls baring teeth at the vehicles behind them. And bumper stickers like: *My pit bull ate your honor student,* or, *Ali'i Status* [royal eminence]. Or, *Got Poi?* Or, *Got Pono?* Or, *Got Ressurection?* [for the Christians] *And, I'd Rather Be Choking You Out* [a jiu jitsu ref]. A few wild cards in there too, like: *Will Work for Dolly Parton Tickets.* A myriad of, *Watchufaka!* [what-you-fucker] And, *Faka Wat!* [Fucker what?]. And, *Ainokea* [I don't care]. Or the elongated derivative, *Ainokea Eni Moa* [I don't care any more].

Then there's the vehicle owner's vibrant ethnic pride messages like: *Tongan Built* or *Hawaiian Built* or *Pocho* [Portuguese] *Built* stickers in arching Old English font. Also, *I Am Hawaiian And I Vote.* Or, *No Hawaiians, No Aloha.* Definitely a lot of *Kau Inoa*'s and *Wai'anae Boyz, Wai'anae Gurlz, Westside, Westsidahs, Pu Insai* [put inside [to have sexual intercourse]], and *Like Poke?* or *Like Slam?* Both stickers asking, "Would you like to have intercourse?" Also, *Hawaiian Superman* and *Bruddah Iz.* And, more increasingly, *Defend Hawai'i,* the two words sandwiching an AK-47. Which replaced last year's popular *F.B.I.* [From Big Island], which replaced the previous year's *Maui Built*, which replaced the previous year's *O.G.* [O'ahu Grown] trends.

Now, the Westside of O'ahu is already a hot place, as are most leeward shores in the Hawaiian Islands, but by the end of summer, it's definitely at its most sweltering. Driving up the western shoreline, away from the emerald, sheerridged Ko'olaus draped in their cloak of clouds, the scenery turns arid, browner, parched. Turning into the handful of valleys at the foot of the Wai'anae range, down the homestead roads, certainly there are lush farms and gorgeous communities, but the façade on the main drag reflects a much tougher picture. One of beat-up liquor stores, vehicles converted into small homes, tennis shoes hanging from power lines, "We Cash Checks" shops, countless lean-tos and homeless tents hanging on for dear life along the juxtaposed pristine shoreline. That, and so many broke-down cars without tires, incapacitated on the roadside, with ironically, a tire shop on the corner of every other block. Along Farrington, the supermarkets look ancient, but the fast-food joints all have bright new redesigns.

Me, Skippy, Gene, Joel, and Kainoa watch this curious slice of life play out before us from the windows of Skippy's Chevy Blazer. Begrudgingly, Skip agreed to drive us in, a condition we negotiated to grant him and his immediate family unlimited free parking. "Immediate," which could probably end up meaning four families, but Skip's out here all the time buying and selling lemons, and we come out here, like, *never*, so a guide in a semi-familiar vehicle in this part of town goes a long way. But even Gene and Kainoa both seem a little rattled by the view.

"Fah-king rough dis town, ah?" exclaims Gene, scratching his chin stubble, frowning in disbelief.

Joel and I give each other furtive *Oh, shit* glances as we watch our "muscle" become intimidated by the environs.

"Dis place is like…Da Wy-ah, yeah?" states Kainoa questioningly.

"Da…why-yah?" I repeat, confused.

"Yeah, haole, you nevah seen Da Wy-ah…on da kine— Home Box Office?"

"I can sell you one passcode fo' HBOGo, brah. My cousin Jansen get plenty," offers Gene.

"Which season you talking?" asks Joel.

"Season Foah, because 'The Vacants,' yeah," says Kainoa.

"Nah, bu, Season Tree, 'cause stay like 'Hamsterdam,' bu!"

Passing Ma'ili Point, we accelerate with the turning light when a shredded, tatted-up man blindly pulls out in front of us while making a left turn onto the highway. His tanned face contrasts with a burst of buzzed, peroxide-blond hair. He's on a rickety moped that looks toy-like beneath him, his massive knees jutting out on both sides like stumpy, unusable dodo bird wings. He has a toddler with matching platinum hair on his lap, holding onto the center of the handlebars, and leaning into the turn, he eyes us out over his right shoulder, flicking his chin at all of us, mouthing, *Wat-chu fakahs!* the shout muted by the shrill whine of his moped. Skippy slams on the brakes to slow us from trailing him or getting us into an unwanted altercation before even arriving at The Bush.

A few miles yonder, up ahead on the right, smoke wafts from an old 76 gas station. Approaching closer, we notice that the smoke is actually rising from a car, incapacitated at the pump. The driver has decided to investigate the problem (one involving heat and smoke), right next to the gasoline pumps. The hood is popped and a shirtless man swats at the smoke billowing from the engine as he glares into the car's guts, attempting to discover the problem. I can't tell whether the car is exactly on fire or not, but it's a pretty good possibility with a cloud that black. Slowly passing the scene, I see that there's actually a young boy sitting shotgun in the car, seat-belted and peering through the window with a look on his face like, *Please get me out of here.* Even Skip looks over and squirms, shaking his fat head and pulling at his collar.

"Should we, like, pull over and say something?" I ask. "That looks like a disaster waiting to happen."

"Wepullovah an what?" says Skip. "Whattya gonna say, *gadje?* Moveaway from da pump or Ima have ta take *your* boy, too?" He laughs hysterically, morphing into a bronchial smoker's cough.

A few miles ahead on the sidewalk in front of Taco Bell, a woman with a body like Cruella de Vil—sunburnt and cackling—wobbles by the highway. Her face is skeletal but her eyes spin in their sockets. She hangs onto a dog by the leash that looks like it's in a lot better shape than she is. The mutt actually appears to be pulling her away from stepping onto the highway.

"Ho, fakah, you see dat?!" shouts Gene.

"The lady?"

"No, da dog. Das one seeing-eyes dog,' bruddah."

"I don't think she's blind, Gene—"

"Yeah, she *not*. But da dog still one seeing-eyes dog, da kine wea da mastah stay so tweaked dat da ting lead dem. See: One Seeing *Ice* Dog. *Cheee!*"

Even four valets and a gypsy can't resist a good pun, regardless of how off-color. The Blazer shakes with our laughter. But just a hundred yards farther, and we watch a homeless man pushing a shopping cart overflowing with plastic bags, dusty blankets, and crumpled-up tarps—hell, his entire life. Oddly, there are even cans with strings tied to the tabs dragging behind the back wheels as he pushes, like those "just married" ornaments on newlyweds' limos. I really can't think of any good reason for this addition to his cart, besides maybe using the noise like that of an ice cream truck jingle, except that his was like, "Crazy coming through," and the jingle was somehow even more annoying and bizarre. As we pass him, he stops and grabs a filthy teddy bear that's riding in the front seat where toddlers would sit. He pulls it out of the seat, raises it to the sky— like Simba from *The Lion King*, or something—pulls it to his chest, and holds it tenderly to his heart, closes his eyes and smiles deeply. Everyone in the car looks at one another and groans, *Awwwww* like a bunch of kids around a puppy. And then following that—a moment of collective silence, as if we're all trying to make sense of this scene, to comprehend the chaos and the heat and the sweat and the suffering and the beauty that surrounds us.

"*Fahk*, dis road is nuts, bu," decides Gene, summarizing our silence.

Everyone sighs in agreement.

36.

Double-crossed shakas

We take a left into a large beach park where teams of bronzed, glistening youth launch colorful fiberglass outrigger canoes from the shoreline. Joel and I refill plastic water bottles from the outside shower faucets while Gene and Kainoa take a leak in the bathroom.

"Baa-rah, get like foa' guys pass-out, jes' tweaking on da floah inside," exclaims Gene returning, shaking his head and zipping up his shorts.

A sight like that, however, isn't terribly shocking. Tweakers on a beach park bathroom floor on O'ahu are about as common as orange chicken on a Chinese restaurant menu. While clean, free tap water and outdoor showers abound at most beach parks, illicit sexual behavior and other nefarious pursuits do, too. I wonder if the state doesn't install mirrors in most bathrooms, as not to reflect the visitor's look of disgust. Most stalls lack any doors, broken from being kicked in not to mention four out of five toilets, on average, are clogged, overflowing with feces and toilet paper, so don't even think about stepping into the place barefoot.

We hop into Skippy's truck and move on. Countless boarded-up, closed-down, and vacant business shops are withering away or deceased on both sides of the road. The buildings, hidden in crude cobwebs composed of graffiti tags, are crowned with "For Sale" and "For Lease" signs like hopeless offers. Most of their former monikers like, "Ke'au's Liquors," "Maile's Restaurant," or "Kenny's Drive-Inn" wear broken smiles with jagged teeth, the plastic sign façades shattered by bottles, rocks, and other hand-held projectiles.

Every few blocks or so, these abandoned stores' vacant lots have been converted into recyclable redemption centers. Reynolds Recycling and other private companies' Mack truck containers occupy the center of the lots, manned by large, no-bullshit-looking men. Surrounding the containers, milling, waiting, leering, lurking, queuing, are homeless and home-withs getting cash back for cans, bottles, plastics, and cardboard, scoured the island over, picked from the murky depths of garbage cans, dug from the sand like buried treasure. Men and women gather around the converted containers, some with shopping carts overflowing with the junk and clutter that defines their mobile lives, and others with just a shopping cart of HI-5 redemption cans. Some with both. Many wear almost rags, filthy and tattered, others wear almost nothing, just swim trunks and slippers, holding industrial-sized trash bags, the same ones they'll reuse to comb the island yet again.

Some collect their money and then quickly wander off, on the prowl. The really loaded ones look zombie-like, and are so impatient for their next fix that they don't even have the time to search long enough to sufficiently fill up their bags. Some stay and loiter, hanging on to that euphoric feeling of "getting paid." Just to draw that sensation out a little. To have that cash in hand—that small symbol of a future—for a little while, before it's blown on lunch or dinner or cigarettes or beer or drugs or sex or whatever one spends their money on when they can't afford to save it. They hang out and talk shit, talk story, rabble-rouse a little and gloat before the burly men manning the containers tell them to shove off.

Still rambling westward, we peer down the random homestead roads and into the valleys at the foot of the Wai'anae mountain range. Near some Section 8 apartments, a small crowd queues at a metallic van, the local manapua man's rush hour. So many dilapidated, grandfathered single-family homes. Many of which have as much as nine inoperable vehicles in the front yard, coupled with a discarded fishing boat and array of sun-bleached furniture. The cars and junk bulge from the garages like strange growths. House tumors. An invasive species swallowing its host body. Such is the clutter.

Sporadically, grown men donning winter beanies beneath the scorching afternoon sun pedal children's bicycles through town with backpacks on, scanning the abandoned lots or un-abandoned, random shopping centers, for who-the-fuck-knows-what. A small band of adolescents, about six of them, pedal by carrying boogie boards, two to a bike, wearing tī leaves as bandanas, some with them tied around a bicep, another even wearing one below his nose, hanging over his mouth like some kind of island outlaw. First time I've ever seen that one before.

"Why are none of these damn kids in school?"

"Still summah-time, haole! Da keeds cannot have fun?" snaps Kainoa poignantly.

"I stand corrected..." I mumble, embarrassed for passing judgment in this place we're all quite unfamiliar with.

We roll by two giant beige Quonset huts that look like airplane hangars. It's the Wai'anae Civic Center, an emergency shelter for the homeless built by the state a few years back to get the communities off the beach. At the entrance gate, guards grapple with a man trying to push his way into the building. A woman emerging from the shelter runs toward them shouting, raising her hands in the air.

"Anybody needadrink...ora candy bar?" asks Skippy. "This 7-11 is da laststop to getanything before the Bush." He slows the Blazer by the convenience store past the Civic Center, looking into the rearview mirror at us.

Shrugs in the backseat, a couple, "Nahs."

Skippy sighs.

Shortly after the 7-11, a man in a clattering, bumperless minivan passes us impatiently and then slams on the brakes in front of us to turn down a street. Not paying full attention, I hit my forehead on the back of the front seat. Kainoa, sitting beside me, looks peripherally and shakes his head. I stare down the road where the van just turned, and the decal on his back windshield is so huge I can read it fifty yards into the valley. *NOAKUP.* (Don't act up). Amen. A final warning for us all.

Farther down Farrington, we catch glimpses of the setting sun between gaps in the koa haole trees and kiawe brush, between the rotting roadside houses, beach paths, and concrete drainage canals—peeks of the falling orb. We had planned to knock this matter out before nightfall, before five, even. We were supposed to get in—Joel and Gene would grab Ulu, me and Kainoa would handle Jojo's thing—and all get the hell out. Perhaps have Gene give Jojo's parents a pep talk while we're there... At the mercy of Skip, our designated driver, "Pick ya up from the Sands at noon" meant more like four o'clock. But honestly, what did I expect from him?

"*Chee!*" shouts Kainoa, grinning down at his phone. "Just got one Tindah match, bu. And stay out past Makaha, maybe in da Bush. What, charge 'um, or...?"

"Chance 'um, bu!" yells Gene. "Frick, I nevah get one match yet, but..." he sighs scrolling through the app.

We watch the sun duck behind a crumbling cinderblock wall that stands in front of a barren beachfront lot, a crude, spray-painted *MAKAHA BOYZ* scribbled across the wall's facade. At the bathrooms across from a lifeguard tower, a homeless mother washes herself and child in an outdoor public shower. She lathers shampoo into a little girl's hair as she shrieks hysterically in delight. A boy of about ten stands on a concrete bus stop bench, holding a neon bodyboard, wearing a shirt that reads, *Hawaiian... Nuff Said.* He glares at all of us in the car, raises two crossed arms to his chest, leans back, flexes his abs, with two fists: slack shakas.

"Ho, fahkin' *mean* dat double-crossed-shaka. I nevah seen dat long time, bu!" Gene exclaims, suddenly impressed. It was pretty damn hard-core.

Shortly beyond Makaha, residential homes thin out. The light is soft and the earth is finally cooling off. We pass a few paniolo ranches advertising horseback tours on crude signs etched in wood on the right side of the road. And then, before we know it, we've arrived, even pass it a bit without realizing. We have come to the tree people, The Bush. Maybe the only way Skippy knew when to stop was from the sight of the clutter creeping into the roadside. Broken TVs sit next to ripped-up couches tipped on their sides, next to metal file cabinets and bed frames trailing from the slum within the bushes. Piles of belongings precariously straddling the line separating "owned" and "please take." I wonder how a city and county garbage man out here even deciphers what's what. Or if they even drive out this far?

Skippy pulls over behind more junk gathered on the road. An old oven with the door bashed in, a stack of bald Goodyear tires, frayed wicker ottomans.

"Muthafucka," he says decidedly, staring at his phone. "There's nofuckinservice out here. I gottacall my clients, fellas."

We all look down at our phones. Right he is.

"That shack right there—dats where Rob stays. Seen dat boy playin' around dere, too. And da pit bull, pretty-sure dats a couple shacks ovah. Guy named Freddy might have it." He points across the road at an indiscriminate tent-hovel in the bushes.

"Fine den, we go. Let's get da dog an da peppahs,"

says Gene, hopping out of the car, stretching his neck and sparring with the air.

One by one we get out and look across the highway. Dogs bark wildly from somewhere in the brush; a dozen dull lights and several fires flicker within the trees. A few men ride children's bikes from one entrance of the bushes to another. Skippy peels out and whips it back around.

"Ima just gonna goback to Makaha, maybe da 7-11, too. I'll meet-cha back at dis spot in 20…Okay?" he yells from his window, barely stopping.

"Just come back, Skip!" shouts Kainoa, "or you no moa free parking!…*Anywea!*"

Skippy nods and speeds away, toward town.

37.
Da Ghost of Christmas Future

Kainoa and I dart across the highway while Gene and Joel start calling Ulu's name. We walk over to the tent where Skip pointed, Monty's letter of consent in hand, but it is hard to decipher where the entrance is through all the debris. Oddly enough, in many of the shacks out here, it's the piles of junk and belongings that seem to separate the rooms more than plywood or siding, acting like walls to the puzzle-pieced disorder. Wardrobes missing drawers, turned on their sides, are used to stack another part of a wall, dirty blankets and bags of cat food act as sandbag pilings, inlaid with sweaters and clothing, held together with a bicycle frame, cardboard boxes, and rusty paint cans. The pillars and columns of a slum mansion. It is beyond—

"Fah-kin' Tundah-dome ovah hea, ah?" mumbles Kainoa.

I nod in agreement. This definitely is *Beyond Thunderdome.*

An elderly woman in a sun-faded muumuu with long, silvery hair hanging down her shoulders like Spanish moss steps through a slit in the canvas and introduces herself.

"I'm Mary," she says, "You guys looking for Rob, yeah?"

We nod and she motions us to follow. The woman leads us on a path of dirty carpet patches, box crates, and upturned industrial dishwasher racks hovering over the sandy earth. Strewn forty-watt light bulbs dimly illuminate the tent home and sway occasionally with gusts of trade winds blowing in from the valley. A generator rattles, its motor turning in anguish while a refrigerator hums incessantly, drowning out the shore break's natural sea song. Mangy, cross-eyed slum cats slink between our legs and let out feeble, sickly meows. I scratch my ankles, my fingernails running over mosquito, or maybe flea, bites. We've only been in this place thirty goddamned seconds, and they've worked me over. The woman stops and pulls out a tackle box from between a stack of board games and a VCR with its cord wrapped around. She unbuckles the box and presents us with an array of mini conches, sunrise, puka, and opihi shells.

"You boys like purchase shells for make necklace? We find 'um right here on da Wai'anae coast," she announces with a soothing smile.

"Uh, das okay, Auntie. We jus' like find Rob an den go, yeah," replies Kainoa.

She sighs tragically and slowly closes the tackle box, deflated. She leads us forward a few more steps around another corner where the backs of two large painting canvases meet at an angle.

"This is Rob's room, when he's here. And he is today, but stay tired all da time. Could be sleeping. Some days are better than others…"

A colorful shower curtain covered in tropical fish hangs as the door to his room, and Kainoa brushes it to the side as we enter. A shirtless man sits cross-legged on a dingy futon beside a young woman lying passed out, drooling with her mouth half open, beside him. The shirtless man tightens a belt around his lower bicep, and next to him a rusty camp stove burns, a blue flame hissing loudly in the small space. The man has earphones on and is mouthing the words to something, still fiddling with the belt. He hasn't even noticed us.

I look around the small, cramped room for any traces of Jojo's existence or past. A teddy bear or children's book or some goddamned kid thing. I look at the face of the two canvases we'd just seen from behind that served as two walls. One is a crude replica of Goya's *Saturn Devouring His Son*, but the colors are brighter and happier, a black light version of the original. The other is an imitation of Picasso's *Guernica*; again, the colors in vivid neon, but almost identical to the original. A small Hitachi television that looks about thirty years old plays a movie in black and white. It's Fellini's *La Dolce Vita*. Next to the television are stacks of VHS tapes: *8 1/2*, *The Third Man*, *Straw Dogs, Do the Right Thing, The 400 Blows, The Seventh Seal*…

Puzzled, I gaze around the room some more, confused. Stacks of paperbacks and hardcovers create another wall to the room. Rushdie's *The Satanic Verses* stacked on

Melville's *Typee* on top of *The Sheltering Sky* on *Tropic of Cancer* on *Island* on *East of Eden* on *Invisible Man*. Chomsky on Mishima on Steinbeck on Camus on Hesse on Baldwin on Bukowski. Another pillar of classics— Whitman, Thoreau, Gogol, Dostoevsky, Nietzsche—hold up a head-high lamp. I wonder if we've come to the wrong room, or tent, or cosmic dimension and look behind at Kainoa, who peers back at me blankly. More works of foreign authors—and in their native tongues—like Calvino, Borges, Grass, Vallejo, and Lorca form another pile in a corner of the confined space. A Scrabble board game lies on the ground next to a few ancient *New Yorker*s and *Rolling Stone*s. Acrylic paint tubes scatter the floor, along with a few artist palettes dotted with drying color blends. A few yellow legal notepads are strewn about, one in particular lying on a pile of old papers with red notations etched in the margins. A few other stapled papers spill from a tattered school folder that reads *Leeward Community College Faculty and Staff*.

I suddenly feel nauseous. What the hell was going on here?

"Ho, you fakah," utters Kainoa. "Feel like da Ghost of Christmas Future wen take us fo see *you* in ten yeas, ah?… Nah-nah-nah-nah," he jokes, slapping me on the shoulder.

The man glances up and swipes the earphones from his head.

"Sorry, fellas, just got enough for her and me," he says, tilting his head to the unconscious, drooling woman at his side. "I dunno who told you I had any to sell, but I will in two days. It's forty for half a gram."

He holds a spoon over the camp flame with one

hand and searches the floor, finding a syringe beneath a Burroughs novel with the other.

"You're not Rob, are you?" I say, picking up a Tim Buckley album I didn't even know existed. "Whose shit is all this—these books and paintings?"

"I'm Rob, man. And all this shit is *mine*. The fuck do you care?" he growls, sucking the bubbling liquid from the spoon with the syringe.

"*You* read the collected works of Jorge Luis Borges... in Spanish?"

"What, a user can't have taste? I fucking *lived* in Barcelona, man...Listen, I got nothing to sell you, so get the fuck out." He holds the syringe needle up to the lamp light, flicks the base, and a bead of dirty fluid drips from the tip. He shakes his head, confused. "*Who* are you guys, man? Frankie-boy might have some shit a few tents down. Try there..."

He motions somewhere to his right and then jabs the needle between his bicep and forearm.

"We got Jojo," blurts Kainoa, impatient and agitated. He whips out his iPhone and starts clicking shots of the room, the woman on the futon and Rob. I nod to him like, *good thinking*, because I'd have totally forgotten to do that.

The man gasps a little, but I'm not sure if from that piece of information or from the rush of the drug. His body sways slightly as if losing balance, and he puts one arm behind him to keep from falling back. His head nods quickly and he looks up, bleary eyed.

"So...whaaat? You wanna fucking arrest me? You guys cops? You...can't—"

"Shut up," I snap. "We could give a shit about you. We

just need Jojo's birth certificate, plus any other papers—medical, whatever—and for you to sign him over. Just give us that and we'll leave." I pull out the consent letter Monty had printed and hand it to him with a pen.

As much as our presence should've killed his high, the drug seems to be winning him over, the man drawing longer, slower breaths, a pale euphoria flushing over his face before our eyes.

"I don't have it, man," he exhales deeply, his gaze losing focus.

"Find 'um den, jack-ass!" shouts Kainoa. He unsheathes what looks like a foot-long, bloodstained Bowie knife from beneath his shorts, and leans into the shirtless man unraveling on the futon. He draws the blade against his clammy throat.

"Ah, man...*fuckkk*, man," he whimpers, "that kid isn't even mine...I just...take care of his mom...and let him crash...here. He's hers," he says, waving at the passed-out woman. "What you...need the birth certif...for anyways?"

"To put him in goddamn school, dude. You, of all people, never thought of doing that?" I say, picking up the syllabus in the folder.

"Man...she doesn't have...*any*thing. Pre...pretty sure he was born in town...Kapiola ...ni...Med—"

This guy was such a waste of good taste.

"What's his last name, then, so we can find out? And... can you just sign for her, then?" I say, motioning to the lifeless body next to him.

"Um...Va...liere. Joseph...Valiere...The kid's like... seven...or eight or...something," he trails off, scribbling some illegible signature on the line.

Behind him, Tom Wolfe leers at us in a cocaine-white suit, framed on the back sleeve of *The Right Stuff*. The hardcover leans against a crate of records, and next to that, the latest *GQ* magazine with James Franco grinning on the cover. Goddamn you, James Franco.

"How could you just leave him in there?" I ask, my voice splintering. "What kind of person does that?"

"We knew...somebody would...find him—eventu..." he sighs. "It was her idea." He gestures to the woman.

"How does someone like you," I say, motioning to the messy culture cluster around us, to the audience of greats, silent in the small room, "get so goddamned pathetic?"

"*I am a sick man...I am...a wicked man...*" he quotes, his eyes rolling backward into his head.

"*No!*" I shout, slapping his sweaty face to keep him awake. But he is out cold.

"If you guys bringing trouble, I goin' call my bruddah dem next door..." the woman warns, appearing from behind us, shaking a finger, "No boddah him...he sick, you. He pay da rent every month..." she scolds.

"You evah wondah what happen to Jojo?" barks Kainoa.

"Jojo stay wit his auntie dem in town," she retorts, and slips away into another room.

I shake my head, disgusted. More fleas assault my ankles. A calico cat hops onto the futon, sniffs the loaded man, steps over his face, and then sits down between the two of them. The cat stares at us, its tail tick-tocking from side to side like a furry metronome.

"Bruddah, we go. Da hospital goin' get da peppahs," says Kainoa, grabbing my shoulder.

I get up, swipe the Tim Buckley disc, and suddenly the

white noise of motors and humming appliances ceases, subsequently causing a total blackout.

"Ho, shet…Auntie wen cut the gener-ray-tah," murmurs Kainoa into the darkness. "GO, BU!!!" he explodes and shoves me forward, the two of us barreling through the tent's labyrinth of shit, swiping away hanging bulbs like cobwebs, bouncing off wardrobes, and hurtling through blue tarp walls till we quickly fall into the dirt by the highway on the edge of the bush. Dusting off, we make out the meeting spot by the oven and stack of tires, but Skippy's nowhere to be seen.

"Haole, how long since Skip left?"

"Long enough to go to Makaha and back. Jesus, what the hell were we thinking coming with him? Like—"

"*Shhh*, you fakah—you see dat?" hisses Kainoa.

On the other side of the road, ambling toward us, are two or three frenetic shadows. Gene, Joel, and Ulu come into form through the darkness. Ulu is jumping up at Joel as they run, nipping and licking his face. They nearly skid to a stop in front of us. Ulu pokes her nose in my crotch and lifts her snout, her version of hello. The two of them are huffing and puffing, like they'd just full-sprinted a mile or something. They look behind themselves furtively.

"Fakah, you get one smoke, bu?" pants Gene to Kainoa.

"Can I get one, too?" wheezes Joel.

Kainoa digs in his pocket and pulls out his vape pen. Gene takes a drag with his fat fingers, followed by Joel. I look down and see that Gene's other hand is bloody, his knuckles split and swollen.

"Bruddah, wea da Gypsy?" asks Gene impatiently, his eyes darting around the darkness.

"Dude, he's not here…and I don't know if he's gonna come back, man."

Kainoa pulls out his phone and shakes his head. Still no service. Gene sucks in an impossibly long drag, exhales, and hocks a loogie. He looks us all in the eyes, very seriously.

"Coz, we get problems now. We gotta go, but we cannot go dat way," he says, pointing east toward town.

Joel begins to rock and sway, popping his neck, revving up a verse.

Two men enter, one man leave, two men enter, one man leave,
We heard Ulu's bark, like a shot in the dark,
But the fists of Mean Gene are faster than a lark.
Two men—

"Joel, shut the fuck up, haole!" shushes Gene. "Bruddahs, I jes wen drop two fakahs fo' get dis dog, and I heard their cousins calling plenty kine boys from Makaha fo' scrap us now. So…We cannot go back dat way."

"Shit, Gene!" I say, panicking. "Now what?

"Only option…is we run hide out Yokes. Den in da morning, pay one lifeguard fo' take us back Wai'anae to one bus stop in his truck…But we gotta go now, coz, guarrens dey get bats or even one gun."

"Where the hell will we sleep?" I inquire, which comes out as a whine.

He shrugs and turns away, jogging toward Yokohama Bay. Ulu jumps after him, panting in excitement.

"Beach park bat-troom, maybe? Or undah-neat da towers," he calls back to us.

It's another few miles, at the very least, from here to Yokohama Bay. I look at Joel and Kainoa like, *Are we seriously doing this?* Kainoa takes another pull of the vape pen, respires, and through a dense white cloud, jogs away, west.

38.

Farther than five miles

Yokohama Bay is certainly farther than five miles. Way farther. Well, I dunno, maybe it is only five, but five in the dark and, with no streetlights, seems farther. We try to follow the coast along the seashore to keep unseen, but that proves nearly impossible, so we stick more or less to the highway. Every so often we see headlights behind us flickering in the distance, causing us to hop into the bushes, or duck behind some beachside rocks to wait for the cars or trucks to pass. It's a stressful-ass trek, to say the least. Not far from the bay around Makua Cave, we notice Ulu whimpering a little, limping as she walks, so we carry her into the grotto's large opening for cover. Joel shines his phone's flashlight on her legs, and there are about seven different kiawe thorns stuck deep in her paws. It takes us about twenty minutes to pull them out with Kainoa's Bowie knife, but we finally make it to the lifeguard tower by the second dip in the road, with no angry mob there waiting, so the four of us plus Ulu stretch out beneath the stand and try to fall asleep, no matter how many, or how few, hours are left before dawn breaks. We're lulled to sleep by the perpetual slush and sigh of the sea, pulsating and devouring the shoreline with each breathy gulp. By the wedge-tailed shearwater chicks crying in their nests through the night like newborn babies. By the trade winds that suck off the beach like faint whispers, carrying their secrets out to sea toward some obscure horizon.

After a grand total of barely twenty minutes, we are awoken by wild barking. Startled, I sit up and immediately feel a kick to the back of my head.

"What the *fuck*!" I say, rubbing my skull, slightly dazed.

A wide flashlight beam illuminates our campsite and Ulu, barking hysterically, is lassoed by a man with a long metal catch pole, stabbing her neck into the sand to subdue her. Joel jumps up frantically. "Dawg, that's my dog! Get that shit off her!"

"Joel," says Gene, "relax, bu. Ulu goin' be okay, sit back down, brah."

We look at Gene, and behind him is a man in a black hoodie and camouflage cargo pants holding a twelve-gauge shotgun to his head. Another man approaches.

"Which one of you fakahs get da Bowie?"

Ulu's pitiful canine whine slices through the silence. The same man pulls out a .22 from his waistband, points it at Ulu, and cocks the hammer.

"He's staying with Palani in town!" blurts Joel desperately. "Don't shoot my dog, *pleeease!*"

The men look at each other, confused. In the beam of the flashlight, I can make out four of them.

"Auntie said somebody get one Bowie knife," says the man with the gun pointed at Ulu. "'Da fuck you talking 'bout stay in town?"

Oh, *Bowie*—not boy—we seem to realize at the same time.

"I get 'um right hea," says Kainoa, nodding to a sheath at his hip. One of the men holding an aluminum baseball bat grabs the knife, and Kainoa sighs.

"Ho, you fakahs, we been looking fo you long time, ah? And wat? You no moa one ride?" he laughs.

"The dog is his," I offer. "It was stolen from him in Waikīkī. We apolo—"

"Haole, I bought dis dog last Tuesday, fair and square. And dis not one dog—dis one pit. We goin' *train* dis bitch."

Joel drops his head and groans, "I'll pay you whatever you want. Just don't hurt her, *please...*"

"Nah, we know dat," says the man holding the .22, who seems to be in charge, "we going ATM and everybody goin' pay. Who's da fakah who broke my bruddah's jaw and wen drop my cousin? Was you, ah?" he says, pointing the gun at Gene.

"What, you like sum, too?" growls Gene.

"Stand up. All you guys. We goin' make one wit-drawl," says the leader. "Plus one special deposit for my bruddah's friends." He grins at Gene wickedly.

We get up and they walk us down the asphalt road, guns at our backs, toward two pickup trucks just behind the night gate. A few yards from the gate we hear a subtle hiss. A sound not unlike that of tires deflating.

"Da fuck!" shouts the man with the .22, grabbing Joel by the collar and looking around.

Fairly hidden behind both trucks, pulled right up to the tailgates, are two identical, lowered murdered-out Scions.

"Ya'll bitches done messed with the wrong queens tah-DAY!" bellows a voice. Tūtū Raymond, decked out in a tight denim jumpsuit with tennis shoes, wearing a blue *Dora the Explorer*-esque wig, steps out from behind the truck holding the old woman from The Bush hostage with a Glock 9. From behind the other tailgate the two handsome young men from her Kaimukī garage step out in matching black slacks and long-sleeve turtlenecks, both holding AR-15 semiautomatic rifles. Lo and behold, Skippy and his brother Steve step out from behind Tūtū Raymond, too, Skippy clutching a large knife, Steve, with what appears to be a snub-nosed revolver.

"Now, I know this is one of ya'll's 'ohana, so slide over the weapons before ya'll bear witness to some vicious tūtū-on-tūtū homicide, mutha-fuckahs." The two young men with assault rifles nod and murmur affirmingly, "*Mmm-hmmm*," beside her.

The man holding the shotgun puts it on the ground and backs away.

"Well, now we all know who's the grandma's boy in this tragic bunch," says Tūtū Raymond. One of the men rolls over a bat, and the leader shakes his head and puts his pistol down, pushing Joel forward as he does. The man with the catch pole handling Ulu releases the wire's grasp, and Ulu cowers over to Joel, whimpering and licking his ankles.

"Get in the cars, boys—and dust off the sand before you get in Tūtū's new xB's!" she snaps, letting go of the old woman. "You need a ride back to da Bush, Auntie?" The old woman nods, and turns back to the Scions to get inside.

"Let this be a lesson to all thugs and future pet owners: always purchase animals with the correct, legally binding paperwork, bitches," scolds Tūtū Raymond, slipping into her car. Her two accomplices keep their rifles aimed at the four men before she snaps her fingers and peels out in reverse. They jump in the other Scion and follow her out.

Inside the car, I look over my shoulder and Skippy is in the backseat with Steve, fiddling with his brother's .38.

"Skip!" I erupt. "What the hell happened?!"

"Ohhh, gadje..." says Skippy, shaking his head. "The alternator gave out onda Blazer by the 7-11. I go in dere for some help, and Ima hearin boys talking about goin' ta fuckup someguys dat stole their dog at The Bush! I call up my bruddah and da only oddah guy I know wit some fire-powah: Raymond."

"That's *Tūtū* Raymond now, Skip," she corrects.

"How do you know *her*?" I ask, nodding at Tūtū.

"Ray— sorry, Tūtū Raymond, gavema wife her first job when she moved ovah from da Bay Area. Worked for ya what—"

"'Bout three or four years, till she had your firstborn," says Tūtū Raymond. She looks over at me, as we pin it through Wai'anae. "Before I left, I texted Mari to see if ya'll were even worth it."

I look at her, my heart dropping into my stomach.

"Girl said Jojo was…" She looks into the rearview mirror and fixes her bangs. "But I knew what she meant." I look at the dashboard and Tūtū's clocking eighty. The Hawaiian Electric Power Plant glides past us after Nānākuli, and in the distance we can see Honolulu's glowing cityscape. Tūtū reaches into the sun visor, pulls out a company valet ticket, and passes it back to me. "She told me to give you this."

I look on the back of the stub and she's written: … *when your love realizes it is part of something oceanic, it begins to move with the whole…I see you, Rumi.*

"Skip, they got a Zippy's out in Kapolei?" asks Tūtū Raymond.

"Last time-ah checked, Ray."

"Ooo child, I could des-troy a Zip Pac right now," she murmurs, gripping the wheel firmly. "Tūtū don't give a *fuck* what tha zumba instructor says!"

39.

"Let it splash inside my chest..."

What do I do with the kid on my day? I used to ask myself that. What do I do with myself, sometimes? I'd ask that, too. We were all a little stuck, all of us a little in limbo. But that kid showed up trapped in a car trunk, kicking and screaming, completely ready to give the world hell—and he shattered that limbo. We'd each have our day with him. Twenty-four hours, and it was never enough. I knew the basics, how he had to get fed, put to bed at a reasonable hour, go to school (eventually), but I didn't know I'd fall in love with him. Or with Mari. Or with this new family that we'd become. Until the boy was ours, I just knew I had be the best father he could have in one day, so it had to be jam-packed. Had to be a day of retribution, a grand consolation prize of sorts, sent through us. A kind of payback for starting the kid off with such tragedy. For that false start of a life. Universe, you owe him.

Now that it's no longer just *one* day with him, and there are a couple more weeks left of summer, I know that I must show him so many places on this island he hasn't seen. Each day must be the antithesis to the one in that terrifying trunk. The heaven to that hell. Each day must be a journey. We'll start in Town and work our way around the island. I'll take him to Kapiʻolani Park, where huge, extraterrestrial banyan trees live with those tentacle vines that drop into the earth and take root. I'll tell him to have at it, to climb and swing and let out jungle calls like Tarzan. Because when you're that age, there's no reason to be embarrassed yet. Plus, school starts in August, so be wild, boy. I'll read him *Quick as a Cricket* again, just like I did with Marisela, and do all the voices at 110%. Yes, I'll read it over and over at his request until his eyelids settle and my voice fades into a dream.

I'm as quick as a cricket, I'm as slow as a snail.
I'm as small as an ant, I'm as large as a whale...

I will walk with him down the Maunawili Trail, point out the guava trees, help him find any fallen fruit, and let him eat something that he picked himself off a tree for a change. We'll cross all the streams to get to the falls, and if we get there and he's not brave enough to jump from the low ledge, I'll pretend like I didn't even notice. Because some heights can eat at a kid for a long time. At night, we'll walk down a beach path to the sea at Waimā nalo Bay. We'll bring flashlights and a bucket and catch the crabs fleeing the shoreline to get to their holes. We'll turn the flashlights off to find the glowing bits of phosphorescence. I'll tell him to pick it up with the wet sand and rub a glowing tattoo on his arm.

I'll teach him surf and I'll paddle out with him at Castles and push him into a few mellow ones to start. Let him feel that special glide and flight of wave riding. We will go to that field out at Sandy Beach where the kites dance and duel with the sun. The ones that dive like neon falling stars. The ones with tails that tickle and writhe across the sky, a mile long. I'll say, "Get 'em, Jojo! Jump and touch the tails for good luck!" And he'll dart into that field of sun, jumping and reaching for the ones that dip low and taunt him, their puppeteers sitting in lawn chairs, sipping beers and smiling.

Don't be stingy, my island home. Give him all the love you gave me, O'ahu, in all your strange beauty. Give him fat rain in blinding sunlight, showers that pass in seconds, the ones that make no sense whatsover. I swear, before the summer's over we'll have done all of this, and maybe even leave some left over for the next. We will leave no stone unturned. We will. I'm sure of it.

I find meaning within Jojo, because he is youth and youth does not question meaning. It just continually discovers, explores, *feels* life for what it is, and not for what it has failed us to be yet. The boy loves anyone and anything so fast, even the ones who have hurt him. Youth forgives in a heartbeat, but I'm tired of him having to forgive so often.

We will keep driving west, toward the sun. Past the snoozing red-dirt stained houses of Waialua town and just keep rolling to the end of Farrington Highway. We'll be flying through the daydream that is Mokuleʻia, and Jojo will be sitting there beside me. I'll look over at him and his mouth will be open, practically drooling at the world, and his eyes will be wide and filled with prop planes and gliders lifting from the earth in flight. Eyes full of people attached to one another, falling gracefully to the ground. Eyes on a beach park inhabited by a cluster of vans and tarps and chickens and children. Eyes on the countryside before him, lying still like a dog on its back in bliss.

And the asphalt will turn to gravel and the gravel will turn to sand, and we will stop and park the car and walk to the edge of the earth. I'll tell Jojo to leave the doors unlocked and the windows down, so if anyone wants snoop around, they can go ahead. He'll comply, and when we start walking down the trail he won't complain because he's been raised to enjoy adventures with no clear purpose. He'll have his baggy-ass swim trunks on that Uncle Gene got him, and he won't be asking, "Are we there yet?" but rather, "When can we *swim*?" It'll be hotter than hell out there, parched *kiawe* bush and ancient lava rocks with no respite, but I'll bring an umbrella because that'd be the kind of thing to do for a boy, who now, more than just one day a week, is my son.

We'll finally get to that point where the water is a color from which all blues are born. We'll get to that one cove out there where it's safe to take a dip. And right before we jump in, I'll tell Jojo, *Okay, bud, when we go underwater, see if you can hear the fish talking. Maybe even a dolphin...* And he'll light up like this was the best thing you could ever imagine, at least at that moment, which for a kid, can be a lifetime. And he'll slosh into the water and submerge himself. I'll think of that one Rumi line *"When the ocean surges, don't let me just hear it. Let it splash inside my chest,"* and I'll follow behind him. I'll open my eyes underwater and look at him. His eyes will be closed in concentration and his hair will be a clump of golden weeds, swaying about his head like sea anemones. Like Marisela's once did. And we will hold our breath, try to listen, and wait. And keep holding. And listening.

THREE MONTHS LATER

40.

"'Ōhi'a lehua, you fakahs..."

imme all your adjectives," growls a husky voice to the back of my head. I flip around, and she's sticking the end of a young tuberose into my shoulder like a gun. She giggles, and I feel a droplet of spit hit the side of my face as she laughs. She's always been phenomenal at sneaking up on me. I grin and look down at the newspaper, sweeping invisible words off the page with one hand to the other like eraser shavings. I hand her the booty.

"Delicious, incendiary, sagacious, ubiquitous, and pensive. That's all I got, I swear," I tell her, playing along, not making eye contact. "Listen, I got an eight-year-old kid. Don't do anything brash—"

"BAM!" she shouts. "You forgot to give me *brash*."

I clutch my heart and sink slowly to the ground behind the rolling valet booth.

Still parking cars? You know I can't leave the game. Nah, the new gig with Graham has been going swimmingly, but I still keep a shift a month at the Sands for some cold, hard cash. Plus, valet parking is kind of like stripping: it's incredible exercise for your core. And let's be real. The publishing game is pretty volatile these days. Wouldn't make sense to burn any bridges if I needed a backup plan. Graham is making good on those travel benefits, though. I'm going to Rarotonga for a story in the spring, and hopefully I can finagle two more tickets for Marisela and Jojo.

Speaking of, Marisela and I patched things up pretty quickly after the Westside debacle. Maybe she was just waiting for that grand gesture, but I also think Tūtū Raymond might've put a good word in for me, too, bless her heart. Mari still slings flowers, a lot less often, though, as she's been busy finishing her first draft of *Basket Case*.

We got Jojo enrolled in public school by the skin of our teeth, too—which I honestly didn't see coming, since there was diddly-squat for any docs at his old spot on the Westside. But Monty advised me to have him along when I went into admissions, and that sloppy, ingenious son of a bitch cited the McKinney-Vento Act, which bypasses a bunch of the immediate requirements to ensure that homeless children get enrolled in school. He even whipped out some photo evidence of Jojo's former living conditions (thanks to Kainoa) and the boy was golden. Needless to say, I'll be using Monty again in the future. It would be nice if he finally passed the bar, though.

"Wow. We're awesome," I say.

"Speak for yourself, nerd. You're awesome; I'm *incorrigible.*"

She places her basket on the counter, looks behind her, and then picks the thong from her ass crack in one swift but not necessarily covert swipe.

"Yah-*huck*! You better wash that dirty little hand, flower wench."

"Meh," she shrugs, slowly bringing her hand to her mouth and biting down on a finger.

"Ew!"

"What? It was my *other* hand. C'mon, what am I, four?" She glances at her cell phone for the time. "You almost off? I'm almost on. How are things going with your latest revision?"

"They're going," I say. "Trying to con a local magazine into publishing a chapter to tease it a little."

"Hmmm," she replies, nodding ambiguously. "You learn lingo like 'tease it a little,' from your trendy new job?"

"I saw that coming as those words left my mouth. You hear back from any agents yet?"

"Uh-uh. Know any?"

"Umm, well—"

"Lemme guess: you could ask Graham?" she grins.

"You really love to keep me on my toes, huh? Wait, where's Jojo?"

"I thought *you* were watching him," she kids. "He's catching geckos in the lobby."

"Naturally. *Dame un beso* then, toots."

"Never say that again, please," she smiles and leans over the valet lobby desk.

Just then Kainoa slides up behind us, puts his hands

on both of our shoulders, and whispers, "'ōhi'a lehua, you fakahs…'ōhi'a…lehua."

Marisela shrugs at me, confused.

"I'll tell you some other time."

She steps backs, looks me up and down, and says, "You know…just because you wear a uniform that looks like you're on safari doesn't mean you can write like Hemingway. Actually, here, I got one for you: 'For sale: valet potential, never realized.' Get it?" she says, slapping her knee.

"Yeah, yeah, I get it. Go hawk your bloodflowers."

41.

Knock-knock

.

So that's how you're gonna end it?" says Kaito. "With a sassy transexual Rambo saving the day?"

"The hell's wrong with that? And c'mon, it's 2018. Try *transgender*, Wolf Quest."

"I dunno, just seems a little *deus ex machina*, if you ask me—"

"I was going to say *derivative*," chimes Ralph, smirking in the front row.

"It is *convenient*," shrugs a girl whose name I don't know.

"More…*eucatastrophic*," adds another.

"I thought the series of events that led to that ending made perfect sense!" I squeak, a little too affected.

"So what, Teach, is Joel giving you sub-scraps now?" hollers Ikaika, sparking a roar of laughter. "Oh, how the mighty have fallen."

Yes and no. I am in fact covering for Joel, who has a

vet appointment today for Ulu. Call it scraps if you want, but Derek did encourage me to discuss my novel in class to somehow hone the kids' long-form game. I kind of framed it like some big, intentional reveal that I'd been planning all along. Like, "*Tah-dahh! We did it, guys! How meta is that?*" I think they saw right through me, though. But some fresh eyes couldn't hurt, right? So here I am in Joel's Freeverse NeoGonzo Journalism class (his name, not mine) with half of my star players present from the summer creative writing course.

"Geez, you guys sure got uppity while I've been gone for a bunch of bottom-of-the-barrel, future college freshman. What've you been learning with 'Professor Joel'?" I air-quote.

"Umm...well..." a few students utter. Someone whistles long and hard like, *Hell if I know...*

"Joel doesn't have a syllabus per se, but it feels like we've been covering a chapter from Joseph Campbell's *The Power of Myth* for, like, a few weeks now?" says Kaito, looking around the room for confirmation.

"It's a pretty fluid curric'," shrugs the same girl whose name I don't know.

"And you guys are cool with that?" I say.

"Beats calculus."

"Yeah, plus we're helping him put together a TED Talk for the spring at UH, which is pretty exciting."

I rub my temples dramatically. I swear to God, they give TED Talks out like parking tickets these days.

"Yeah, and at least Joel has the decency to include us in his creative process *and* give us credit," says Kaito.

"Credit? It's credit you want?"

"Dude, we were the goddamn motivation to your transformation, man!" hollers Ikaika.

"That's debatable, and *language*, guys."

"Yeah, I feel like we pretty much constructed your character arc," adds Ralph.

"And we want workers' comp, bitch!" yells Kaito.

"Dude, the *boy* transformed me, not you," I correct.

"We're still not totally convinced the boy is real," says Ralph.

I pull out my iPhone, scroll through a few pics, and pass it around. "Happy now?"

Everyone has a look. "Still didn't feel good getting *Truman Show*'d," mumbles Ikaika.

"I feel like you haven't actually seen *The Truman Show*."

"We've seen the trailer. It's the one with Will Ferrell and his life's getting written—"

"Nope," I say, shaking my head. "Not that one."

The clock hits 10:55 and the class unravels, everyone fleeing their desks.

"Ralph," I say, waving him over. "Couple things. You gonna be able to hit those deadlines on our department pages? I don't want to overload ya, bud. You've been doing such great work lately, and Christ, the time it takes you to transcribe? You're an animal, man."

He looks up blushingly. "No, I can handle it."

"Seriously, though, thanks for making me look good in the office, Ralph. Even Graham said he's never seen an intern as talented as you in New York."

"You kind of owed me the job, anyway, right?"

"Lil bit."

"*Knock, knoo-oock...*" croons a voice behind us.

Aw, fuck off, Derek. But when I turn to look, standing in the doorway is not him, but rather, a vaguely familar face above a blue college sweatshirt that reads UCLA.

"I'm Ron, Ralph's brother," he says, sticking out a hand commandingly. "Had to stop by my old stomping grounds." He looks around the classroom thoughtfully. "Are there really a bunch of 3-D printers in the science and tech lab? That can't be safe…"

"Ronald's back for Thanksgiving break," adds Ralph. "He's here a week earlier to lead a couple writing workshops on campus."

"Nice. Yeah, I've read some of your work, Ronald, *excellent* stuff," I grin, as if I'm the only one in on the joke.

"*Haaah*," he makes out, staring at my chicken scratch on the whiteboard. Then says, without even turning to me, "Ralph told me about his story. As if I'd care. '*What a good thing Adam had. When he said a good thing, he knew nobody had said it before…*' Quick, Teach, who said that?"

"Umm, was—"

"*ERRR!*" yells Ronald, cutting me off. "Mark Twain. But seriously, who doesn't lift a thing or two off their favorite authors? Sure, a blatant cut-and-paste is just obnoxious, but even the story he took…most of it I just ripped from Chang-Rae Lee's *Native Speaker*. And *Native Speaker*? That title's clearly a rip off Wright's *Native Son*… Really, it's like: '*To copy others is necessary, but to copy oneself is pathetic.*' Second chance, Teach, go!"

"Picasso," answers Ralph.

"I was gonna say that!" I bark.

I was definitely not going to say that.

"Well…" says Ron, looking at me and around the

room some more, increasingly uninterested. "It was good to meet you, *amigo*, but I gotta get to that workshop." He looks down at his wrist and taps the time where there is no watch and scurries away.

"Your brother's kind of a dick, huh?" I say, still staring at the doorway.

"*Kind of?*" says Ralph, shaking his head and packing up his bookbag, as a new class of seniors trickle in toward us.

Glossary

akamai *[ah-kuh-mahy]:*
smart, clever

'aumākua *[ow-mah-koo-ah]:*
familial deity in traditional Hawaiian
culture

boto *[boh-toh]:*
penis

brah *[brah]:*
short for bruddah, brother, bro

bruddah *[bruh-dah]:*
brother, bro

'bu *[boo]*
short for brah, bro

bumbai *[bum-bahy]:*
otherwise, or else, later

cho-cho *[choh-choh]:*
slang for vagina

coz *[kahz]:*
short for cousin, term of endearment
for friend

da *[duh]:*
the

das *[dahs]:*
that is

dat *[dat]:*
that

da kine *[duh-kahyn]:*
the kind…of place/person, vague word
to be inferred

fakah *[fuh-kuh]:*
fucker, a term of endearment

frickah *[frick-uh]:*
milder form of fakah

hakam *[hah-kuhm]:*
how come?

haole *[how-lee, -lay]:*
foreigner, usually Caucasian, white
person

hāpai *[hah-pahy]:*
pregnant

hapa *[hah-pah]:*
half, short for hapa-haole, mixed
ethnicity

kāne *[kah-nay]:*
man

keiki *[kay-kee]:*
child

lai dat *[lahy-dat]:*
like that

manapua *[mah-nah-poo-ah]:*
savory pork-filled bun

moemoe *[moy-moy]:*
to sleep, lie down

nightmarchers:
the undead spirits of Hawaiian
warriors said to march in the night

'ohana *[oh-hah-nah]:*
family

ono *[oh-noh]:*
delicious, tasty

pilau *[pee-lou]:*
smelly, rotten

spock *[spahk]:*
to spot or see something

suckah *[suh-kah]:*
milder form of frickah

stay:
it is

susu *[soo-soo]:*
breasts

tūtū *[too-too]:*
local term for grandmother

wahine *[wah-hee-nay]:*
woman

Acknowledgments

My wife Rachel, Mom, Dad, Aaron and Jordan Kandell, my editor John Paine, Ryan Chun, Matt Thomas, Trina Orimoto, Noa Emberson, Taylor Paul, Dana Valdez, Michelle Mak, Pete Arnold, Chas Smith, Lisa Yamada, Jason Cutinella, Ara Laylo, Joe Bock, Matt Dekneef, Bill and Annie Hart, Michelle Mitchell, Danny Van Nostrand, Rhett McNulty, Eric Wehner, Kevin Whitton, the gang at Enchanted Lake Starbucks (Tim, behave), the many valets I've worked with around Oʻahu, and the village of Bir, India, where the very first draft was written.

About the Author

BEAU FLEMISTER is an award-winning writer from Kailua, Hawai'i. After graduating from the University of Hawai'i at Mānoa, he worked in the valet parking industry on O'ahu for eight years, taught creative writing to high school students at a renowned private prep school, and traveled the world extensively (off valet tips), reporting for publications along the way. A former editor at *Surfing Magazine*, he has been published in *VICE*, *Complex*, *Outside*, *FLUX*, *The Surfer's Journal*, and *Hana Hou!* magazines, among others. His journalism and travel writing has covered stories from indentured sex workers in Paris to a hidden sovereign nation-state within Hawai'i; from being attacked by bears in Nepal to camping with nomadic tribes in Mongolia. He resides with his exquisite wife, Rachel, in Waimānalo, Hawai'i.